A Volcanic Affair

'You said your slave will be back soon. Would it enhance your pleasure to have him watch us?' he murmured as he ran his teasing tongue over her lips. 'Is that why you took a chance to stimulate yourself when someone could have come in?'

'Oh, Juno and Minerva be my witnesses, I don't know!' she moaned. She pushed herself against him, but he held her still with a tight hold. 'Please, please finish it.'

She knew he was teasing her on purpose – deliberately heightening her tension to make her beg, but she didn't care. All she cared about was the need for sweet release.

A Volcanic Affair

XANTHIA RHODES

BLACK
lace

Black Lace novels are sexual fantasies.
In real life, make sure you practise safe sex.

First published in 1997 by
Black Lace
332 Ladbroke Grove
London W10 5AH

Reprinted 1999

Typeset by CentraCet, Cambridge
Printed and bound by Mackays of Chatham PLC

ISBN 0 352 33184 4

Chapter One

Pompeii, Italy AD 79.

*H*er loins were on fire.

She looked up towards the high, cone-shaped summit of Vesuvius and felt the tremors for the second time that morning. Powerful ripples surged through her legs, reaching upwards like silken fingers to caress her breasts and neck. The earth movements ruffled her hair as gently as the hands of a lover, greedy for sensual delight. Involuntarily, she put a hand to her face and stroked her cheek in the seclusion of the dark barroom.

'The gods are angry.'

She glared at the old man for interrupting her blissful dreams of freedom.

'Like the mountain, Marcella, you are filled with pent-up energies and passions. Who is going to erupt first?' he continued, as he balanced a heavy wine container between his knee and the marble-fronted food counter.

'You are exaggerating, Terentius; the mountain will never blow up,' she replied, choosing to ignore his reference to her private longings.

'Which is more than can be said for you, miss,' he persisted. 'The town is full of muscular men from all over the Roman world: Thrace, Tripolitania, probably even Britannia. In your imagination, their bronzed torsos

1

and rippling shoulders are quivering in anticipation of a woman's touch. Your touch.'

She threw a cleaning cloth at him but he dodged easily.

'Every day, when they visit the public baths,' he continued with relish, 'they get the slaves to burnish their skin with fragrant oils, but by the time they arrive here in the evening, they have indulged in all manner of licentious pleasures – with other women, not you! You can't bear that thought, can you?'

She closed her eyes to blot out his taunting words but he had put the voluptuous images clearly into her head and she began to tremble slightly.

'And the situation won't change unless you do something drastic, because your aunt and uncle watch you like jailors. You may have no dowry, but you'll make a better match as a virgin than a wanton.'

'Oh, Jupiter hear my prayer and take me away from this dingy back-street tavern. Make something exciting happen!' she prayed under her breath.

He leant against the counter and crossed his arms, looking at her seriously.

'You'll have to do something positive about your life, Marcella. If the gods spare you, you will need to decide between respectability and adventure. You can't have both and the indecision is leading you to ignore important warnings like earthquakes.'

'What can I do?' she asked with sudden despair. 'Women are fated to marry or work for a pittance in menial jobs. Adventures cost money.'

'You'll find a way of getting what you want,' he said flatly. 'Whether it will be in line with social convention is another matter.'

He disappeared into the store room, and she fidgeted on the low bar stool. She had left off her underclothes because of the excessive heat, so the material of her flowing dress rose provocatively into the cleft between her legs. The fire inside her was smouldering in the most uncomfortable and insistent manner.

'That's the last one,' Terentius declared, as he let

another wine container down from his shoulders and set its pointed base into the floor. 'Have you ever noticed how wine amphorae look exactly like huge phalluses?' He stamped the loose earth around its base and winked at her.

'You may take a break,' she said sharply, unable to endure his company any longer. 'Why don't you go and gossip with some of the other slaves?'

For a moment he looked as though he was about to argue, but, to her relief, he replied, 'It is too hot for any sane person to be out, but I could do with a change. Don't forget to tidy up. You'll have to have something to show for your afternoon.'

She listened to his footsteps echoing along the deserted street and sighed with relief at the silence, the solitude and the semi-darkness of the bar. The material of her dress rode up further, somehow contriving to bunch up so she was desperate to give herself the relief she craved. She concentrated on remembering the sweetness of release when her fingers were inside her secret places.

A shadow fell across her from the door to the street and an impish face appeared. 'Greetings.'

'Lydia!' she exclaimed. 'I am so pleased to see you. Terentius has driven me crazy with his dirty talk and his innuendos and I'm stuck here until my uncle returns, on the off-chance one miserable customer will break the siesta and order a drink.'

Lydia laughed. 'I cannot stay long, Marcella – I came to say that if you want some fun later on today, we can sneak a preview of the wall paintings my mistress commissioned for the dining room. The artist finished this morning.'

'I've heard gossip – people say that they are really explicit and lewd,' replied Marcella, her spirits rising. She filled two beakers from a bronze jug of well-watered wine and handed one to her friend.

'The steward complained that they were so obscene they were fit only for a brothel. He didn't say how he knew!' Lydia giggled.

'At my age, I should have been married years ago and then we would have the answers to the things we want to know,' remarked Marcella wistfully.

'You could have settled down several times but you refused.'

'Perhaps I should have given in to what society expects, but the little runts they chose for me could never have given me the erotic satisfaction I need. Married women have babies, work and no fun!'

'Women don't have to have babies nowadays,' said Lydia, sipping her drink. 'My sister uses a little sponge that soaks up the spend inside her. She says it helps if you soak it in olive oil, too. She covers her husband's prick with peppermint and honey in water as an added precaution.'

'That can't work,' said Marcella in disbelief.

'They enjoy it. She always had a sweet tooth!'

'The feeble dimwits they had in mind for me wouldn't have been able to keep their dicks up long enough for us to find out if any of it worked,' replied Marcella despondently, rocking back and forth on the stool, hugging her waist tightly.

'May the gods be my witnesses, I can't wait much longer. I can't endure the agony of not knowing what it is like. The artist sounds gorgeous – do you think he uses his own prick as a model for the pictures?'

Lydia sniggered. 'He'd need a mirror!'

'Imagine! If he has painted the murals, he must have seen similar scenes in real life!'

Marcella leant forward, her womanhood now totally enflamed.

'I feel so naive, Lydia. I know in theory what men do to women, but exactly what sensation does that produce?'

'A couple of fingers or some long instrument like a cooking spoon cannot possibly be the same,' agreed Lydia ruminatively.

'People speak about a man being hard,' pursued Marcella, 'But just how hard is that? Cupid is cruel – he has fired all his darts at me and none at a suitable man.

4

Why can't I be invited to an orgy where people are openly lascivious and carnal? Where is Venus? Can't she hear that I am praying to her to bring some decadence into my life?'

Simply thinking about the parties and the paintings made Marcella's breasts feel swollen and tender. The soft folds between her legs were beginning to moisten.

'My dear friend, you are in a tavern, in the centre of a small provincial Roman town, in the reign of the emperor Titus,' said Lydia prosaically, putting down her empty beaker. 'Get used to the idea that nothing is going to happen.'

'But there must be more to life than this,' Marcella wailed as Lydia left.

A few shafts of bright light came through the tiny, high windows from the street and the half-open door let in some of the midday heat, gently illuminating the dark red walls.

Idly, she straightened some of the flagons and beakers on the shelves behind the bar and rearranged the low tables and stools. Dice and playing checkers were strewn across the gambling table from the last game. She collected them up in a hurry and hastily brushed some pastry crumbs to the floor. As she kicked them under a bench, a hard piece of bread lodged itself between toe and shoe leather and she swore out loud.

She sat on the stool behind the bar and crossed and recrossed her legs so that the dress material pulled on her clitoris. Hugging herself, she let her arms brush against her nipples so the rough linen grated against their peaks. It was easy to imagine a man's touch on her breasts, kneading and teasing before he brought her to orgasm. She wanted strong, male hands between her legs, the fingers moving rhythmically.

She shifted her position on the stool and with her eye on the door, sneaked a hand under her long skirt. She felt the satiny skin with one finger, as though she were a child trying out forbidden food that was destined for an adult party.

5

The smell of her own desire was subtle and sweet as she brought her finger up to her lips to taste her need. Her buttocks felt hot as the wooden seat rasped against them. She pushed her legs out in front of her and pointed her toes, supporting herself with one arm behind her. Working her leg muscles hard, she pushed towards her hand, rubbing faster and faster.

She leant back, her long skirt pulled high, her fingers sliding over her smoothly-shaven pubic mound. The slave girl at the baths had missed a few hairs but all thoughts of complaining fled as her fingers plunged straight to the centre of her need.

She rubbed herself decisively back and forth, concentrating on the sensation and excluding everything else. She flexed her legs again so her ankles were arched. As the first mild explosions of pleasure began to erupt she rubbed her legs together and half-closed her eyelids, surrendering to the pulsating waves of pleasure. Her internal muscles were crying out for penetration and possession.

She pushed two fingers into the warm depths, but at that angle the stimulation was unsatisfactory so she circled her clitoris and brought her finger down the sweet length of her secret folds.

'The best taverns function on team work.'

She looked up, startled.

Her eyes focussed on the man who had entered the room and was now standing silhouetted against the bright sun.

He was powerfully built, with strong, wide shoulders and a sturdy torso which tapered to narrow hips. His shapely calves showed that he was physically very active.

She sat back, her face flushed, as anger and disappointment flooded over her. She calculated her position: he couldn't know what she had been doing, because the food counter hid the lower part of her body.

She sat forward, the unsatisfied ache between her legs now spreading to her entire body.

6

She glanced at the wax tablet he was carrying.

'You are on official business?' she guessed. 'You will want to talk with my uncle.'

'Come here.'

He stepped into the tavern and half-closed the door.

She sighed. 'If there is some discrepancy with an official return, I'm afraid I can't help you.'

She slid off the stool and reluctantly walked round to where he was standing, smoothing her skirt as she went.

As she drew close, she was aware of the subtly powerful perfume of his masculinity. He exuded a musky scent that was redolent of passion and potency, ability and vitality.

'I've just got time, if you like,' he said, casually placing the wax tablet on the counter. 'Stand still and part your legs. Who needs introductions?'

She stared in astonishment.

'You are all primed up for love and lust, aren't you? Nobody will come into the bar at this time of day and you hardly need a lengthy foreplay. Let us seize the opportunity that Cupid has sent us!'

'Here? Now?' she asked, in a whisper.

'Here. Now.'

He looked very decided. His hand was under his tunic, loosening his loincloth, and his face was set in a business-like mould that was softened by a faint, flickering hint of amusement.

'I certainly do not intend to go anywhere else. I'm quite ready to pleasure us both – feel.'

His invitation increased her curiosity. She put her hand under his clothing and felt that he was huge and hard. At the same time there was a soft pliability that was inviting. The warmth and the gently-cushioned effect proved that her experiments with the harsh wooden handles had been, as she guessed, totally unrealistic. His size surprised and excited her: she wanted this symbol of manhood right inside her, pushing hard, and buried up to the hilt.

7

'Don't be shy – you can move your fingers. A cock feels good. Just as you do, but very different.'

She tugged at the material, pulling it aside so she could see his penis more clearly. It sprang up so that she jumped slightly in surprise. She moved eagerly forward, holding it in both hands as though afraid that it would run away or fly skywards.

The marvellous feel of heat and the promise in its strength overwhelmed her. She rolled it gently between her palms, revelling in the sensation. Delicately, she put a finger to the tip, smoothing the heavy hood with a circular motion. With infinite sensitivity, she squeezed the bulbous top, using her thumb and forefinger. She knew she was exciting him because the stem sprang slightly, giving her a huge surge of desire. It was harder than it had been when she first touched it, and looked even bigger, though it still retained the marvellous silky texture. She thought how easily it would slide inside her.

He drew her towards him, put his hands on her breasts and kneaded them slightly. He firmly pulled the loose, rounded neck of her dress downwards to release the bursting mounds with a practised movement so they jutted in front of her, pushed upwards by the tightness of the material. He had firm, enveloping hands that caressed softly. His fingers moved to her nipples with a confidence that made her feel deliciously secure.

'I know how frustrating it can be,' he murmured. 'You stroke and rub. Sometimes I'll bet that you keep up the manipulation for an hour or so, and your hot little maidenhood gets swollen with the anticipated pleasure. Then you have to wait, don't you, till the tiny bud that is the source of your greatest joy of all, is throbbing with want and the sensations are sharp once more.'

'How do you know these things?' she whispered.

'I talk to women. I know how they feel. In the darkness of your bedroom, you tease yourself, deliberately taking your hand away as you near the height of your bliss. I can see it now. I can picture your soft breath coming faster and faster. I'll bet that after some of the night-time sessions, you are almost bruised from the rubbing, and even then you don't always manage to reach your zenith.'

She hid her face against him, overawed by his knowledge.

'As you grew older, you guessed that this was because you needed something more than your own hand and fingers to produce the ultimate ecstasy. You need a man's hard cock, don't you?'

As his hands cupped her breasts, he rubbed the nipples between forefinger and thumb. He was using the same movements she herself used, but he was producing an infinitely more pleasurable sensation of physical bliss. His hands were slightly roughened, almost grazing over her smooth soft skin. Brazenly, she pushed her chest towards him, and moaned quietly as he increased the pressure. With a delicate lightness of touch, he flicked her nipples before rolling them between his fingers with a firmer touch.

'You are impatient, aren't you? But it takes two to make a real team. I want to savour you more fully than this. You have seen me – I want to look at you.'

She threw her head back, feeling his hardness against her stomach.

'The slave will be back soon,' she murmured. Suddenly she felt shy and innocent – she was only too aware that what he wanted to do was totally against all the moral and social codes she had been brought up to follow. The semi-public situation made it unthinkable. Diffidently, she put her arm around his neck. He smelt faintly of some highly expensive unguent that complemented and enhanced his own, basic male odour.

'You haven't done this before, have you?' he observed as he grasped one of her thighs, and pulled it up to his waist. Under her apparent reticence, she was blazing with desire and her body was shaking with the need to end her torment. She could feel her secret, folded places opening like a flower in the sun. She licked his neck and

9

teased him with her tongue. She knew that, regardless of caution, there was no going back: she was choosing adventure, not respectability.

He lifted her leg higher so she was suspended above the ground and she had to hold on tightly to his body. His strength entranced her and she wrapped her other leg around him so his hands could reach under the mounds of her buttocks. He kneaded her there, pinching her gently and making her cry out with the delicious pleasure. He pulled her upwards and angled his body under hers so she could feel his engorged manhood nudging at the smooth mound. He deliberately slid it along her secret opening that was now lubricious with the juices of her desire. At last, she felt the sweet sensation of a hard, silky penis on her soft yielding folds. He nudged the cleft, looking into her eyes and smiling gently.

'You like that, don't you? It makes you want me. You are ready aren't you, little fire furnace of desire! But I shall make you wait longer yet. I told you, I want to look at you.'

She groaned as she licked his neck and pulled his ear lobe into her mouth.

He slid his hand down along the crack of her bottom, and stroked the swollen folds that she could feel were glistening with the dew of her passion. He pushed his finger inside her, sliding slowly, then faster until he was stretching her. He gently broke the slight resistance.

'You really are a little innocent, aren't you? I shall have to initiate you into the things you want to learn. How have you lasted so long without a man? Haven't they all been overcome by your beauty and your sensual, potent femininity?'

'They were all incompetents,' she said. 'I only want the best.'

He carried her effortlessly to the gaming table and put her down, scattering the piles of dice and playing pieces. Her legs were still splayed outwards from embracing his waist. With a restraining hand on her knee, he prevented her from closing them modestly.

'Put your hand to yourself.' He sounded very much in command.

She turned her head sideways and bit her lip, suddenly confused.

'So you are nothing more than a voyeur after all!' she cried, disappointment clouding her mind. She glared furiously at him.

'Do as I say.'

'Why?'

He laughed. 'I enjoyed watching you as I stood at the door. You looked so contented and at peace, as your fingers gave you pleasure. I only stopped you for selfish purposes – I thought you might not want me if you came to your peak. Besides, I never let a lady do all the work.'

'You were watching for a long time?' she asked, flushing with deep mortification.

'Long enough.' His smile was kind, his eyes sympathetic and understanding. 'Don't be embarrassed. It is so rare to find a woman in this prudish society who knows what she wants and admits to her needs. They purse their lips and pretend to disapprove.'

'Are you too afraid to do it for me?' she asked challengingly, still fearful that he was simply an observer.

'I want to know what gives you pleasure. How else will I know what to do? You want an individual treatment don't you? Or would you prefer me to initiate you with a ready-made formula that will probably work on ninety per cent of women. Suppose you are one of the ten per cent? You would definitely be disappointed, and I never disappoint a lady. It isn't in my nature.'

Feeling reckless, she slid her fingers to her throbbing vulva, keeping her eyes on his face, as he gazed on her softness.

'You are beautiful. It isn't only your long black hair, the shape of your face, the dark lustrous eyes and that straight, determined jawline: you are beautiful here – like a pink flower opening to the sun,' he murmured,

11

kneeling in front of her on the floor so his head was close to her pleasure zone.

He grasped her fingers and moved her hand aside. He stroked her labia firmly, moving from top to bottom, first on the outer edge and then moving further inside with each stroke. She could feel she was glistening with the oils of desire and that he was aware of it. He used light, flickering movements to lubricate her further before stroking her clitoris with a gossamer-soft touch.

'You are like a sweet flower with nectar, ready for the plundering.' He brought his lips to her, licking the sweet drops.

She shuddered from the warmth and the gentleness. The fire within her blazed more fiercely than ever before. To the depth of her being she wanted him and the pleasures he offered. His tongue moved sensuously on her inner creases, sometimes fast, sometimes in long, languorous sweeps. It returned and circled her clitoris, gently taking the liquor from her as though it were life-giving water.

'You taste better than a fine wine. Even the emperor himself does not enjoy such a feast.'

He took her labia into his mouth and she moaned at the heat and the greedy manipulation of his tongue as he tenderly sucked. He pushed his tongue inside her with a sudden, thrusting decisiveness and brought his hands over her stomach and down along her thighs. She was aware of the wealth of his experience, for he was massaging and kneading the very muscles she used in helping to gain her private pleasures.

He gently brought her hand to her clitoris again and said, 'Continue. I like to see the look on your face when you do that. You are a woman who enjoys intimate physical recreation. It is so unusual to find a real connoisseur so young and so inexperienced. Like any other fine art, the gift is given young or not at all, though a good level of expertise can be learnt the slow way.'

She opened her eyes as she lay back, delightfully aware that she was presenting the most shameful and wanton image to him. Her legs were splayed wide and her head was thrown back voluptuously in the semi-darkness. Her shoulders and breasts were arched towards him as he stood in front of her, his manhood ramrod straight. His tunic hung each side like a banner, paraded through the streets of Rome at the ceremonial Triumph of a military hero.

The sudden sounds of a hurried pedestrian in the street made her freeze.

'Stay where you are,' he said resolutely, never taking his eyes off her secret place. 'You can't be seen from the door and I want to watch you. Keep stimulating yourself so I can see your pleasure.'

'Is the tavern keeper around?' A male voice rasped into the silence.

'Not for a couple of hours.'

Her companion turned his head. She realised that any signs of his arousal or her wantonness would be obscured from the newcomer. The thought excited her further and her fingers moved faster.

'I need to speak to him soon.'

The intruder swung the door as he left, so it was nearly closed and the darkness increased.

His footsteps receded and the tall stranger moved closer and knelt between her legs. He pulled her knees upwards, so her heels nearly touched her bottom. Her aching womanhood widened in full invitation.

'It looks as though we may be running out of time,' he said.

He gently inserted a finger and probed the inner cell of her secret place with a casual familiarity that was entrancing.

She sat up and grasped the stiff stem of his virility. She began to squeeze gently, revelling in its hard strength. It seemed huge.

'I want you inside me,' she murmured, made reckless through need.

He fumbled under his tunic and gently laid her down once more before pushing a finger inside her as though

13

tucking something away. His touch was sensitive and went far deeper than her own penetrative explorations had managed.

She could feel him stroking her, sliding over the inner wall firmly, then fluttering fast so she was impelled to push against him with the extreme urgency of her desire.

'What are you doing?' she whispered in an agony of suspense.

'Making sure you are protected.'

'I want you inside me, not just a piece of sponge. Now, now,' she groaned.

He laughed softly and moved his body, adjusting her position so her legs encircled his waist and she could feel his penis sliding with heavenly sweetness along the forbidden entrance of her body.

She pushed herself upwards, unable to hold back for a moment longer. He moved inside simultaneously, so they came together in one deep powerful movement of mutual pleasure.

Marvellous new sensations flooded her brain and she felt faint, yet she would not allow herself to pass out and miss any of the delights. She was totally filled with pleasure as he moved his hard, potent strength further inside her, producing wildfire sparks of intense delight. She no longer had coherent thoughts; she was aflame, arching herself against him, pulling his body towards her, pushing her bottom high off the hard table in a frenzy. Her nipples were burning.

She ran her tongue along his jaw and he bent his head to her face. She parted her lips and he entered her for the second time, his tongue now keeping up an insistent rhythm in time to the movements of his penis deep inside her. She was being possessed and taken to sensual heights she never even dreamt were possible.

'You said your slave will be back soon. Would it enhance your pleasure to have him watch?' he murmured as he ran his teasing tongue over her lips. 'Is that why you took a chance to stimulate yourself when someone could have come in?'

14

'Oh, Juno and Minerva be my witnesses, I don't know!' she moaned. She pushed herself against him, but he held her still with a tight hold. 'Please, please finish it.'

She knew he was teasing her on purpose – deliberately heightening her tension to make her beg, but she didn't care. All she cared about was the need for sweet release.

She deliberately compressed her internal muscles from a point deep within her and felt the ponderous shudder of his satisfaction. She pulled his head towards her, and kissed him, pushing her tongue into him and letting out the pulses of fire. She was goading him now, knowing that she was at last gaining partial control from him.

'You said this was team-work. Well, work yourself, pull your weight.'

She whispered her impatience and flicked her tongue over his ear-lobe.

'Jupiter, but I should like to have you to myself for a few hours, somewhere where nobody can interrupt, and if they did, they would either watch quietly or go away without disturbing us.'

He pressed into her fast and hard, using a force that threw her body into delicious spasms. She marvelled that male strength should be used to counter her own in order to produce such bliss. The force of his pelvis against hers was the most satisfying and complete feeling she could remember having. She grasped his torso with her arms and held on tight, bracing herself against the onslaught of passion that overtook them both. She matched his every forward movement with one of her own.

Her body was exploding, shattering into a thousand points of pleasure. Blissful relief pounded into her muscles. She shook in his arms and he held her tight as his hardness increased. Finally, with a massive shudder, he slumped as if exhausted, and supported himself above her on his elbows.

He kissed her gently, his lips barely touching hers in the sensuous aftermath of satiety. The energetic, intense frenzy of the preceding moments was a thing of the past, replaced by a tenderness she had not expected. She smiled shyly at him in the semi-darkness and stroked the sheen on his brow. His finely-formed face had the look of a bronze statue.

There was a noise from the street and the thrill of being caught with a stranger's prick actually inside her brought on a further spasm of pleasure deep within her body.

She looked over his shoulder towards the half-open door, half-expecting someone to enter.

'Maybe you are right,' she murmured. 'Maybe I wouldn't mind being watched – so long as I didn't get into trouble later!'

'There is nothing wrong with wanting other people to know about your talents, even if they do lie in an area that is frowned on in polite society,' he replied with a slight smile.

His expression changed as a small earth tremor shook the building. 'Leisure-time over,' he said briskly as he lifted himself away from her. The smooth departure from her body made her feel as though a part of her had left.

She straightened her skirt and saw that his tunic was caught up on his tumescent penis.

'Let me do that.'

She knelt in front of him and grasped the material in her hands. She put her hands under the tunic and felt for him. His stem was still slightly springy and she held it in both hands before moving her fingers to his balls.

'You haven't finished yet, have you,' she asked, wonderingly. Her fingers worked against the silkiness, feeling him spring against her touch.

'For the moment, certainly. Give me an hour. There isn't a woman on earth who can satisfy me entirely, as you might have guessed.'

He retied his loincloth and straightened up, instantly in control again. He pulled her to her feet.

'Nothing doing in the Forum – it was dead, as usual,' complained Terentius as he pushed the door wide open

16

and came in. 'Just my luck to be given time off when there's nothing to do.'

Marcella felt heady with the change in pace and the total transformation of the atmosphere.

'Is that a challenge?' She looked at the stranger who was now her lover.

'I don't make a habit of setting women impossible tasks, but you may choose to interpret it like that.'

He had reverted to a formal manner, but she wanted to savour the aftermath by lying next to him and taking in the scents and textures of his body that she hadn't had time to enjoy properly. She wanted to try other experiences. She particularly wanted to take his penis into her mouth as he had enveloped her feminine folds.

In the semi-darkness, after the bright sunshine, she calculated that Terentius' eyes would take time to adjust, so she would have time to compose herself. Her face felt flushed and her body was heavy and languorous. Her hidden cleft was still swollen – so much that she could feel the folds when she walked.

'Everything is in perfect order,' her lover said in a clipped fashion, as though they had been discussing business. He picked up the wax tablet.

Marcella felt both more content and more alert as she moved fast into the real world after the mild dream-like state she had been in.

He walked to the door and turned.

'I don't know your name,' she said, panicking.

'You'll find out, I'm sure,' he said shortly. 'If you are interested enough.'

'You aren't the usual official from the town council are you?' she asked with sudden suspicion.

'I'm a very unusual town official.' He sounded amused.

Totally appalled at the thought of not seeing him again, and never enjoying the delights of his body in the future, she repeated haltingly, 'That was a challenge, wasn't it?'

'Certainly.' He gave a short laugh. 'But be warned – you will not be able to meet it.'

Chapter Two

As the bar filled up with customers, Marcella gradually recovered from the onslaught of her senses that
the passionate encounter had produced. All outward
signs of her wild abandonment disappeared, and her
body was replete with a marvellous new sense of well-
being and peace. It reminded her of her childhood before
she had been tormented by libidinous urges.

The gaming table had been straightened and two
gamblers were being cheered on by their friends.

'Another beaker of your finest.' A filthy building
worker shouted his order, wiping his runny nose on his
tunic.

'Keep your hands off me,' she snapped contemptuously. 'Didn't you understand when my uncle warned
you off last week?'

'I certainly did. You weren't pleased!'

He guffawed.

'Well, you are wrong – I don't have to stoop so low as
an unwashed, lecherous bricklayer on piecework.'

'Your uncle is out in the street, chatting. You can safely
give me a quick one.'

He put his hand under her skirt and she slapped him
away.

'You were fast enough to back down when he chal-

18

lenged you,' she said. 'Being able to drink in this bar is more important to you than an amateur fumble!'

His friends laughed as he rubbed his cheek.

'The bordellos are full of girls who will give me what I want for a few coins. You aren't that special. Any two tits and a steaming crotch are all I need.'

'You are all louts,' she shouted in revulsion. 'You are the kind of scum who are forced to pay for your women. You are not connoisseurs, prepared to enjoy only the best. You have to pay because there isn't a female on earth who will let you touch her for love, lust or even pity. I can do better.'

She flushed at the catcalls, but deep down, she felt too relaxed to challenge the patrons further.

'That man wasn't an official.' Terentius chuckled in his rasping way as he decanted wine from one of the new amphorae into a mixing bowl.

'He must have been.' She shrugged to show a lack of concern that she certainly did not feel.

'I never saw a bureaucrat with muscles like his, nor a manual labourer who was so well-groomed. He must spend hours in the gymnasium and the baths – even his ears and his finger nails were spotlessly clean. You probably noticed.'

She decided to let that pass.

'That means,' he continued, 'he is rich enough to spare the time and to maintain slaves who attend to his personal appearance.'

He added water to the wine and stirred the mixture carefully. 'He was a man of action, not a stylus pusher. His face was plucked, not shaven. That means he doesn't mind the pain and he probably travels around a lot and can't be sure of getting a decent shave every day. Besides, I know all the puny creeps who come here. He was not one of them.'

'Then who was he? You must know his name at least,' she replied, her anxiety growing.

'Of course I don't know who he was,' he said as he ladled the mixed wine into a jug. 'I never set eyes on him before. He was a passing stranger wanting a cool drink during the heat of the day. He was probably going to the harbour on his way to Greece. He didn't speak like a local, did he?'

'No. He had a Rome accent. He was no plebeian. He had a certain presence,' she mused, now seriously worried about how to find him again.

'Out of your league, then.'

She flashed a look of loathing at him and snatched up the filled flagon.

'I was simply interested in who he might be. He left before I could ask. There is no question of any other type of interest.'

'No, my lady. As you say. Naturally, you were totally unmoved by him. Naturally, you don't want to see him again. You also don't believe the mountain will erupt soon. Let us see which of us is right!'

'If there was any danger of an earthquake we would have been told by the town officials,' she snapped. 'Why else do the augurs consult the entrails of sacrificed animals? There have been no indications of a disaster.'

'There were no warnings seventeen years ago and look at what happened!' He pointed to the huge crack that ran from the ceiling across the tavern wall. Spiders had filled the crevice with webs and dead flies. 'They've still not repaired all the damaged buildings so the town is little more than a huge building site with a handful of luxury houses and new public buildings! This time the disaster will be worse.'

'I was only a baby at the time, but I know you are exaggerating,' she snapped as her impatience welled up. 'I'm going to meet Lydia.'

As she passed through the door to the street, she could not resist a peek through the gap along the hinged side. The end of the gaming table was visible. The very area where her nude pelvis and moist, throbbing maidenhood had been lying, was exposed to gaze.

'I had a very interesting time off this afternoon – thank you for asking,' Terentius said in a low voice, as he brushed passed her. 'You thought it was just your good luck, didn't you, the two of you finishing a few moments before I returned? I had been back for ages.'

She shuddered at the thought that he had ogled her soft folds, watched the primeval nature of the coupling and vicariously savoured her orgasm. More repulsive still, she knew that he must have been imagining that he was the handsome, virile man who had repeatedly plunged his pulsating stem inside her.

'It's been years since I set eyes on a crotch so young and unused. Quite a novelty. I enjoyed it.'

'You repulsive piece of low-life! I have nothing to be ashamed of – nothing at all.'

An hour later, Marcella and Lydia knocked on the heavy wooden door set under an ornately carved stone lintel, which was the main entrance to Lydia's employer's home. A mosaic of a fierce canine warned, *Beware of the dog*, and a loud barking came from inside as bars were drawn across.

'Do pricks get fatter and more muscular with use?' mused Marcella. 'Or are they simply the same general shape as the man they spring from? I can't wait to see these pictures.'

'Keep calm, Marcella. They will suspect us of mischief if you look this excited,' replied Lydia restrainingly.

The doorkeeper let them into the cool, marbled interior. Columns around the hallway gave the house a stately atmosphere in complete contrast to the homeliness of the apartments behind the tavern where Marcella lived.

Silently, but walking slowly and trying to look as though they were innocently on their way to sun themselves in the courtyard, they drifted towards the forbidden room.

The steward appeared from the staff quarters, loudly complaining to some unseen member of staff. The girls froze as he noticed them and looked critically at Marcella, taking in every detail of her plain dress and outdoor shoes. His expression was hard, but there was something about it that made her feel naked and vulnerable.

'I have a major crisis on my hands,' he said to Lydia. 'Who is this? Can she wait at table? What are her qualifications?'

Marcella stared at the rapid change of events. 'She works in her uncle's tavern in the town,' replied Lydia, reacting fast. 'We have been friends for years.'

'The master and mistress have arranged a party at short notice to show off the murals and we will be seriously understaffed. The work isn't hard. You have to look good enough not to put the guests off their food, but not so good that the women are jealous.'

Marcella nodded, trying not to show her excitement.

'No showy earrings, no bangles, no rings. The most important thing is not to flirt. Can you manage that?'

She cast her eyes to the ground and clasped her hands in front of her, trying desperately not to think about the size and shape of his prick. And the lewd scenes she was sure she would witness.

'What happens if a man gets too friendly?' she asked demurely.

'If I haven't already noticed and come to your rescue, you come to me. I will order you to go and help the cooks, as if they have some pressing task for you. We manage these things diplomatically.'

She nodded again.

'You seem suitable,' he pronounced. 'Lydia will fill you in on the details.' He cast a flickering glance at Marcella's skirt before holding her gaze for a fraction too long. Her private places began to moisten.

He disappeared in a flurry of shouted instructions to others and Lydia collapsed in giggles.

'With the new paintings to encourage the guests,' observed Marcella carefully, trying to conceal her intense excitement, 'we might see some interesting sights! It might turn into a real orgy. I can't wait.'

Lydia opened a door and revealed the stuffy, window-

22

less dining room. Bare of furniture, the floor was strewn with pots of pigments and many brushes and rags, a pitcher of water and a sack of unmixed plaster.

Marcella strained her eyes to pick out the details which were painted in light green, white and yellow against a base colour of dark red.

As her eyes became accustomed to the dim light from two wall lamps, she could see shadowy painted figures. The walls were divided into sections of painted columns and draperies, and between each was a small scenario with figures.

'They are just standing there doing nothing,' whispered Lydia, disappointedly.

'No they aren't. Look!'

Marcella stepped forward and peered at the figure of a young man in a brown tunic who was leaning towards a woman in a blue dress.

'I thought at first that she was bending down picking flowers, but her frock is around her waist and she is supporting herself with her hands on a low wall. Look at the size of the man's cock. It's huge!'

'He's standing behind her!' exclaimed Lydia.

'He is about to enter her orifice from the back.'

'You can't see her intimate parts.' Lydia sounded discouraged again, but Marcella was excitedly looking at the rest of the scene. Next to the couple about to enter into a frenzied rut were two others. The woman was bending backwards over a table with one leg in the air, like a dancer. Once more the man's penis was prominently depicted as he bent to thrust it towards her body.

'Look at the woman whose breasts are falling out of her dress,' she murmured. 'The one with long hair flowing down her back.'

Lydia leant forward to inspect the picture. 'You can see all the details,' she whispered.

With subtle skill, the painter had depicted the painted woman's secret cleft. The leaf-like creases were just visible as she raised the leg on the far side of her body, to her partner's waist. The pictures were inspiring Marcella so much that she was half-peaking, her clothes pulling uncomfortably against her clitoris. She glanced at Lydia and saw that her face was slightly swollen and flushed with desire. Her nipples were already hardening under her thin frock.

'It's strong stuff – imagine all those fat merchants having dinner here and getting stiff by the end of the meal! They won't be able to keep their hands off the women. This party is bound to be really hot.'

Lydia moved to the other side of the room.

'Here are three in a love clinch – look!'

A man with an erect stem stood behind another man who was about to enter a woman. The painted female turned to the viewers with a bold stare and an idiotic grin on her face.

'That isn't very realistic,' pointed out Marcella.

'What isn't?'

'That grin. She'd be too busy thinking about her own pleasures. She wouldn't have time to smirk at other people.'

'How do you know?' Lydia stared at her in the semi-darkness. 'Marcella! I do believe that you have had a man inside you! What did it feel like? Did it hurt? Was it very hard and long?'

Marcella turned away, aware that she was annoying her friend.

'Tell,' demanded Lydia. 'We always agreed to share everything!'

'I don't know who he is,' she admitted at last. 'Or where to find him. How will I know if the delights he showed me were real? I might have exaggerated them because it was my first time.'

Lydia turned back to the paintings.

'I think you are making it up, if you don't even know his name. If he was that good, you'd have asked. This picture is even more blatant – look.'

A man and a woman were entwined, the woman with her feet off the ground, her partner deeply penetrating her.

'That must feel so very, very good,' Marcella said, her breath coming faster.

She closed her eyes and clutched her waist in a tight embrace. Once more she could smell the musky warmth of her lover.

She was still mentally reminiscing when the painter slipped quietly into the room.

He was young – though not so young as Marcella had imagined. His curly hair was cut short, framing his face as though he were a marble statue. He was finely built, with narrow hips and waist, but his calves and shoulders were less muscular than her lover's. He had long, tapering hands like a musician.

'I am Petronius – Petro to you captivating ladies. I have seen you in the house occasionally,' he said to Lydia, who blushed. He returned his gaze to Marcella. 'I tried to paint as many variations as possible on the universal theme of carnal love. I have spent a lot of time in Rome to get my ideas.'

'You mean that you look at other people's paintings and are inspired by them,' she asked. 'Isn't that rather dull?

'Not at all. I paint from life. I have witnessed all the scenes I have painted in this room, and many more besides. It isn't possible to paint while it is all going on – men in particular, aren't willing to pose while I paint. Besides, it would be asking too much of them. Their erections would wilt if they had to stand around while I mixed the pigments and applied them to the wet plaster.'

Lydia sniggered behind her hand and immediately afterwards tried to look demure. Marcella could tell that she, too, was excited by this matter-of-fact discussion of libidinous matters.

'I never thought about that before,' she said in a slightly strangled voice. 'Carnality is a major part of your trade. In the past I thought only pimps and prostitutes would consider erotic matters as business propositions.'

'How kind you are,' he murmured, with a twinkle.

25

'The practicalities of painting obscene murals do seem to be a hurdle,' she went on, resolutely. 'I suppose you must have seen a lot of orgies.'

'These are hardly obscene,' he protested. 'They are quite tame compared to some scenes I have witnessed. It is difficult to live in Rome without being invited to a few wild parties, though of course, there aren't nearly so many since the emperor Nero died. The new dynasty has generally preached restraint in most things, though Titus is more fun than his father, Vespasian, ever was.'

'But you can't stop people doing what they like behind closed doors,' she suggested hopefully.

'When I knew I had this commission, I didn't turn down any invitations,' he replied with a slight smile. 'But I didn't have to look very far for my material either.'

Marcella looked at him with frank jealousy. 'We don't have any social events like that in Pompeii.'

'Parties can get quite hot in this house,' Lydia said unexpectedly, 'But we haven't had a full-scale orgy yet.'

Petro smiled at her, 'That will change. People don't pay for murals like these if they want to impress staid prudes!'

Marcella glanced triumphantly at Lydia.

'Full-scale orgies have become less popular in Rome,' Petro continued, 'But Pompeii is a small provincial town. I think the idea is about to catch on here! So, have I pleased you ladies then? Do you approve?'

'You have a wonderful way with women's bodies,' said Lydia. 'The techniques you use to show the breasts and the – er, other areas – are very suggestive.'

Her eyes were shining as she smiled at him. He returned the smile as he picked up a paint brush and began to wipe it with a rag. His fingers caressed the wood with heavy sensuality as his eyes followed the contours of Lydia's face, dwelling on her lips before moving down to the soft curves of her breasts.

Marcella looked curiously from one to the other.

'I approve,' she said decisively. 'The pictures are exciting me. And Lydia is on fire – I have never known her like this before. I presume that is the intention? These are not the cold, statuesque pictures of the goddesses that you usually find in formal dining rooms in this stuffy town. These are real people.'

'They are tributes to the power of physical love. If I have managed to stir your blood, then I am well pleased,' he said, coming closer to them. Some pigment had lodged on the back of his hand and he rubbed it slowly, with obvious pleasure.

She could smell the faint musk of his body under sweet unguents and perfumes. His hair was still slightly damp from the afternoon baths, which gave it the quality of a sculpture. She could see that he was aroused under his tunic.

'I have one more figure to paint before I return to Rome,' he said, transferring his gaze to Marcella. 'It is a board painting of Venus on her seashell, with an attendant water nymph. I blocked in the background when I was waiting for some of these murals to dry so I could put in the finishing touches. I can do it all from memory, but you have a beautiful, seductive figure and unusually arresting, lustrous eyes. I could use you as a model for Venus, with Lydia as the nereid.'

'I cannot get the time off work,' Marcella murmured automatically, casting her eyes down to hide her eagerness. The idea of undressing and showing herself to this man was exciting because he knew female and male beauty so intimately that he could capture it in a painting.

His eyes were burning into her skin and she was aware that he was mentally undressing her. She could almost feel him touching her nipples and encircling them with his fingers.

'I lodge a few streets away,' he said casually, picking up another brush. 'If you decide to be the inspiration for a painting, drop in tomorrow morning.'

27

Chapter Three

Marcella spent an uncomfortable night thinking about her adventures and finding that her own hands did not satisfy her even a fraction as much as her mysterious lover had.

'Did you feel the earth tremors?' asked her uncle as she walked into the kitchen next morning, feeling bloated from lack of sleep.

'We get little quakes like that all the time,' she said dismissively, thinking only of her body and the pleasures she had enjoyed and was determined to enjoy again.

A few hours later, after telling her aunt two outright lies, and failing to find out anything more about her mysterious lover, she climbed the stairs to Petronius' lodgings.

'Lydia came by earlier and said she wasn't free to pose until later on today,' Petronius told her.

His two rooms were sparsely furnished. The first was a muddle of painting materials, with a paint-spattered couch in one corner next to a storage chest and a small table. She could see through the half-open door that the other contained only a bed and two wooden storage chests.

'You live so high up!' she exclaimed. 'The street noises are barely audible.'

'That is one of the few advantages of a cheap tenement,' he said, smiling. 'Have some wine. It isn't Falernian but it is quite good. It will relax you – most first-timers are a little nervous. Are you tense?'

'It will seem strange to take my clothes off in front of a man,' she acknowledged, acutely aware that she had no intention of leaving things there. His body was enticingly different from her lover's and she was avid to gain experience in carnal matters. She was determined to meet the man from the tavern again and she wanted to bring something more to their relationship than the charm of innocence.

'Even the most experienced models sometimes get the jitters thinking about the social disapproval there would be if they were caught,' he said calmly, handing her a cup.

She sipped the wine cautiously. 'It is good,' she said. As the liquid pulsed through her veins she began to feel a little calmer.

Petro was slightly built compared to the man in the tavern: his mouth was looser and his facial features less regular, but his eyes were large and soulful and she loved the idea of having him between her legs in intimate embrace.

'I get good fees, but I'll never be rich,' Petronius said, with a slight note of bitterness. 'In return, I create paintings that will give my patrons salacious enjoyment for years – so long as they don't throw too much food at the walls during bouts of drunkenness.'

'You have a low opinion of your employers,' she replied, walking round the small room. She clutched the beaker tightly and her head began to swim, making her feel slightly reckless.

'They want wall coverings and cheap titillation, not art. I could paint them something really tasteful, or I could do something very explicit and frankly erotic. But they want this half-way stuff that merely teases them into finding each other attractive.'

He was standing close enough for her to smell the

masculine tang of his body, along with the faint but not unpleasant aroma of plaster and pigments.

'You don't think they are attractive people in themselves, then?' she asked. She was wondering whether her legs would seem too short to him, or the tangle of underarm hair too wild. Would the slope of her stomach be elegant enough to meet with his approval?

Feeling more daring, she deliberately gulped down her wine, far too fast. The effect was of instant and delightful liberation. She began to feel seductive and fascinating, sophisticated and mature.

'Most of them are plain,' he said sweepingly. He too took a long draught of wine. 'The thing I hate most is when they want me to paint their lumping horse-like daughters in the guise of Venus or Diana. That stretches my talents! They would look far more attractive as themselves, instead of inviting comparison with goddesses.'

She swayed her hips and glided over to sit on the edge of a wooden chest. Surreptitiously, she watched his eyes follow the svelte line of her hips. 'You are different,' he continued. 'Your voluptuous beauty is exactly right for the Goddess of Love.'

She smoothed her dress over her knees and adjusted her tie belt with deliberate informality, knowing that she was drawing attention to the swelling of her breasts. She moved her legs slightly so that the dress material fell in soft disarray into the delta of her femininity.

'And all the time I have to pretend that I'm doing it from imagination and have never seen a woman naked or felt her quiver with desire around my cock.'

She drank deeply from the wine cup, exhilarated by his frank earthiness. The strong liquor was giving her a wonderful hazy feeling. She wiggled her hips a little as if settling her dress and stared at him, wanting so much to be the woman who would give him such delights.

He continued lounging against the wall, beaker in hand.

'Perhaps we should start without Lydia,' she suggested boldly, holding his gaze and wondering how much more encouragement he needed.

He smiled slightly, narrowed his eyes and appeared to be calculating the lines and angles of her curves.

She put the wine down carefully. 'I've never done this before – shall I sit like this?'

She undulated across the room with swinging hips and sank to the couch. The swollen creases between her legs were already aching.

'You will have to take your clothes off. We can't have the Goddess of Love looking as though she has been shopping in the fish market, can we? This is a fantasy painting. She doesn't need real-life fashions. Besides which,' he added with a slight smile, 'I want my pictures to last for ever, and only the naked, unadorned human body has timeless beauty.'

He moved towards her and deftly removed all her clothes. As she watched, he placed them on the wooden chest with the neat movements of a maidservant. He picked up a small dish from the table.

'This is my own invention,' he explained. 'Like most other artists I use egg white to bind the pigments, but for painting the more exotic pictures, I like to add some cream and perhaps some honey. Lie down.'

A subtle lubrication surged deliciously between her legs, but she was conscious of growing anger and chagrin as well as physical frustration: did he really intend to do nothing at all but paint her?

She lay down in blatant invitation, staring at him challengingly.

'I want to see the artist naked. I want to make sure you have painted the men realistically,' she murmured boldly.

He smiled as he scooped up some of the liquid. He drew his creamy fingers over her breasts and down to her stomach, leaving a trail of sweetness. He gently touched the tips of her nipples with his forefingers.

'And I need to know the real woman before I can paint the Goddess in you, don't I?'

31

He bent down and began to lick the white liquid off her skin with long lascivious movements. He flicked his tongue and turned her loins to fire.

She pulled him towards her by his leather belt and undid the heavy buckle. It clattered to the floor and the tunic fell straight, so the pleats no longer concealed his arousal. She pushed her hands under the garment and felt the long, thin stem of his manhood standing proud and erect.

'You are a luscious, delectable temptress. Completely worthy of being painted as Venus. I have never seen a woman who better symbolised the shimmering expectation and the sensual promise of the Goddess of Love.'

He pushed his hips towards her and she raised his tunic over her head. His penis was warm and heavily musked as she closed her eyes and rolled it between her hands, consideringly, comparing it with that of her lover. She felt him move involuntarily as she brought her fingers up to encircle the bulbous glans. She couldn't feel the little sponge her lover had placed inside her, but she knew it was in place. From now on, she vowed, she would never be without it – or another like it – since it would be impossible to tell when opportunities for erotic research would appear.

She grasped the stiff rod and began to rub it, moving her hands one after the other from bottom to top. She circled the tip, each time applying more pressure. His hands were on her head, kneading her long flowing hair under his tunic, massaging her neck and around her temples with the expertise of a masseur.

'Lie back,' he said.

He took the bowl and poured some of the liquid over her stomach. He watched it flow slowly down her curves to fall each side of her legs like two rivers flowing to the sea. Picking up a thick paintbrush he began to stroke the liquid over her body.

'We need some more,' he pointed out, his breath coming faster. She could hardly wait for his touch.

He put the bowl close to her and poured the liquid

over the tiny pearl of her clitoris. Taking hold of one of her ankles, he pulled her leg to one side so that her foliate secrets were displayed and she could feel the oils of her arousal exposed to the air. With his tongue between his teeth, he brushed her most intimate folds with long, careful movements and she felt another surge of heat. The half-hidden lips of her womanhood were swelling by the moment, as she anticipated his touch. He moved his gaze downwards as the cream slowly made its cooling path to the crevice between her legs.

'I don't often have the opportunity to paint this sort of thing because the women become upset and the men are so aroused they don't get any work done,' he observed, watching the liquid closely. 'But it would make a wonderfully powerful image – the white cream set against the dark petals between your legs. A few men would pay highly.'

'Do you often have such commissions?' she asked, writhing towards him, desperate for the feel of his tongue on her heated clitoris. She could imagine him licking up and down her silky folds. Why else had he covered her with the cream if he did not want to suck it up? She felt she could die if he did not give her that relief now. The memory of another man's mouth over her quivering labia was searing into her soul.

'Occasionally a libidinous recluse will ask for a painting – on a board, not a wall of course.'

He sat on the couch and continued to brush the liquid as it slowly streamed downwards, as though her body were a painting. She could feel it in the crack between her bottom, and opened her legs more fully to let it in, shamelessly inviting him to enter her with his body, not simply his ardent gaze.

'I do occasionally accept that sort of commission,' he went on. 'I like doing the paintings, but the men sometimes get jealous when they think of me with the models. The kind of man who wants to buy titillating art likes to feel that the woman in the painting belongs to him alone.

He will look at her in the privacy of his library or bedroom.'

She became increasingly impatient with him as he played with her body, lost in his own reveries. At last, he grunted, put down the brush and gently encircled her wildly pulsating clitoris with his fingers. She pushed towards him, feeling the relief at last, but wanting so much more.

He moved his hand faster, his finger moving from side to side before plunging between her flushed, labial creases and into the hidden depths of her desire. She clamped her thighs around his hand, relishing the penetration, but still craving to be pleasured by more than his fingers. She was very disappointed that he wasn't going to taste her, but she consoled herself with the fact that his cock was nice and hard and she knew that it could give her relief as well as pleasure.

He drew his fingers in and out, faster and faster in the cream and she bent her body towards him with her eyes closed.

She wriggled and turned under his hand but wherever she moved her hips, his hand followed. He kept up the tortuous stimulation of her senses however much she tried to dislodge him and force him to enter her with his prick.

'Faster, faster. Harder,' she nearly screamed at him, beating her hands on the bed in a frenzy.

She gave a low guttural cry as her climax came, and he nodded, studying her face closely.

'That was good for you, wasn't it, my lovely artist's model?'

He picked up the brush again, dipped it into the cream that had collected on her stomach and lightly skimmed her nipples.

'You haven't had your pleasure yet.' She was panting heavily, trying to regain control. 'This time I want to be on top.'

He peeled off his clothes and lay down on his back

next to her with his penis ram-rod hard. She liked his slim physique.

'Straddle me. Once my prick is inside you, I can give you what you want. Then perhaps I can have some peace in which to paint.'

'There is no need to make it sound as though you are only pleasuring me in order to be able to get on with your work,' she complained as she crawled over his hips.

He pulled her into position with her knees bent towards him.

He was not as ardent as she wanted, but her need was too great to let him off the hook now. They were naked, he was erect and they were alone. This was too good an opportunity to miss. She pushed herself on to the hard member. It felt very good.

She moved her hips from side to side before rotating them. Her body desperately needed to be pounded and massaged by a strong, erect cock.

She ground her hips towards him and rocked rhythmically, bringing herself to a near-peak and willing him to touch her clit and give her the perfect relief. He lay there with his eyes closed, groaning.

There was a slow clapping from the doorway.

They both looked up and Petro smiled.

'Greetings, Lydia. Lovely to see you! Come on in!'

'How long have you been there?' demanded Marcella, her cheeks rosy. She hadn't expected her friend to see her like that. She threw her long hair back out of her face and sat up straight: the movement reminded her that he was still inside her, though his erection had partially subsided. She was bathed in a light glow of sweat. Until that moment, she had no idea that she had been working so hard.

Lydia came into the room and shut the door behind her.

'Don't get up, Marcella,' she said softly. 'You two haven't finished with each other and I don't like to interrupt you. I can see that you did not exaggerate yesterday, when you said you had shared physical delights with a man.'

As Marcella and Petro watched, she slowly took off her clothes. She had a slight figure that Marcella knew well from the women's baths. In the studio, under the diffused sun from the small window, her breasts looked bigger than usual and Marcella realised she had deliberately oiled them.

She stepped elegantly away from her dress and moved towards them.

'You look exactly like a water nymph,' said Petro, his eyes smiling. 'I was quite right to pick you for the nereid. One day, I would like to paint you with Neptune.'

Marcella could feel his penis hardening inside her. It was such an exquisite feeling that she moaned with delight. His rod felt as though it were alive, pulsating without rhythm this time, as he watched Lydia move towards him. Marcella knew that his senses and lusts were aroused at the sight of her friend because he was radiating a further musk.

'It is your turn, Lydia,' she said. She was loathe to leave him, and was by now yearning for the delights his body could give her. At the same time, she did not want to leave her friend out in the cold.

'I know you don't mean that. I am very inexperienced. If you don't mind, I would prefer to watch quietly this time,' replied Lydia.

'Come closer,' said Petro. 'We can all have a good time.'

He put his hand to Lydia's mons and palmed her. Marcella felt his penis give a jolt of excitement inside her. She responded with an involuntary tightening of her muscles, because she knew exactly how his touch would feel to the inexperienced Lydia.

'You are ready for a man,' he observed. 'It would be a shame for you to watch and not join in. And after this I shall be tired for a few hours and unable to pleasure you as well. Come closer and let me taste your breasts.'

The girl blushed deeply, but she squirmed against his

hand and pushed herself forwards, standing very close so he could put one hand around her little bottom and the other to her mound. Her rounded breasts swung down towards him and she leant over him so he was able to take one tight little nub into his mouth and suckle.

Marcella could contain herself no longer: she began to move up and down on his penis, steadying herself with her hands on his torso. She watched his slender fingers manipulating her friend's clit, moving round and round, slowly at first and then faster when the glistening drops began to appear. He tightened his grasp on Lydia's bottom, running his fingers into the crack. He pushed two long fingers inside her.

Lydia moaned and began to push herself against his hands, jutting her hips forward, throwing her body back so he was no longer suckling at her but simply watching her breasts as they bounced and wobbled in time to her own rhythms.

Marcella could feel his manhood throbbing inside her as he thrust upwards. She bore down on him hard, grinding her hips towards him and savouring the feel of him, deep inside her.

'Come closer,' he said hoarsely and pulled Lydia so her mound of love was near his face. He pulled her bottom towards him and pinched the cheeks in his grasp. His body was twisted sideways and Marcella had to hold tight to keep up her rhythm.

'I love the smell of you, you delicious creature! Do you taste as good?' he asked and thrust his tongue to Lydia's clit. He moved it down to her petal-like folds and thrust it deep inside her, before sliding it up to her clit once more. Marcella could hear Lydia breathing faster and faster and giving little cries of ecstasy. The couple's ardour fuelled her own desires, despite her anger at being ignored.

She watched as Petro tongued Lydia with fast flickering movements and pushed his fingers into her with a strong, pounding insistence till the girl was shrieking with pleasure. Her breasts were bouncing as she bucked towards him and he sucked greedily at her love juices.

Marcella climaxed first, almost willing herself to end the episode, determined that she would not be done out of her satisfaction simply because these two were too impolite to consider her feelings. Almost immediately Petro exploded inside her and Lydia gave one last, gasping shriek and collapsed on his chest.

'Where did you learn to do that?' Lydia murmured, looking at Petro. They seemed to be oblivious of Marcella's presence and her anger grew. She had given him a magnificent performance, riding him as though he had been a prize stallion, matching her movements to his and squeezing his stem with her own tight muscles. She had endured an hour of his ineffectual talk and allowed her body to be covered in honey and cream as he studied shades and lines. The least he could do was to acknowledge her presence instead of staring into Lydia's eyes. The girl had done nothing at all except let him do all the work. Marcella felt used.

She remembered the touch of the man in the inn.

She had climaxed twice in the past hour, but it was not nearly enough. She needed a man who could match her, and whose interest in the erotic act was as a pleasure, not as a route to painting better pictures. She required a man who would want her and not be turned on solely by watching another woman's naked body.

The ache for the man in the tavern grew as she rolled off Petro's now pathetically limp prick and began to dress. There was now nothing to look foward to except the party where at the very least, the steward was likely to increase her knowledge of carnal matters.

Chapter Four

Women in brilliantly-coloured dresses walked past, as if floating on the hot, scented air. Their breasts trembled under diaphanous materials which showed the buds of their nipples, already firm from anticipating the evening's delights. Their breath was softly scented with cinnamon fresheners.

'Even the plain girls look lovely tonight.'

Marcella and Lydia paused for a moment to watch the guests arrive.

'Look at that gold-embroidered material!' The metal thread caught the subtle light from terracotta lamps that were set high in wall-niches.

'They can afford the finest oriental silks,' replied Lydia tersely. 'For Juno's sake, Marcella, stop acting as though you've never been to a rich party before.'

'I haven't,' said Marcella simply. 'I had no idea that you worked for people like this. From the way you talk, I assumed they were stodgy and dull.'

'You try working for them for a couple of weeks and you'll soon stop admiring their selfishness and start worrying about how much your feet and back hurt,' replied Lydia brusquely.

A middle-aged woman glided past, her dress swirling as if in wanton caress of her svelte, beautifully cared-for body. The material caught on the curves of her buttocks as she moved with limpid grace. Her fine bone structure was perfectly enhanced with powder and khol. Delicately suspended gold ear-pendants swung against her neck, guiding the eye downwards to the necklace which nestled between her full breasts.

Lydia pushed her hair out of her eyes with the back of her hand and balanced a silver platter on one knee as she talked. 'This promises to be the party of the year in Pompeii, Marcella, but it is all show. It is fantasy for them. They like to pretend that they are almost as perfect as the gods and goddesses.'

'Don't be so bitter,' chided Marcella, 'Just think how we would look if we had access to such riches.'

'I am not resentful. I'm a realist and thankful I was freeborn. You will get twisted up and cynical in the end if you don't get things straight. The tavern is reality. We have no place in their world except as servants.'

Lydia readjusted the heavy plate to rest against her hip, causing some of the honeyed sweetmeats to wobble dangerously.

'Give up all thoughts of competing, Marcella. Your aunt and uncle permitted you to come tonight only because they knew this household has a reputation for being strict with its servants and slaves. The guests may get up to all sorts, but we have to work. And stop dawdling. The steward will be around this way soon and you can't afford to be caught slacking.'

She walked away, looking self-righteous.

A woman's silk shawl brushed against Marcella as she drifted past, her expression dreamy.

'Wonderful, isn't it, darling?' she said to her companion in low, husky tones. 'Haven't they been clever to capture such a talented artist? I hear the drawings and murals are perfectly divine. I can't wait.'

She put an arm around her companion and kissed her on the neck. The other woman pulled her close and returned the kiss, on her lips.

Marcella stared.

40

'I can't wait either, but to be honest,' the companion replied, 'I am more interested in the dicks than the decor. And since when have you been an art lover?'

'Since I discovered that art doesn't always mean pictures of columns or outdoor scenes painted for no other purpose than to make stuffy little rooms seem bigger.'

The two women laughed. One paused to readjust her slipper: the delicate, gold-decorated leather showed off her beautifully manicured toe nails. Marcella saw, with surprise, an unmistakable bulge between her legs. She glanced at her companion and realised that they were both men, heavily made up and expertly coiffeured.

Marcella continued to watch avidly. She could hear the minstrels and players warming up: swift bursts of melody stopped abruptly and then restarted, only to be succeeded by snatches of other tempos and tunes.

'Go to the front door and take their cloaks. Put them in the doorman's lobby,' the steward hissed at her as she stood listening to the pipers and tambourine players. 'You are not here to dream.'

The stern look on his face did not seem genuine and Marcella glanced across the hall where a number of servants were openly trying to listen to their exchange. His voice was seductively low and she felt her breasts heave with the excitement of knowing her power. He was breathing slightly too fast and his eyes flickered over her body as though she wore nothing at all. After the offhand way Petro had treated her, she was more than ready to respond to the advances of any man who showed a red-blooded interest in her.

'I was catching my breath for a moment,' she whispered back and moved so her breasts touched his arm, as if by accident. He patted her bottom with gentle assertiveness and pushed a finger between the cheeks, pushing downwards to the sensitive, secret places. She shivered with anticipation. He squeezed her left buttock slightly and she flexed her internal muscles, wondering what it would be like to have his prick inside her. Her nipples began to harden and she turned towards him, her lips slightly apart. She wondered where he would make a serious move on her – and when.

He moved away without meeting her eye, but she caught a slight gleam of satisfaction in his expression.

She walked along the corridor in a daze. The scents of expensive toiletries were wafted in the heat, as further beautiful women sauntered past her, laughing with equally well-groomed men.

When most of the guests had arrived, the steward ordered her to take food into the dining room. He stroked her breast with a movement that to anyone watching would have looked like chance. Her loins leapt at the touch and she could feel herself dampening in readiness for a man.

'Don't touch the paintwork – it isn't completely dry yet,' he murmured as they passed each other between the dining couches.

'If I am not allowed to reach across the guests or interrupt their conversations, I will have to brush against the walls,' she whispered boldly. 'You imposed the rules, not me.'

'Wait till I get you to yourself, later this evening. We'll see who breaks rules I make for the permanent staff.'

He groped between her legs, this time barely concealing his actions.

'More wine over here.'

Reluctantly, Marcella turned to the man who had called.

He looked at her nipples through the soft cloth of her dress, his eyes half-glazed. Leaning towards her, he put a hand on her left breast as though he were a greengrocer in the market feeling the ripeness of melons.

She stiffened and glanced back to the steward, as she filled the goblet.

'Darling!' cried a woman with a particularly ornate hair-do.

The man turned and instantly tipped the woman's full

breasts out of her neckline. He tongued them wetly before straightening up.

She screamed with laughter and slapped his hand playfully. 'Naughty, naughty. What will you think of licking next?'

'Your crotch, my sweet. I am hungry. Let me taste your ambrosia. Now.'

Marcella gasped.

His free hand moved straight to the woman's deltoid mound.

'Sweetness, you think only of your own needs, she said petulantly. 'I too, am almost faint with thirst. What do you suggest we do about this?'

He dipped a finger in his wine and slid it into her mouth. She sucked, tilting her head back, her eyes openly inviting his advances.

She put her long, elegant fingers to his hand and stroked it up and down, suggestively. Bending slightly, she ran her other hand under his white tunic. He smiled.

The steward walked past and gently touched Marcella's buttock. 'You did well. Keep up the good work.' He slowly ran his tongue along his upper lip, holding her gaze.

A mild quake shook the ground as she walked away. A strong libidinous thrill started in her feet, rippled upwards and forced itself between her legs till she felt she would erupt from the tension of suppressed energy.

Some of the other guests noticed the tremor and laughed.

'Oh Minerva and Juno! What a bore this is becoming,' drawled a woman with gold-impressed ivory combs in her glossy hair. She snapped her fingers. Her glossy nails made her hands appear extra long and elegant.

'Over here,' she said to Marcella.

She wore several rings: two with huge round, emeralds and another with a small sapphire cabochon which shone dully under the lights.

Obediently, Marcella moved towards her and placed in her hand an opaque glass beaker, subtly shot with green lights. The woman ignored her and smiled up at a tall, thickset man who flicked a glance at the row of tiny ringlets that framed her face.

'I see you have been to Rome and told your maid to copy the Court style.'

He sounded bored and she simpered up at him, all fluttering eyelashes and quivering bosom.

'I always did like tight little curls. This female habit of shaving the crotch is pointless. In the provinces lots of women don't shave at all.'

The woman flushed slightly and replied, 'As it happens, Caballius, I haven't been shaved for several weeks now.'

She threw him an arch look. 'Perhaps you would like to give me your opinion?'

'You may find you get more than merely my opinion,' he said, after a short pause and she giggled uncertainly.

The dining room was emptying fast as guests began to make their way to a large ante-room where the musicians were performing.

A girl with ample curves lolled on a couch, her breasts falling out of the low neckline. A man sat on the floor beside her, drinking from a bronze flagon and holding its neck rather than its handle. A number of discarded beakers and drinking cups lay on the floor beside him. As the wine spilled down his chin, the girl laughed and leant towards him. He caught one of her ripe nipples between his lips and she shrieked with laughter.

Encouraged, he fumbled for the second breast and tweaked it expertly. The girl's upper body shook so her breasts wobbled. She pouted as he fell back.

He selected a piece of exotic fruit from the huge silver platter nearby and began to cut it into a phallic shape. Marcella stared in fascination as he rapidly produced a magnificent dildo. He pulled at the girl's skirt and revealed her pink, glistening folds below her shaven pubic mound.

He sucked her nipples noisily and then placed the phallic shaped fruit between her legs. She moaned as the juice ran down each side of her crotch into the deep crack of her bottom. He wiped it along her inner thighs with his fingers and then licked the trail.

She pushed her hips towards him and he took the juicy phallus in his mouth, holding her thighs in position. Still holding it in his mouth, he pushed the fruit into her body and she writhed with enjoyment. She began to moan in time to his rhythms and climaxed quickly. The man pulled the fruit out of her and began to eat it as the girl lay back, looking exhausted.

Marcella drifted back to the man called Caballius. With another man and a woman he was scrutinising the wall painting of a threesome that had intrigued Lydia.

'That fellow with the long dick isn't going to get anywhere like that, is he Caballius?' the woman said thoughtfully.

Marcella was astounded by her matter-of-fact manner – she sounded as cool as if she were discussing the latest prices of bread.

'Not much penetration,' he agreed.

Marcella felt slightly scared by the air of suppressed energy he exuded, as though the proceedings were trying his temper to the limit and he would soon explode.

'Trios of that nature are always tricky, I grant you that,' the other man replied, slurring his words badly.

'She'd have to bend over far more. See – at least this far.'

The woman bent over, her bottom in the air, her dress lifting at the back to reveal a pair of shapely calves.

'A demonstration,' suggested Caballius in a bored drawl to the drunk. 'Show us all how it is done.'

The man lunged, fumbling with his toga, but the thick woollen material became caught up on the couch and he fell heavily to the floor.

'Too tipsy to manage! You lover of the Bacchanalia!' the woman cried, unable to conceal her contempt.

'It is easy to see that you worship Bacchus more than Venus,' said Caballius.

'I make no secret of the fact that I am a Bacchant at heart. There are no thrills so great as those you get from the grape.' The intoxicated man straightened himself out on the floor and closed his eyes. 'Vines must be properly grown on good soil, watched over by Silenus. Then the grapes must be left to ripen in the sun, by the grace of Apollo. The household gods and Hestia take over for a while, and finally Bacchus has to take over responsibility. Wine requires many deities. Lust is looked over only by two – Venus, and her son.'

His speech was still distinct, though it was obvious to Marcella that he was seriously drunk.

'We would be ungrateful if we did not do justice to the elixir. I love the sheer sensuality of the heavenly droplets and the bitter-sweet taste as they caress the tongue,' he said to nobody in particular. 'Even now, I can feel the heat as the liquid reaches into every muscle of my body. It is incomparable! It is the only way to live. The only real pleasure. Everything else is a poor and feeble substitute. With enough wine, all senses are heightened and pleasures become ten-fold.'

He grabbed the woman's leg and she burst out laughing. Her voice was high-pitched as the liquor began to affect her too, but Marcella detected a definite tone of some extra frustration or need that she did not recognise.

'Come my sweet, come down here and suck me.'

'No.' Her tone ridiculed him, though he appeared not to notice. 'I know you prefer boys but you might do me the courtesy of having a go at shafting me from the back! It can't be difficult.'

'I know it isn't difficult. I do prefer boys, so I do know,' he said apologetically, his eyes still closed. 'Get the serving girl to suck you up,' he added. 'That works for anybody. One tongue is as good as another.'

Marcella stiffened in horror.

He grabbed her legs so she fell awkwardly across his prone body, the flagon of wine in her hand tipping dangerously.

She struggled into a sitting position and found he had

twisted round so he was kneeling in front of her. He held his tunic high to reveal his limp penis.

'Fix me up first.'

Marcella glanced around the room. Apart from the couple on the couch, there was nobody else around. In the distance she could hear that the musicians were well into a fast little number that involved the cymbal player stamping loudly and often. The pipes shrilled above the hubbub of the revellers.

'I know something you will like,' she said slyly, with a note of promise in her voice. She was aware that the other two were watching intently.

She took his long, thin cock in her hand and dipped it in the wine that was left in the flagon, swirling the liquid round so it gently hit the bronze sides. As she brought out his stem, she blew on it and then dipped it in again. She had one eye on the doorway, fearing the steward's return.

She took the penis between her fingers and rolled it gently. It began to harden almost imperceptibly at first, but increasingly as she blew through pouting lips.

'A first! A first! That's never happened with a woman before, has it?' observed the woman thoughtfully.

Marcella felt a surge of excitement and pride.

'I am glad, lord, that I have been able to ease your physical discomfort,' she said, in as casual a manner as possible.

She didn't like him because he smelt too much of pomade and was drunk. Her experience in the tavern suggested that he was wrong about drink heightening the senses: it seemed to render most men totally incapable of any action. He was no connoisseur at all, she thought contemptuously. She had not sunk so low that she had to take everything that was offered, no matter how flattering. She had to escape without losing her dignity.

She winked lasciviously and swung her hips as she rose.

'Come, lady,' she said invitingly. 'He is ready for you now.'

The woman glanced from her to the hardening stem, her face flushed. Involuntarily, she licked her lips as she sat on the floor next to the drunken man and took his stem gently between her teeth, flicking it expertly with her tongue in a way that fascinated Marcella. The drunkard groaned his appreciation.

A male slave walked past, collecting discarded tableware. The frenzied woman grabbed him and pointed to her crotch. He fell to his knees in front of her and lifted her skirts to smooth her pubic mound with his palms. She moved so her legs were parted and her swollen labia and vulva gleamed under the dim lights. The slave took a long look before bending his head to nuzzle. He spread out his hands over her lower stomach so that his thumbs massaged a fraction above her clitoris.

'Get over here,' cried the drunk rather hoarsely and Marcella jumped. To her relief, he was not talking to her. Still tonguing the woman's crotch, the servant moved his groin so that the drunk could take his already-erect cock in his mouth. The slave thrust towards the guest so he was deeply embedded. The drunk brought his hands to the prick and began to suck, his eyes closed in enjoyment.

The three lay in a triangle, lapping and nuzzling at each other as Caballius watched closely with a dark intense expression on his face that unsettled Marcella. She walked hurriedly out of the dining room door.

Two magnificent men were leaning against the columns. The taller was black skinned, with the thin, lithe figure of an athlete, though he was not so muscular as a gladiator. There was something civilised and feline about him – a natural grace that came from long hours spent in sporting pursuits. He had the air of one who exercised with the express intention of making his body attractive to the eye and who regarded his physical strength merely as a by-product. The lines of his body were smooth and elegant.

48

His companion was a complete contrast – an almost white-haired blond with medium blue eyes that reminded her of sunny days in early summer. He was thicker set, but still without the physique – or the scars – of a fighter or a charioteer. He had strong chest muscles and well-developed thighs.

She was able to savour their beauty in detail because they wore nothing at all except dark leather thongs, a few heavy gold rings and light cloaks which were flung carelessly over their shoulders.

They stood aloof from the party. A couple of semi-clad women were hurrying past towards the music but the two men remained unaroused.

She had a sudden urge to approach them both and put her hands in their thongs. She wanted to watch their cocks spring out so she could manipulate them till they stood erect and proud.

She wanted to rub each prick on her nipples until she felt the hot spend dribble over her breasts. She wanted to rub herself with their juices and bring herself to a climax by massaging her clit and watching them put their hands to their own stems.

Her fantasies were cut short by a low giggle. The murmur of a man's voice drew her nearer to the garden. Water gently trickled from a pitcher held by an antique Greek statue of Eros and she was shielded from view by the trailing plants which twined around the trellis and columns. A faint spray of water moistened her face as she strained to hear the words.

'Julia, my dearest woman, I would stay if I were able. In any case, this isn't my kind of party. I prefer something more intimate, you know that.'

Marcella felt she had been struck by Jupiter's thunder-bolts – the distinguished-sounding voice belonged to the man from the tavern, her lover.

She edged round the trellis to get a better view. The woman with him was stately and elegant. Her coiffeur was perfect despite the lateness of the hour. Her superb figure was draped in a dark blue dress of high quality

Indian cotton, that was simply held at the waist with a cord. Her well-shaped arms were enhanced by a few plain gold bangles around her wrists and one on her upper right arm.

She wore the iron band of a married woman on the third finger of her left hand and even in the semi-darkness, Marcella could see that she was exquisite.

'My darling, Gaius, you know I find it so hard to be without you.' Her voice was low and beautifully modu-lated. 'These interludes with you are all that keeps me from insanity.'

His reply came in the form of a low chuckle that surprised Marcella because she had never heard him in light-hearted mood .

'These interludes, as you call our relationship, are a delight to us both, but all the more charming because they are unexpected. You would soon tire of me if we were able to meet on a regular basis like a couple of illicit lovers at the Imperial Court.'

She laughed lightly in return and laid a hand on his arm. Her ring glinted dully in the reflected light from the water.

'I didn't expect you to be at this vulgar social event,' she said. 'I must be the only woman who isn't dishev-elled or nearly naked! I wondered why my husband was so keen for us to come but I never guessed that you two were using it as a front for a business meeting.'

'It was arranged at the last moment. I could hardly send you a message openly, could I Julia?'

'How could you be so cruel?' Julia continued. 'Why didn't you let me know you would be here? If I hadn't come out of the music room when I did, you would have disappeared without even a greeting, wouldn't you?'

In reply he put his lips to hers, his hands lightly touching her cheeks. Marcella was consumed with an intense anger and passion that left her shaking.

He put an arm around Julia's shoulders and said, very clearly, 'Tonight, you shall have as many physical delights as you want, if you will be patient. I promise.'

Totally distraught, Marcella stumbled back towards the dining room where she was intercepted by Lydia.

'You look upset.'

'I feel betrayed and humiliated.'

'Some man has insulted you?'

'I have seen the man from the tavern. I should have known he had other interests,' she said.

'Tell me everything!' Lydia demanded, pulling Marcella out of sight, behind a pillar.

'The ease with which he brought me to a climax on my first time should have told me he was a master of his art. Of course he has other women! Of course, his mistress is a patrician, able to converse in an educated fashion! Of course, she is beautiful!'

'I did try to warn you that the guests are out of our league,' said Lydia softly. 'It is pointless pining for such a man. He will have a life of his own and probably won't even remember you.'

'You are right, of course,' Marcella said reluctantly. 'I have to move on and form new relationships. I will always be grateful to him, but I mustn't let the joy of his touch spoil me for other experiences.'

Feeling slightly more emotionally secure Marcella left Lydia and was almost immediately swung round by the shoulders and pulled back into the cool of the courtyard garden.

'Come on, you little tease – you got them all excited in there but you left me out.'

She saw that her abductor was the man called Caballius. She wanted to strike him down and hurt him because he wasn't the one she craved. He was heavily built and thick around the jawline and his hand hurt her arm as he grasped her firmly.

'Come on. Suck me like you did that drunk in there.'

'I didn't suck anybody,' she protested angrily.

'So suck me now,' he whispered loudly. 'They've become boring. I lost interest when the stupid woman couldn't climax even with two of them working away at her. The two men have ejaculated all over the place –

they had no staying power at all. On the other hand, my dick is already hard and you've got tits like ripe fruit. I'd like to come between them. And a lot of other places, too.'

Despite his coarseness, she was suddenly consumed with interest.

What did his prick feel like, taste like? Just how big would it get? How hard would she have to suck?

She looked at him with mute curiosity and growing excitement as the tempo of the music increased and clapping began, to encourage the dancers. Her body was already ripe for sensual encounters and under his gaze, it leapt into a new dimension of excitement and anticipation.

Chapter Five

'*T*hat sounds delicious,' she whispered as Caballius pulled her into the deserted fountain area. Their footsteps echoed on the gleaming mosaic floor and the painted and burnished walls of the corridor.

'This will do,' he muttered as they reached the pool. 'I can't hang around while we find a bedroom. Besides, most of them will already be taken and I certainly can't be bothered with a foursome just now.'

She gasped.

The tempo of the music in the background increased and people began to clap louder. She felt her heart beat faster in response to the rhythms and to the situation she was in. After years of enforced celibacy, it seemed to her that she had broken through the barrier of forbidden pleasures and every man she met was apparently willing to satisfy her libidinous needs at a moment's notice.

'The dancers are warming up,' she said, panting slightly from the exertion, her breasts rubbing against his toga. He let her go and impatiently began to discard it in a heap on the floor.

'I've seen scantily dressed women gyrating to a bunch of street musicians before. I've seen more cunts displayed in public than you've had spiced sauce,' he muttered, stepping away from the material and pulling her towards the water.

'I haven't,' she pointed out. 'It must be a real spectacle since there is no one left in this part of the house. Listen!'

'So some small-time actor has just taken the stage,' he said dismissively.

A howl of approval rose from the audience, followed by cheers and shouted comments that could not be heard clearly.

'It promises to be as good as the theatre,' she said wistfully. 'I never have the opportunity to watch private shows. I hear they can be very lewd and explicit.'

'You seem to be regretting coming here with me, now that there is a live show to watch. This will be much more explicit and lewd, let me assure you!'

Caballius pulled her roughly towards him. She felt the tingle of illicit excitement well up inside her breasts and between her legs. She dare not be caught or she would be turned out of the house and paid not even a paltry copper coin.

'We can watch the dancers when we have finished here,' she said, hopefully. She suppressed her wishes and concentrated on the immediate future: what would it be like to suck him off? How long would it take? Would it be messy?

He picked her up bodily and almost threw her into the pool. The cool water reached past her knees and she gasped with the shock. He climbed over the side to join her, his movements cumbersome from the drink. His tunic caught on an ugly concrete repair where seventeen years ago the earthquake had cracked the low wall.

'I don't know your name,' he said, slightly slurring his words. He adopted an exaggeratedly reasonable tone that she found strangely threatening. 'I like to know who I am fucking, but first I want to be sucked.'

He pushed her down into the water by the shoulders until she was kneeling and the water lapped around her waist. She tried to struggle free, but he lifted his tunic and displayed his stem near her face.

Despite her growing revulsion for his personality, the sight of his penis attracted her. It was thick and powerful, listing slightly to the left, with a vast knob that looked full to bursting. Curiously, she took it in her hand and felt the power in her palm. The faint, bewitching odour of musk wafted to her nostrils and she moved nearer.

Delicately, she held the pulsating rod and moved her head towards it. Her hair fell from the combs that held it in place and he gripped her shoulders in anticipation.

She put her tongue tentatively to the tip and felt it surge in response. His grip increased.

'More. Really suck me, deep, deep down.'

'Will you do the same for me?'

'I'll suck you like an orange ripe from the tree,' he replied hoarsely.

She plunged her mouth down on him. It tasted hot. She had expected some potent tang – perhaps salty, or fishy maybe, from the descriptions she had been given – but the taste was nowhere near so pungent. She could smell frankincense amongst the oils the slaves had rubbed into him earlier in the day. The rare, exotic scent pulsed towards her from his pubic hairs where it was trapped.

She moved her tongue and lips around him and heard him groan. The water lapped under her breasts and she could feel her labial folds blossoming at the thought of this powerful stem inside her.

She held her hands around him and nuzzled. Slowly and lingeringly she took her mouth away and worked him with her hands, emulating the feel of her own internal muscles on her lover.

Gaius. The memory of him was sweet, and yet so bitter.

She fought back negative emotions and mouthed Caballius again, pulling at him with renewed vigour. She concentrated on the man who was in front of her and put everything else out of her mind. The gods had been good, sending her this opportunity and she intended to make the most of it.

For long moments she knelt in the water savouring the new sensations as his hands worked at her scalp.

Very suddenly, he pulled away.

'That is enough. I want to take you properly now.'

'But you haven't climaxed.' She felt cheated. 'How will I know what you taste like?'

He hauled her to her feet so that her dress clung suggestively to her lower limbs.

'I'm tired of watching the top of your head. There are other places I like to see when I ejaculate.'

'You obviously have great self-control,' she said in confusion.

'I am well known for it,' he replied tersely, turning her round.

'What are you doing?'

'Getting you ready for a decent fuck. The only real pleasures are to be gained from the back. Are you ready?'

'Yes,' she murmured as her excitement grew. She bent over, exposing her wet bottom to him under the dress.

He exclaimed in annoyance at the folds of material that impeded his progress. Finally he held her in position and she supported herself with her hands on her knees. With a practised thrust he was inside her and she gasped at the suddenness and at his size.

He began to push rhythmically and her senses were kindled. She throbbed with the need for fulfilment and her breasts, pendulous over the water, were aching for a male touch. He held her hips with a tight grip and continued to push so hard that her body rocked at the force.

She pushed backwards and urged herself to pleasure by squeezing with her inner muscles. Her wet dress was pulling on her clitoris, but the pressure wasn't sufficient. She wanted him to put his fingers on it as he pushed but he seemed to be lost in the rhythm, so she surrendered to it. He rocked her body with a well-rehearsed economy of movement, his solid male power working at her inner muscles, his body pressing against her bottom. He changed position slightly, moving under her so she could feel his hardness deeper inside her. She bent over a little more and he grunted and increased the strength of his efforts. It felt good. She felt as though she were in the sea with the waves of movement lapping over her with ever-increasing power.

She began to moan. After each thrust inwards, he pulled out, taking his rod to the very edge of her body. She was taunted by his power as he withheld her immediate pleasure and slid in and out effortlessly. Her vulva became increasingly hot and swollen with desire.

As abruptly as he had started, he pulled away. She staggered to the side of the pool and leant against it weakly for a moment, before beginning to straighten her dripping skirt.

'You bastard,' she said under her breath. 'You deliberately stimulated me and then let me down.'

'Stay where you are.'

His voice was harsh and she looked round in anger, but also with a little apprehension. He was still completely erect.

He lifted her dress again and bent her body over. 'I haven't finished,' he said sharply.

Relief flooded over her.

'You simply like to tease a woman, withdrawing and entering until she is consumed with need, don't you?' she asked. 'Do you want me to beg?'

She felt the tip of his stem nudging against her buttocks, and he opened the cheeks with his hands and thumbed her anus firmly. The tip of his penis nudged further down, pushed towards the focus of her inner desire, and was partly enveloped by her silky vulval folds.

'Yes, that is what you want,' she sighed, glad that she had found the key to his personality and therefore to her own pleasures. 'Yes please – now. I beg you.'

The sensation was so soft that it almost tickled and

she pushed back with her hips, desperate for his penis inside her – deep inside once more.

He thrust hard and she cried out with the joy of relief, as she settled back into the rocking rhythm.

Without warning, he withdrew again and she felt the spurt of his semen over her backside.

'You can beg all you like,' he said harshly. 'So long as you learn that that I am not here simply to attend to your whims.'

She distinguished a definite note of cruelty in his low laugh. 'Neither you nor any other woman has any right to gain pleasure from the acts of lust.'

'You scum! I hate your guts, you pathetic bastard.' She bit back a long tirade of abuse as a sudden fear welled up. She tried to straighten up but he held her down with cruel, hurting hands.

'I want to watch. I want to see the seed run down into your crack. You are a little whore, nothing more, and you shall not have the pleasure of getting your satisfactions from me. Your function is to please me. And that you shall continue to do until I am tired of you.'

She tried to move away, but he held her thighs firmly under spread hands and massaged the semen into her bottom, pushing a finger into the tight orifice. She clenched herself in disgust.

Anger and humiliation coursed through her as she felt the liquid flow into her most intimate creases. Her hatred and contempt for him burned with a fierce intensity. She stood still, furious that she had allowed herself to be manoeuvred into the situation.

'Now we know one another, we can do this often. You will come to my house tomorrow and we can indulge ourselves again.' He pushed her away.

She straightened up and pulled her dress down, sinking deeply into the water so the spend would be washed away.

'I wouldn't cooperate with you if you were the last man on earth, Caballius,' she cried, keeping her voice down, acutely aware of their surroundings. 'I loathe the sight and smell of you – and only a few moments ago, I was desperate with desire for you!'

In the background, the music was still wild and the spectators indulging in a fast hand-clapping that suggested that the dancing was nearing a climax.

The ache, deep inside her womanhood, was subsiding and being replaced with anger.

'You will come and see me at my house – or you will lose your job and the respect of everyone you know,' he said nastily. His voice had a strident tone and he was beginning to slur badly from the excess of wine.

'You bastard. That is nothing but blackmail. Do you really live your life on such a low level? Have you no pride?'

He shrugged. 'Blackmail, as you so quaintly call it, is the quickest way to winning in this life. I have found it is the only sure way to victory.'

'You piece of scum!'

Her words echoed into the corridors, despite the deadening effect of the fountain water. Shaking with horror, she climbed out of the pool and stepped on to the mosaic floor.

'Tomorrow you will come to visit me, you bitch,' he said coldly.

'I will be there,' she lied firmly as she walked briskly away from him across the stone floor. She wanted nothing more than to get away from him and regain her sense of equilibrium.

Chapter Six

'You look as though you've been in a thunderstorm. What happened?' asked Lydia, looking exhausted as she slumped against the wall with a half-empty bronze jug in her hand.

'Some drunken fool threw me in the fountain.'

'There are fresh dresses folded up behind the lobby door.'

Marcella fought her wish to weep with the agonising mixture of anger and sexual frustration. 'It was humiliating,' she confided. 'I couldn't risk a confrontation because I was afraid he would turn seriously violent.'

'Give thanks to Juno that you were not in a deserted place where he would be free to do what he wanted. Some men can be vicious if there is nobody to hear except their own slaves.'

'It has taught me one thing very clearly,' replied Marcella as she slipped into a dry dress, 'The man I met in the tavern was special. He is worthy of my admiration and desires. That other bastard turned my lust to sheer hatred in a few moments.'

Much more composed, she made her way to the dining room, and paused to watch the last moments of the dance routine. She caught sight of Gaius. He was alone and she could see no sign of the lady Julia. He looked broodingly angry and her heart stood still, hoping that they had quarrelled.

He walked up to her and said, in a tone of complete contempt, 'It seems I was mistaken. You are no connoisseur, after all. What a pathetic sight you were! You should have resembled Venus arising from the waves, but instead you were like a beached fish.'

His scorn was almost physical in its intensity and she recoiled. In her distress at hearing the harsh words from the man she craved most, she blurted out the first angry retort that came into her head.

'You know nothing about it. What were you doing? Eavesdropping?'

As the musicians finished their performance with a flourish of cymbals and pipes, all she could think about was: how much had he seen?

'I thought you were different,' he continued. 'Who was he? I didn't see him clearly. Scum, you said to him, and he called you a bitch. What a charming couple! Why did you agree to meet him?'

'I had to say something to get rid of him. Besides, it is none of your business,' she retorted defiantly. 'I don't have to defend my actions to you or anybody else.'

The dancers were now holding hands to take applause and shouted admiration. The woman was almost naked except for a few diaphanous scarves that were draped over her shoulders. Gaius leant against a pillar looking at Marcella with a hard, calculating expression. She stared back, her own eyes challenging.

The steward looked sharply at them both as he walked past carrying a huge silver dish of savouries. 'Marcella,' he said briskly, 'you are needed to serve food. Immediately.'

As she hurried away, he winked at her.

The fountain courtyard was empty as she paused for a moment to collect her thoughts and look over the place where she had been so humiliated. She bent and scooped up some water to refresh her face.

She rinsed her mouth out and spat into the water, wanting to wash off the memories in the public baths and to sweat out the disgusting odours. She vowed she would spend hours in the hot room, forcing out the last vestiges of Caballius' smell.

The ultimate outrage was that the one man in her life she hungered for most had witnessed her disgrace and now had nothing but contempt for her. She felt a hand on her hip and whirled round in anger, her hand poised to hit and hurt.

'Don't you dare touch me . . .'

Gaius caught hold of her hand gently. 'You are missing the floor show.'

'What floor show? I thought the dancing had finished,' she managed to say.

'There are other shows. This is the time when people's imaginations have been fired and they perform for each other, for free. The paid actors and musicians were just appetisers.'

He put his hand to her shoulder and turned her to face him squarely.

'It seems that you discovered that lust and lechery aren't as simple as they might seem at first.'

Still smarting from the humiliations that Caballius had forced on her, she looked away.

'It hasn't all been drinking ambrosia on the slopes of Olympus with the Immortals,' she said.

He looked at her for a moment. 'I apologise for thinking badly of you, Marcella. You lied to him so beautifully that I was taken in.'

The slight crinkling at the corners of his eyes seemed to imply that he had looked out on many things he did not like seeing and that he would understand how she felt. She desperately tried not to think what he and the lady Julia might have been doing together for the past hour while she had been with Caballius.

He smiled at her. His expression was kind and the heat of his hand on her pelvis burned into her with an impelling intensity.

'You have found that the men at this party haven't been what you hoped?'

'I am not allowed to hope for anything – the steward is very strict,' she replied tightly.

He gave a low chuckle and the intimate sound made her heart turn over.

'The fellow with the convenient problems in the kitchens and a nice line in lewd winks? And I suppose that he hasn't even hinted that he wants to get his cock between your pretty legs and rut till he drops?'

She blushed at the unexpectedly coarse expression, but she guessed that he had deliberately used it to defuse her tension.

'He has suggested that I should be available to him at the end of the evening.'

'Exactly – the man has a cause to plead. I can hardly condemn him for trying. Let us put him out of our minds and concentrate on more interesting things. Tell me your adventures.'

He stroked her cheek and brought his hand under her chin, passing one finger lightly over her full lips.

'The bastard,' she said quietly, as she savoured the sensuality of his touch, 'humiliated me.'

Her anger and hatred were now subsiding and being fast replaced by single-minded desire.

'And Petro was no better,' she added. 'That was like masturbating with the addition of a man inside me. I had to do all the work.'

'Wait a moment. Who, in the name of Hades, is Petro?' He looked amused as well as frankly admiring. 'You have been busy in the past few days. You were a virgin when I met you but you are getting through men faster than I got through women in my novice-hood.'

'I met him after you left me in the tavern. He is very sweet, but he prefers my friend, Lydia. The other man was a thug. Luckily, he was drunk or I might have been in real trouble. I have to be more careful in future.'

'That is true,' he said grimly. 'I am glad you have learnt that lesson. You need to choose carefully, my desirable little friend.'

His hand lay casually on her shoulder, but it was

causing excitement to boil up inside her. She wanted him to move his fingers down to her breast, and bring his mouth to hers. She craved his touch on the mysterious, forbidden places of her body. The fever was on her and she moved slightly under his grip.

'I seem to be fated by the gods to meet you when I am in a tearing hurry. You haven't offended one of them have you? I am already late for an appointment that cannot wait.'

'I understand,' she mumbled, desperate to keep control so she could find out where he lived and make an assignation with him, but fearful that the appointment was with Julia.

She felt she could get through the next few hours and days if she knew for certain that she would feel his hands on her stomach, his mouth on her most intimate places, and his firm manhood inside her, working at her needs once again.

'So, what did he do that was so offensive?'

He brought his hands to her waist and pulled her gently towards him. His mouth was warm and tender on her lips and his tongue tasted like an elixir. He had discarded the heavy woollen toga he had been wearing, and she tried not to think that he might have done so in the privacy of a bedroom, with Julia. Had he taken off his light, white tunic as well? It was totally unmarked and uncreased. Had he lain naked on a cushioned couch in the semi-darkness, helping the lady to lose her air of cool sophistication as they took forbidden pleasures in vigorous, practised copulation?

'Well?'

She looked up and met his eyes a little ashamedly and explained haltingly.

'In that position, a woman has special needs or she will, as you do now, feel very frustrated afterwards,' Gaius reassured her.

She nodded. She had longed for her breasts and her clitoris to be caressed as Caballius had worked on her from behind.

64

Gaius' lips brushed hers, infinitely softly, so she could feel his sweet-smelling breath in her mouth.

'He meant me to be frustrated,' she said with certainty, but the incident was receding into insignificance against the onslaught of need and desire that Gaius produced in her body. She could think of nothing that wasn't his touch. There were no pleasures in her imagination that did not include him.

'Some people get their enjoyment like that.' He stroked her brow and smiled down at her with a mildly affection-ate expression that turned her inside out with desire.

'Turn around,' he murmured. 'I can spare a little time in a good cause. I can't have you spoiled for the next time. You will only go and brood about it and possibly even get bitter.'

The promise of future bliss caressed her troubled mind. She felt as if a halcyon breeze had wafted from Olympus, perhaps stirred up by the passing wings of Eros himself.

He turned her around and lifted her skirt to the waist.

There was a soft, shuffling sound and she looked across the courtyard to see the two magnificent men she had noticed earlier.

Gaius called in muted tones and the men walked towards them. 'The lady needs a little special help.'

She felt herself stiffen with sudden anxiety.

'Don't be afraid,' he murmured. 'They won't hurt you – quite the opposite.'

He kissed her neck gently and she felt him lift his tunic and nudge her with his erect manhood. The fam-iliar way he touched her body quietened her senses. It seemed totally right, even though they were screened from public view only by plants and pillars.

'This is Albinus – he comes from the Danube border-lands. And Numidius was born in Mauritania. They occasionally cooperate in taking my partners to the heights, if the need is great. And I think the need is very great at the moment.'

'Greetings, Lady,' they said, almost in unison.

'Greetings,' she whispered, unable to trust herself to say more, her imagination working double-time as she wondered what sensations she was about to enjoy.

The flaxen-haired stud knelt in front of her and put his hands on her shoulders gently pulling her towards him.

'Let your weight rest on Albinus,' said Gaius. 'His shoulders are softer than a stone column and you will find it less tiring than supporting yourself. What you are about to do will leave you exhausted, I promise. I am not leaving until you have had the last ounce of desire and frustration wrung from you.'

Her anxiety fled as the blond brushed her lips with his, sneaking a taste of her mouth with a swift movement of his tongue. She allowed him to continue to kiss her – a gentle, uninvasive fluttering of tongue on lips. She felt a flood of desire between her legs and the nerve endings on her nipples went wild.

Gaius began to caress her velvety womanhood with one hand, the other cupping her mound from the front. He put a lazy finger inside and then withdrew it so she moaned in pleasure, wanting him to repeat the process. She needed so much more.

Then she felt her dress and under-tunic being gently drawn upwards. Albinus withdrew his lips as Numidius took it over her arms and head leaving her completely naked. She could see the appreciation in their faces as they ran their eyes over her curves, lingering on her breasts and between her legs.

Numidius edged himself under her at an angle. She turned her head to one side and saw the huge bulge under the leather thong. He took one of her breasts in his mouth and lightly caressed the other in a circular movement that seemed to be working in unison with Gaius' intimate caresses.

The waves of pleasure broke over her as the three men fondled her most private areas with the knowing expertise of masters. They worked in complete harmony, their own desires suppressed as she rose and fell in a fever.

Albinus took his mouth from her and ran his hands

lightly over her back. She felt Gaius stoop to stroke her labia from behind, his hands each side of her thighs, holding her firmly, securely and safely. She felt weak: if it had not been for the strength of the men she would surely have collapsed under the pleasures.

Gaius stood upright again and pushed a finger inside her, massaging the inner walls of her femininity with a repetitive movement that made her shiver in anticipation. He put both hands on her mound and rubbed the ultra-sensitive place, a fraction above her clitoral bud, until the juices ran freely. Numidius slid down under her and took the little pearl in his mouth as Gaius continued to massage her mound at each side.

The Mauritanian lapped at her, pushing his tongue over the centre of her desire, flicking it with sensual, all-enveloping lips. He sucked gently and then moved up her stomach, kissing her softly with fluttering movements.

Gaius put his hands on her clitoris again and she braced herself, flames of liquid fire shooting through her body. She began to move higher into a plane where everything was pleasure and delight. He pushed a finger inside her and a series of involuntary internal spasms took her soaring higher and higher. At last she could bear it no longer and she screamed out her pleasure and fell across Albinus' shoulders in exhaustion.

Gaius put his hands under her and adjusted her bottom so she was squarely presented to him. She felt exposed as his hands gently parted the cheeks of her body and then ran up and down them with exquisite softness. She could feel the dark strength of his virility nudging her as he slid down to the moist centre of her femaleness. He pushed her torso, so she was bending over more fully, and she felt him pushing the entrance to her bliss with his hot penis.

She cried out and Albinus kissed her face, his hands on her back. Numidius resumed sucking her nipples and her desire rose fiercely.

She pushed her bottom towards Gaius, moaning gently.

'This is what you want, isn't it?' he murmured in her ear. 'It is what I want too. What I have been waiting for since I left you in the tavern.'

Decisively he pushed deep inside her and began to rock her. His fingers slid to her clit and began rapidly vibrating it, his finger lying along its internal length. She pushed and writhed, her breasts on fire as Numidius sucked and kneaded. Her breath came fast as Albinus scattered light caresses on her cheeks, her forehead and her neck.

She panted and pushed, savouring the depth of Gaius' hardness deep within her as it pushed at the innermost recesses and expanded against the sides. She felt she would burst. His finger worked faster on her pubic mound, his hand bracing her body against the force of his own power and of her own responding thrusts.

She began to moan and cry out in rhythm, unable to stop herself or to think of anything but the beauty of the sensations.

He slowed down, taking his penis almost to the brink of her womanhood and then pushing it slowly inside till it was up to the hilt. As she began to cry out with need, he pushed hard and fast, so she was breathless from the exertion. She clung to Albinus and buried her face on his strong shoulder, tasting the sweet musk of his body.

She climaxed again, her body shuddering against theirs. Gaius did not withdraw.

'When you have caught your breath, we will come together. This time I want to feel your spasms of passion at the same time as my own,' he murmured.

He began to move with a different rhythm. His penis felt very hard inside her as it moved smoothly up and down, creating a delicious friction. She revelled in his deep penetrative power within her. She felt his muscles contract as he neared his peak and the thought was thrilling. She found that her own body responses totally matched his: her breath came at the same pace and her cries of pleasure matched his quiet grunts. As she felt the first shudders of his satisfaction, her own bliss increased into waves of ecstasy that rippled out and over her entire body. The tension left her with slow undulations. Ripples of pleasure shot through her legs and her loins, moving to her breasts and shoulders. The top of her head was immeasurably sensitive as Albinus stroked her hair. Softly, she sighed with joy, as her need was quietened and her tormented body became less tense.

She felt Gaius' body relax in orgasm, a fractional moment after the last ripple of peace reverberated through her. His pulsating stem became almost imperceptibly less hard and insistent within her. He pushed a few more times and she moaned with delight. Numidius stopped sucking her breast, uncurled himself from her body and stood beside them. She tasted the salt on Albinus' neck, smelt his skin and glanced down to see that he was bulging with an erection. She thought with satisfaction that it must have been due to her: had the two men been lovers, he would surely have climaxed with his friend's body so close to him.

Gaius caressed her pubic mound once more and slid a hand across her clit which was now alive with a myriad sensations. She pulled back and he kissed her neck.

'You have had enough, then?'

Albinus curled his legs under him and with his hands on her shoulders, gently forced her upright as he stood up. Gaius slid out of her body.

'Julia is waiting for you,' he said to the two men. 'Go and make her happy.'

They smiled and turned quickly, both clearly willing and able to pleasure the lady.

'Are they your slaves?' she asked, watching their neat, strong buttocks as they walked away. 'No,' he said, turning her round to hold her close. 'They are freedmen. They are under no obligation to do what they do. They enjoy their work and their pleasures. Sometimes, like tonight, I find I don't have time, or perhaps a lady needs a special treat. Normally a woman I am intimate with, has my sole attention, but sometimes a little variety is a good thing.'

'It was wonderful.' The words seemed inadequate.

'Have you recovered now?' he asked and she nodded, resting against his chest, exhausted and sated.

'Next time, we will take our pleasures alone, together,' he whispered into her hair. Her emotions leapt at the implication that there would be a next time.

He gently moved a wisp of hair from her damp forehead. She sighed and touched his hand with her lips, kissing him gently.

'That would be wonderful,' she said. 'I feel so good now.'

They stood together for a long time. She felt relaxed and happy and totally at one with his body. She felt she was moving into a sphere of pleasure that only the gods could truly understand.

'Don't ever be sad again, Marcella. You have a magnificent talent and you must use it for your enjoyment and for others. No good will come in spending your life crabbed and inhibited. You will become unkind, maybe even cruel.'

She saw that he was thinking of something, or someone, a long time ago. She wondered what, or who, had caused him to feel this way.

'I won't ever forget you,' he said at last. 'Not even the diversions of Rome will make me do that!'

Her heart felt like stone. He had wanted to see her again and explore their exciting talents, but something from the past had come between him and his desire.

She thought in anguish that the diversions of Rome would certainly all be female.

'You are naked. That won't do at all,' he said, briskly. 'You must have clothes. Come with me.'

He took her hand and led her along the corridor to a room with a half-open door. A very matronly and correct woman sat within.

'This lady needs lots of new clothes. She's even lost

her jewellery. She needs a great deal of pampering to make up for her traumas.'

'That is why I am here, lord,' she replied and held a hand out towards Marcella. 'Come my dear, you don't need to feel upset. It happens all the time. Things get spilled, or an admirer gets a little too boisterous. Men will behave so wildly won't they?'

'But I am not . . .'

She stopped herself from saying she wasn't one of the guests, as the woman put a cloak around her shoulders.

Marcella turned to speak to Gaius, but he had disappeared. Perhaps they would never meet again. The thought left her appalled and desolate.

Chapter Seven

'You have pretty colouring, a lovely complexion and a seductive figure. I think you can wear bright colours which would make some women look sallow,' the attendant said as Marcella sat down, defeatedly.

A young female slave held up a huge polished silver mirror and Marcella saw that her face was slightly swollen from her passions. She stared bleakly into the depths, seeing herself reflected against the youthfully feminine decor. The golden light from the lamps made her look ethereally pale against the amber-painted walls.

She glanced round and saw that dresses were laid out on couches and wooden storage boxes. Neat rows of slippers had been arranged on the sophisticated black and white mosaic floor.

'Guests often spill wine or food and need clean clothes,' said the woman easily.

'I am not a guest,' said Marcella, depressed. 'You talk as though setting naked females at their ease is part of your everyday duties.'

'It is,' the woman said simply. 'You would be surprised what happens in some parties. When I was younger, I belonged to a family in Rome. In the reign of the Emperor Nero, there were all sorts of goings-on.'

She selected a couple of dresses from a box.

'Try these. This one is of very fine linen with embroidered silver braid around the hem. There is a silver-embroidered waist tie to match it. It would need silver jewellery, of course.'

She stepped over to a side-table and found a pair of earrings. A delicate bead of glass was suspended on a silver wire from each tiny hook.

'I still have my own earrings,' Marcella pointed out, thinking how Gaius had caressed her and nuzzled her neck in a way that had sent shivers down her entire body. Just the memory now disturbed her.

'They are very pretty, my dear, but they won't go with any clothes we have here.'

'I can't take them – they are far too costly,' she cried in anguish. 'I am only a hired servant. If they catch me at the door wearing clothes like these, they might accuse me of stealing. I cannot bear to think of the consequences!'

'There is nothing unusual in this, believe me,' said the woman. 'When a cherished guest gives orders, my mistress would punish me if I didn't carry out his wishes. She would not wish to offend anyone like him.'

'The doorman won't know that!'

'The doorman knows better than to question a guest who is leaving. His duty is to ensure that nobody gets in without authority. How they happen to be dressed when they leave, is not his concern.'

'You obviously know Gaius' identity. I know only his first name – and it is the most common in the world,' Marcella said eagerly. 'What are his family and clan names?'

The woman suddenly looked ill-at-ease.

'I'm sorry. If you don't already know, then he must want to conceal his identity. I dare not tell you.'

Marcella sighed with impatience.

'What is so secret about him?'

'Nothing. You know that the patricians get ideas in their heads and ordinary people like me have to conform with their wishes. I dare not tell you. But rest assured that if he wants you to be well dressed, then that is what has to happen.'

'It makes me feel cheap to accept such gifts,' she said.

'Cheap you will certainly not be,' said the woman briskly.

She held another dress against Marcella and scrutinised the effect.

'He isn't compensating you for some licentious favour or even paying you in advance, if nothing has yet happened,' she added thoughtfully.

'Then what is he doing?' demanded Marcella as she pulled the cloak around her and marvelled at its fine texture. She wandered around the room, the material caressing her neck as softly as Albinus' kisses had done.

She hugged herself, running her hands along her hips where Gaius had held her in the throes of passion. She ran them to her waist and gently over her breasts. Her nipples felt raw and tender from Numidius' insistent tongue.

'It is quite normal,' replied the woman. 'A gift or two from a friend. He never pays for his pleasures, that one. There is no need. On the other hand, he comes from a section of society that constantly gives gifts. Rest assured that sooner or later my master and mistress will receive gifts from him that will more than recompense them for this little service.'

'Little service,' repeated Marcella faintly, fingering some material that was decorated with braid. It had been embroidered in gold thread with a riot of birds and flowers, trees and small animals.

'You would do the same if a guest spoilt her dress at your house – wouldn't you? You would certainly not let her go home a mess. You would lend her one of yours.'

She held a short string of amber and jet beads around Marcella's neck. Held together on thin gold wire, they caught the light and gave her skin a warm glow.

'That must have cost at least two denarii,' Marcella protested.

'More like ten times that amount,' said the woman

dryly. 'Take the necklace. It suits you. I think you should find a dress to suit the jewellery, rather than the other way round.'

Marcella held a silk dress to her face and felt Gaius' touch once more. She closed her eyes and sniffed deeply to recapture the scent of passion. Mentally, she relived the moment of tenderness when he had run his fingers over her moist brow, gently calming her after the surfeit of pleasures.

She felt totally sated. Her body was slow and relaxed from the marvellous sensual experiences. She could still savour the male odours that clung to her skin. She did not want to wash or put on scent; she wanted only to prolong the delights.

Deep within her, the spasms of pleasure that had shaken her to the depths of her femininity, still reverberated quietly.

'It was good wasn't it?' murmured the attendant in her ear. 'You are fortunate. Your lover is a connoisseur of women. If I were not so old and with my own memories, I would be jealous. And the girl is too young. That is why we are here instead of in the dining room. It is the consolation of old age and youth that we can listen to the music and re-dress the beautiful women who need our help.'

Marcella dragged herself back from the memories of passion to admire a gown the attendant was holding. It was saffron – the colour for a bride's shawl.

'I love this dress.'

The amber and jet beads gave it a decisive sophistication and brought out the lustre of her hair.

She slipped into it and the young girl moved the mirror up and down so she could see her entire length. The soft material swirled alluringly around her breasts, her waist and her hips before falling softly to skim the floor. She swayed slightly and admired how the frock accentuated her womanliness, subtly drawing attention to the delta of her private secrets. She could imagine Gaius' expression as he saw her. She wanted him to see her now. She longed for him to take the dress off, lingeringly, before he possessed her body once more in a frenzy of sensuality. Next time, she wanted him alone so she could return his caresses.

'You look breathtaking,' said the attendant. 'Now, all you need is some make-up and nobody will recognise you. You will be able to take your place with the lords and ladies and watch or join in with their games.'

'I've had enough physical pleasures for one night,' said Marcella. 'Unless it is with him.'

The woman laughed. 'You need a pair of light leather slippers with gold decoration, and a belt embroidered with gold threads.'

The little slave girl ran to a box and brought out an exquisite belt which she tied loosely round Marcella's waist.

The attendant scooped Marcella's long hair on to the top of her head as the girl held the mirror.

'That makes me look really elegant!' Marcella exclaimed in delight.

'I'll pin it up securely in a while. It is a pity we don't have time to cut and curl it. The most fashionable ladies are wearing it very short at the front, curled tight to frame their faces. At the Imperial Court they use hair pieces piled high on their heads, with lots of ringlets. Put on this bangle and this ring. No woman with your looks must be without that sort of accessory.'

The bangle was solid gold with an intricate little decorative motif. It matched the ring which was set with a fine piece of jet.

'This outfit would cost years of wages from the tavern.'

'If you are to take your place amongst the ladies and gentlemen, you have to look the part,' the woman repeated.

'How can I take my place amongst them? I am nothing. A mere nobody.' She could hear the bitterness in her tone, but it was tempered by the growing knowledge that her appearance compared very favourably with the most beautiful of the guests.

'Whether he meant it or not, your friend has made sure that you have suitable clothes to go to the places where you might meet him. Don't be so negative.'

'That is very devious,' she cried. 'I can't believe he meant it like that.'

'I know the way the men think. He is running away, but you have enough clues to enable you to follow, don't you? He knows that!'

'You mean he is testing me?'

Marcella began to laugh.

'It could be that. Take the dress and a couple of others too. Hide them under your cloak. Yes, I know you haven't got a cloak. In case you hadn't noticed, that is not a problem in this room. Remember me with kindness when you have taken your place in society, won't you?'

Marcella sauntered through the corridors of the great house, unrecognised by anyone, including Lydia. She walked haughtily through the rooms and corridors, her eyelids heavy with cosmetic ash and charcoal. Her face was lightly powdered into a sophisticated pallor, warmed with amber lights, and she was perfumed with jasmine and orange flower oil. She practised walking with elegance and charm, finding that it was easy to glide and twirl in the light leather slippers. The dress material swirled between her legs as she moved, gossamer soft as her lover's hands. The softness of the expensive breast and loin cloths, and the undertunic, was a delight after the harsher material she normally wore. She knew she looked stunning.

When she saw Caballius playing dice in an ante-room, she put on her haughtiest expression and moved away.

The party had died down into a slumberous calm. A number of couples were entwined and half-asleep. Marcella floated past them as if she were in another world and made her way to the front door. She knew that Gaius had left and that she had a challenge on her hands if she wanted to see him again. There was no doubt in her mind – she wanted to see him again.

'Are you ready to leave, lady?'

She nodded at the doorman, unable to trust herself not to give away her common origins.

He opened the door deferentially, called to some litter bearers who were waiting in the street and gave them a few coins.

'Thank you,' she said quietly as though such service was the most natural thing in the world to her.

She crept into the tavern without waking her aunt or uncle, and hid her new clothes in her storage box. She removed the thick make-up with some olive oil from the bar.

She fell asleep almost immediately. The memory of Gaius' touch was still on her skin and his words of tenderness were still in her ears. He had fled but the attendant had said he probably wanted her to follow him.

She awoke thinking that her aunt was shaking the bed to waken her, but it was the entire room that moved. She frowned as she recollected Terentius' warnings.

She found her aunt and uncle in the street outside the tavern, gazing up at the mountain. The first, faint flickerings of dawn threw pastel tints over the sky, a subtle background to the grey-green leaves of vines: but there was something more ominous in the air.

'There is smoke coming out of the top – look. The gods of the earth are angry. Vulcan and Pluto are offended. We must do something to appease their wrath.'

She stared and could make out a faint wisp above the line of the olive groves and vineyards.

'It will be some farmer burning rags,' she replied dismissively, her mind on more immediate problems. Her lover's name was Gaius and he spent time in Rome – but she needed to know far more than that.

'Will you lend me some money?' she asked without preamble when she had climbed the stairs to Petronius' rooms an hour later.

'Have a heart, lover,' he said. He was lying in bed, the rumpled sheets twined around his body as though he had spent a disturbed night. 'I'm hung over this morning. They had me drinking in the staff quarters for hours after the main party had broken up.'

She poured him some water from a jug on the side table.

'You look terrible, but one thing I have learnt from living in a tavern is how to cure a drinker's headache. Have you any eggs?'

He groaned. His cock was flaccid, half-covered by the bedclothes. His hand lay limply over it, as though he had fallen asleep masturbating.

'Of course I don't have any eggs.'

'Artists paint still-lives – eggs and dead birds or hares. And you sometimes use egg white for binding the pigments together, I know that for a fact!'

'We don't leave them lying around afterwards – we eat them. If we are lucky. Mostly the patrons take any decent food away with them,' he added ruefully.

He drank some of the water and made a face.

'You are the only person who can help me,' she said seriously, squatting by his prone figure.

'Where did you get to last night?' he asked as his hand moved idly over his prick. He rubbed his thigh as though it were itching and then felt his balls. 'The steward was in a filthy mood. I wouldn't hope to go back for another job if I were you. Apparently there was a complaint about you from one of the guests. You pushed him in the pool.'

'That pig,' she said, watching in fascination as he casually held his drooping stem and passed it from one palm to the other.

He began to harden and she felt a familiar tingling in her breasts that came with the certain knowledge of the pleasure a man's body could give her. She moved her position slightly to see him more clearly.

'You look better. Finish the water and help me. I need to get to Rome.'

'You were missing from the end of the party and now you want to get to Rome. It is my betting that you met a man.'

'Your imagination is too fertile,' she snapped. 'Stick to imaginative pictures, Petronius.'

He laughed and grasped his now erect penis firmly. 'The boyfriend must be a patrician,' he persisted, 'Because a mere knight could have lands anywhere, but senatorial families have to be in Rome at least part of the year.'

He began manipulating himself up and down with one hand and she took note of what pleased him so she could do the same for a man one day. Preferably for Gaius.

'I'd give a day's wages to find out what you were up to. And a week's rent to paint it in detail! Your nature is over-flowing with lust.'

'Don't be ridiculous,' she said sharply, but she was thinking back over the exhibitionism she and Gaius had displayed. They had taken their pleasures in a public place, oblivious to who might be watching. She felt a thrill of forbidden rapture at the thought.

He lay back and closed his eyes, his hand working more firmly on his penis. His balls began to tighten and she put her hands on his thighs, lightly running them up and down the silky skin.

'I need some capital to get myself started in business, if I am to make a better life for myself,' she said in a lighter tone. 'There are bigger markets in Rome with more profits to be made than in Pompeii.'

He opened his eyes and looked at her, still pumping his hand up and down. She put a finger on the tip of his glans and he smiled. She liked the feeling as he pushed the bulbous softness against her hand.

She pulled her breasts free from her dress and thought of Gaius' two freedmen. She had wanted to do this to them. She held one nipple against the end of his cock and then gently put her breasts around it, enveloping it completely. Petronius pushed himself towards her.

He looked at her for a moment and then slid away.

'I want to do this myself, by hand, looking at you,' he said. 'Lift your skirts and let me see you. You are very sweet when you want something, Marcella. You have a lot of personal charm as well as physical attactions.'

'Tell me you will help me!'

'Come on, lover, let me see you,' he replied, his hand working hard on his prick. His voice faltered slightly.

She lifted her skirt and stood by the bed, her crotch close to his face. The stimulation at seeing him pleasure himself had turned her to a quivering fount of desire.

'That's better,' he said, looking straight at her labia. He lay back and worked his hand hard and fast around his cock. She could feel her inner muscles throbbing with anticipation under his gaze. His breath was coming very rapidly and his eyes had a slightly glazed look. She shifted position by bending her knees and parting her legs, so he was given a wider glimpse.

He licked his lips and continued to stare at her as he furiously massaged his prick.

'Please, Petro – please help me.'

'I haven't been paid for the murals,' he said faintly. 'The rich never pay up on time.'

Marcella looked at him in dismay.

His eyes continued to glaze over with his pleasures as he stretched out one finger to touch her clitoral bud. She pushed herself towards him and he massaged himself vigorously for a few seconds, his energies totally concentrated. Without warning, he erupted and the ejaculate shot over his chest in a soft burst as she watched.

'There is one way we could help one another, and you could earn real money,' he said as he lay back with his eyes closed.

'Tell me how!' she cried eagerly.

'You might not like it.'

'Petro!'

He ran his hand sensuously over his penis.

'At the moment I have three commissions for board paintings, in addition to the Venus. One is complete – a straightforward portrait that is waiting to be picked up and paid for.'

'What about the other two – why are they so special?'

'The subject matter is a little – shall we say – delicate. I had expected to have to return to Rome before painting them, but if you are willing, then the situation might change.'

'Delicate?'

'Explicit. Compared to the wall paintings you saw, they will be hot. Some patrons like to toss themselves off in private, looking at a board painting of some woman's cunt. Or in the case of the second painting, she has to be tied up as if she is unwilling.'

She stared. 'What kind of men pay highly for that?'

'Rich men sweetie, rich men. Also slightly weak and ineffectual men because they can't get their fun with real women and just bottle it all up. Of course, if you are not interested . . .'

She thought back to Gaius' expression of sadness when he talked of suppressing natural urges beyond endurance and finding that people became bitter and cruel.

'I have heard that some people repress their desires beyond what is natural,' she said slowly.

'You have just proved you don't mind being looked at in detail for a man's personal pleasure rather than your own. I enjoyed that a lot, Marcella. Think how many other men could have such pleasure. And you could benefit financially!'

'You mean that you were interviewing me for a job just now?' she cried out, astounded.

'The prudes of this world object, so I have to chose my models carefully.' Petro wiped himself with a cloth and sat up. 'I often have to paint from memory but this client is fussy and wants realism. If you are truly interested in earning some ready money, you have only to say.'

She looked at him squarely. Her physical desires were fast receding at the thought of an opportunity to move out of her mundane life.

'Paint me.'

'It's a deal,' said Petronius, as he fumbled around for some clothes.

'Lean back against the cushions and throw your breasts outwards.'

She shifted her position for the tenth time, bored with his constant changes of mind and his assumption that she would obey his every whim.

'Are all painters this temperamental?'

He ignored her. 'Splay your legs out a bit more.'

She threw herself into the most wanton pose she could think of and he smiled. 'That's fine. After a short break you can take your clothes off and we'll get down to business.'

Gracefully, she rose to her feet as he poured himself some wine, watered it well and chewed on a hunk of cheese.

'You seem on edge, Petro.'

He shrugged. 'I'm always tense. It is a testing time for me.'

'Lydia won't arrive unexpectedly to embarrass us, if that is what is worrying you. She will be busy clearing up after the party.'

She picked up a board painting from a stack in the corner and looked idly at the subject.

'I thought you specialised in fantasy scenes. This looks like a very realistic portait.'

'I started out painting portraits. The rest just followed. People wanted me to paint them with their own faces on the bodies from some statue of a god or goddess. Then the business just escalated.'

'It is good,' she said, marvelling at the sensitive way in which he had portrayed the lined, world-weary face of an old man.

'There is real money in it, if you can tap into the right social circles. I like to paint the up-and-coming as well as the already-established, because they will ensure I have enough commissions in my old age!'

He picked out another painting and held it up to the light to show her.

'This is a very good example. Gaius Salvius Antoninus will go far in his career, so it is said. If he does, he will further my career too. When people see this in five or ten years' time, they will come to me for their own portraits.'

The man in the painting was her lover. There was no doubt about it. She ran her finger across the brow and the tousled hair of the painted face.

Gaius Salvius Antoninus. She repeated the name to herself several times, committing it to her memory.

'Come on then, we have work to do.' Petro was suddenly very business-like. 'We'll make this a short sitting. I'll use a light style which will be quick and easy for mapping out the general shapes. I'll fill in the details tomorrow.'

She lay back on the cushions, her thoughts suffused in happiness.

He scowled. 'Take your clothes off!'

'Sorry.' She giggled, feeling light-headed in her joy. 'Do you think I need to take them all off at once, or can I just lift up my skirt when you get to that bit?

'Don't play around, Marcella. Of course I can't. I need to see the line of your stomach. And I want your breasts pouting upwards in that alluring way when you throw your arms back behind your head.'

She took her dress off and stretched out on the couch, her legs wide in overt invitation.

Petronius frowned. He moved towards her and moved one leg so her foot was on the ground. Her labia were spread wide but unaroused.

'You are too dry.'

He took a piece of damp cloth and squeezed some water between her legs. She wriggled.

'That is better, but not good. We need to get you excited, I think. Try putting your hand to yourself.'

'Certainly not! I don't do that sort of thing for just anyone.'

'Aha! So you have done it for someone special! The story gets more complex. So, who is this patrician who watches while you arouse yourself?'

'There isn't anyone,' she said flatly.

He smirked as he began to paint.

She closed her eyes and wondered how large Rome was and how easy it would be to find a particular person. Now she knew that Gaius belonged to the Antoninus family and the clan of Salvius, the task would be easier.

Her mind wandered in delicious fantasy to the moment when, sometime in the future, she had found him and he would take her to his bed. She could feel his touch and his breath. In her imagination his voice was still mouthing the words of passion. Time ceased to have relevance.

'Done.' Petronius interrupted her dreams with rude lack of sensitivity. 'Now get your clothes on, Marcella.'

She rose, stretched away the day-dream and wandered over to the board.

'May Juno and Venus preserve me, I don't look like that, do I?'

'I am not credited with being a bad painter,' he said stuffily.

She looked with unease at the flushed features of the girl – very recognisably herself – on the board. He had painted her with heavy breasts and dark nipples that spread lazily outwards.

'Someone might recognise me!'

'Nonsense. I have painted your face in a blur. The only details are between the legs. There is no doubt that this will excite any red-blooded man, no matter how inhibited. You are a terrific model.'

'I had no idea the painting would be this explicit,' she said unhappily as he tidied up his paints.

'I can tell when you are thinking about your boyfriend because the effect on your body is astonishingly immediate!' he said with a smile. 'And the look on your face is quite different from your everyday expression. Tomorrow, we'll do the pose where you are bound up. This is the start of a terrific business partnership!'

85

Chapter Eight

*T*he blunt nose of the mountain top thrust into the sky as if trying to free itself from the vineyards and villas which clung to its slopes. As Marcella returned home after visiting the public baths, she had to edge past people who were looking up at the wisps of smoke near the summit. A patchy white and grey cloud was forming and there was ash in the air.

At the tavern her aunt bustled round vigorously, her wide hips wobbling.

'We are leaving for a few weeks, until the threat has gone. I shall stay with my youngest sister, in Apulia.'

'It is nothing more than a large bonfire that has got out of control,' Marcella maintained staunchly.

'I agree, there is nothing to worry about.' Marcella's uncle sounded resigned but acquiescent. 'Your aunt is getting the whole thing out of proportion. We survived the last quake when thousands of people had huge repair bills.'

He picked up one of the larger amphorae and began to pour wine into the mixing bowl.

'Where is Terentius? You will damage your back. That is his job. He is slacking again,' said Marcella.

'He has run away,' replied her aunt brusquely as she pulled pots and pans down from the shelves. She began to sort out the best into a pile on the food counter.

'He can't have! He is a slave. The penalty is death.'

'If we get him back, we can't afford to throw away good money by punishing him that harshly. Besides, he's been with us for years and I am fond of him in an odd sort of way. But it does show the extent of his fears and I, for one, intend to take him seriously.'

'He is exaggerating,' persisted Marcella.

'For days he has been telling us to get out. I wouldn't listen and neither would anyone else. If he is willing to risk maximum punishment, then I am convinced that he really believes what he says about the mountain.'

'I can smell ash and something else unpleasant on the wind.' For the first time, she began to have real doubts about their safety.

'The first moment we can take a vehicle through the streets without being prosecuted, I am off.'

The woman picked up a handful of the best knives and pushed them into a leather bag along with their best red ware bowl and a small glass beaker. A knife fell from her slightly shaky hands and clattered to the floor.

'You are overreacting,' chided Marcella.

'You would do well to listen to me. Pack a bag. What does it matter if I am proven wrong? If nothing happens, we haven't lost anything and I will simply be seen as a silly old woman. I would rather be that than a stupid dead one. I am not taking a chance. I'll wait for a short while at the Nucerian Gate, at dusk. If you aren't there, you are on your own. I will pack some essentials for you, if you won't do it yourself, you lazy girl.'

'I will do it,' Marcella agreed hurriedly, thinking of the gold jewellery and fine gowns that were carelessly concealed in her room. 'I will take my bag with me this afternoon so I don't have to waste time coming home before meeting you.'

'Perhaps we should leave,' Marcella confided to Petronius as she lay on the couch in his studio an hour later. Her legs were wide apart and bonds secured her arms to her sides so her breasts were pushed high.

Quick footsteps echoed on the paving slabs far below them and a couple of heavy doors slammed on the floor above. 'There is a lot of shouting in the street. It is like the hour before an important event at the racing circuit – the kind when they have boxing, sprinting and wrestling as well as chariot races and everyone is hurrying to get the chores finished in time to secure the best seats.'

'I want to finish this picture now we've started.' He spoke absently as he studied her body with detachment. 'I don't want you running off to Rome in a lustful panic and leaving me with something incomplete. Now, I want your hands between your legs – you have to look as though you are reluctant. Don't obscure your cunt because you must appear to be trying to defend your virginity.'

She giggled uneasily.

'After all the trouble I had losing it in the first place, that is a joke. Do some men really find this sort of artwork exciting?'

'To the point of paying very well for the material. I haven't noticed you complaining about the money I'm offering, Marcella.'

She put her hand on the newly-shaven skin between her legs. The warmth and pressure turned her thoughts to sensuality. She felt her feminine folds dampening at the memories which were so recent and so sweet.

'Don't rub yourself off, you idiot,' he said impatiently. 'In the name of Eros, Marcella, put some of the right emotion into this. Yesterday was amorous expectation: today we want horror and disgust. This is a job that you must take seriously or I shan't be able to paint you. You are supposed to be reluctant, not panting for it!'

'I'm sorry.'

She put her hands near her legs, spreading her fingers without obscuring her labia.

He shook his head. 'That is even worse.'

His fingers brushed against the board. With lingering sensuality, he wiped the pigment off with a cloth.

'Don't worry. Lydia won't walk in on us,' she said with more certainty than she felt.

'Apollo only knows what we will tell her if she does,' he muttered, glancing over his shoulder to the door.

He undid the bonds and retied her hands across her chest, so her breasts pouted with the pressure.

He painted in silence for well over an hour until the sharp cries of the people in the street were partly blocked out by a low rumble.

'Is that a wagon?' she asked incredulously.

'It sounds like it. They are so afraid of a puff of smoke and some earth tremors that they are breaking the rules and bringing vehicles into the town during the day. They are hysterics. What could possibly happen to a huge place like Pompeii?'

'My aunt is leaving. She thinks there is a threat.' She wriggled uncomfortably. 'May I have a short break Petro? My arms are tired from the bonds.'

He sighed and shrugged. 'Oh, very well. But only long enough for you to stretch your legs.'

He untied her and she sat rubbing her arms, listening to the people shouting. Increasing numbers of carts were being pulled over the paving slabs. Occasionally a horse whinnied.

A sharp knock on the door made her whirl round in surprise as a man entered and looked expectantly towards Petro. She felt weak with fear as she recognised her tormentor from the party.

'Caballius Zoticus! I didn't hear you come up the stairs,' Petro, said smoothly, moving forward to greet him.

'You said to come round at about this time, Petro, and I am impatient to see what you have to offer.'

She sat down with bowed head, so her hair fell over her face.

'One painting has been completed, Caballius,' Petro was saying. 'It hasn't dried out yet, but I used egg white as a binding and in this heat it should be completely hard by tomorrow. I think you will like it.'

Marcella picked up her dress and started to edge her way to the door.

'By Jupiter, I know that girl! So that is what her cunt looks like! I'd never have guessed.'

There was lascivious greed in Caballius' voice as he studied the picture. Marcella gently pushed the door to Petro's second room, shaking in her desperation to hide. It creaked loudly and the two men turned.

'It is you! Come here, you little slut. I want to talk to you. You ran out on me last night.'

He was standing between her and the door to the stairs. His bulk seemed far greater in the cramped studio than in the elegant rooms of the town house.

'I didn't run out on you – you passed out from the drink,' she improvised with a languid drawl. She knew that she must keep cool and fight off any antagonism, no matter how many lies she had to tell. 'But now we have met up – I'm glad you admire the painting.'

'So much so, that I am going to commission another.' He stared hungrily at the board.

There was a hard cruelty about his mouth that she had not noticed in the soft lights of the party. What, in her innocence, she had taken for sheer enthusiasm for lechery she now saw was a repellent form of perversion.

'That is very gratifying.'

Petro's ingratiating tone disgusted her.

She was shaking with apprehension. Half-naked and vulnerable, she slid through the door into the bedroom. She flung on some clothes as she listened to the two men talk.

'I can finish another within the week,' Petro said and she winced.

'From the back. I want you to paint her from the back – naked of course, but with the bum showing. Nice and open, with the cunt flaps quite long and floppy like dewlaps and the asshole rosy.'

Marcella was appalled by the loathsome, degrading way he was describing the female form. She was shocked that what had seemed no more than a relatively innocent piece of dare-devilry, was turning into something far more threatening. She realised that the man was a pervert as well as a blackmailer.

'Rose-red costs money,' began Petro.

'I don't care about that. You can put the rouge on her bum if you need inspiration,' Caballius interrupted, his voice raised against the hubbub in the street. 'I know it will cost me more, but I like the effect. Where has she got to? I'll show you in detail exactly which pose I want her in.'

Marcella drew herself up and walked with dignity into the studio.

'Both Petro and I are fully aware of what you want. I am familiar with your particular needs and interests,' she said with a contrived composure that sounded haughty.

'So show me now. It is always best to be certain that painter, model and patron are in complete agreement.'

He walked up to her and grasped her, his fingers digging painfully into her shoulders as he pushed her round to face away from him. He put an arm over the back of her neck to bend her forwards. She wrenched herself away so her arm was twisted painfully.

'I'll show you tonight – we have an assignation. Remember?' she said fiercely. She stared into his eyes over her shoulder and willed herself not to be over-whelmed by the depravity and brutality she read in his expression.

'I need Marcella here this afternoon if you want another painting,' said Petro mildly.

Caballius let her go so abruptly that she fell to the floor. She scrambled up with as much composure as she could muster.

'You won't get away again, you little trollop. I have some very special things in store for you. I made the steward tell me your name. I know where you live. You will meet me tonight, or you will regret it. You don't want your family and friends to know about what you get up to on the quiet, do you?'

'They wouldn't believe you,' she cried uncertainly.

'They would disown you and there would be nothing else for you but to go into a whore-house. I shall have no qualms about making sure that you end up in degradation and disgrace if you don't do what I want.'

'Perhaps we should leave this for now,' suggested Petro as Caballius' footsteps receded on the wooden staircase. 'I would like to go into the street and sketch a few scenes.'

'You knew he would be arriving.' Marcella was shaking with fury and fear.

He walked over to her and put his hands around her waist, pulling her towards him.

'It was a mistake. The noises from the street were too loud for me to hear him come up the stairs.'

'You specifically told him to come at this time, when you knew I would be here,' she said. 'He is an evil bastard.'

'I wanted some money off him. That has worked to your advantage too because I will be able to pay you sooner.'

She moved away and hugged herself to stop herself shaking. She felt as if she had been violated simply by Caballius' thoughts.

'In that case I'd like the money now.'

'You are a schemer, Marcella. I'm not paying you before the painting is finished.'

'Then finish it now.'

Her recent fear and embarrassment was being replaced with cold anger: she would get even with Caballius some way. Any way.

'I'm not leaving without my money. You have completely misled me, Petronius. The kind of man who pays for obscene paintings is not always a sad and gentle inadequate, as you suggested yesterday.'

'Not always,' he agreed evenly.

'Caballius delights in mild cruelty when there are

people around. What do you suppose he is capable of in his own home?'

Petronius looked at her curiously.

'I think you are exaggerating it all. He just talks dirty and tough. Your infatuation with your boyfriend has simply made every other man seem less desirable. However, rather than have us both lose out on this, I'll finish the painting, and pay you now. You will hardly be able to run out on me, bound up and naked.'

He gave her a small pouch of coins which she immediately placed safely in her bag before she undressed and he retied the bonds over her naked body.

After her terrifying experience, the sweet desirous thought of Gaius flooded her entire being. She knew that she was swelling and glistening as her body became ready to possess his. She closed her eyes and lay back, dreaming of being pleasured and sated.

Petronius pulled the bonds very securely and she winced.

'Not so tight, Petro!'

He grunted.

'That is much better, Marcella. Keep that expression! I was afraid you would be lying there all seductive and provocative, instead of acting out the part.'

'It's too constricting,' she complained furiously. 'This is ridiculous.'

'But it is giving you that wonderful look of natural hostility that I am seeking,' he replied without passion, as he pulled the bonds even tighter.

She shrieked, 'That hurts!'

'In this pose, you are supposed to be on the verge of being raped, Marcella. Think of the Greek legend of the marriage of Pirithous of the Lapithae. Imagine you are his bride Hippodamia!'

She frowned as he began to paint. To her horror, she saw that he was erect.

'That is a horrible myth. The Centaurs got drunk and tried to rape her and her attendants. The incident led to the war between the Lapithae and the Centaurs. I didn't know you painted such sinister subjects.'

'It is a common enough subject in art.'

'Women attacked and their men killed for pleasure by wild creatures! It is a horrible story, not titillating at all.'

'But marketable,' he replied prosaically. 'Imagine you are the defenceless girl about to be assaulted by creatures who are half-man, half-beast. Their baser natures have got the better of their sophisticated and civilised veneers.'

She shivered again as his words graphically conjured up the threat.

'You should have been a story-teller.' She kept her voice even with difficulty.

'It is an allegory,' he said lightly. 'It is not to be read at face value. It is to remind us all that there is both good and bad in human nature. It is up to each individual to make their own choices.'

She felt totally vulnerable in the half-light of the cool studio. She was acutely aware that the street noises were so chaotic that any cry from her would go unnoticed.

'You led me to believe this was to be an erotic painting, Petronius. I don't call this titillating. Cupid is a charming god – the son of Venus. He is usually thought of as a playful and light-hearted child.'

He shrugged, squinting at her before glancing back at the board.

'Many rich men would consider that to be silly, effeminate rubbish. They want something more robust.'

'I hate you for this, Petro. You misled me and I am in real pain. Untie me now!'

'The bonds need to be tight enough for realism. You were looking hot enough to seduce a thousand men.'

'Petro.' Her voice sounded strangely hoarse.

'Marcella, darling, you look completely horror-struck! Absolutely right for these purposes. You are quite the little actress aren't you? Perhaps you should think of that for a career. You are wasted in the tavern. You will

94

have to go on stage – with your talent you could play the theatres of the world.'

'This isn't acting. This is real. I don't like it. I've changed my mind.'

There was something sexual about the way he was lovingly spooning out the powders: he looked close to orgasm. She felt sick.

'It is all very well for you,' she said with difficulty. 'You aren't in this vulnerable position if someone comes in. Suppose that pervert comes back?'

'Stop panicking and lie back. I want to see your crotch properly, as we arranged before.'

She willed herself to keep calm. There was nothing to fear, she told herself. Petro's lack of concern was a mark of how little threat he was. His needs were passive – he was getting his pleasures simply looking at her while playing with the paints. There wasn't any danger and he didn't mean her any harm.

But with every second that passed and with every panic-stricken shout from the street, her terror welled up.

'Please, Petro. I want you to untie me. Now. I don't want this any more!'

'You asked to be painted.'

He surveyed her minutely, concentrating on shapes and forms and colours and then put his tongue between his teeth and tenderly brushed some paint on to the board. The action clearly gave him considerable pleasure – she could see his eyes glazing over.

'No, I don't want this, really I don't.'

She struggled on the couch, her legs wide apart in order to gain her balance. Her arm and chest muscles strained against the bonds.

'Lie back and think of the money,' he replied with an easy smile that told her he had finally ejaculated. 'Your expression has been superb and it has been there long enough for me to capture it perfectly. You can relax now because I've reached the shoulders and arms.'

'You manipulative low-life scum!'

'If you feel like that, Marcella, I hope this man in Rome is worth all this discomfort.'

She felt the folds between her legs relax and moisten deliciously at the very thought of Gaius Salvius Antoninus.

'He is worth it.'

She lay back resignedly, willing herself to be calm by thinking about her lover. She recalled the softness of his touch; the hard penetrative insistence of his penis; the way his two freedmen had added to her pleasure without expecting anything in return. She could taste and smell the marvellous perfume of his skin. He had been rigid with need as he pushed into her, holding her thighs tightly, and yet so gently. She remembered with such sweet pleasure how his fingers had vibrated her clitoris as she neared her climax.

Involuntarily, her internal muscles began to contract as she imagined his thrusting power inside her. Her stomach contracted and her breasts pushed against the bonds. Her nipples were distended with anticipation. She thought of the fast and furious finish to her climax in the party and relived the tender moments when Gaius gently allowed her to recover after withdrawing from her body.

'There, all finished!' Petro sounded triumphant.

She opened her eyes and saw a tall, powerfully-built man silhouetted in the doorway behind him.

As he moved into the room, she saw a scowl of anger darkening his face. He looked ready to destroy anything that stood in his way. Lines furrowed his brow and between his eyes. His mouth was set with uncompromising rage.

Marcella stared mutely and then closed her legs quickly into a more modest position.

'Gaius.' She said the words softly and saw the look of open contempt he gave Petro, before he returned his gaze to her.

'Well, my little lady, so this is how you like it, then?'

'Don't you dare call me that,' she said with a harshness that was born of fear.

Petro turned round in surprise.

'What the – ?'

'So you have some sort of education, have you?' Gaius snapped at Marcella, ignoring the painter and striding towards her. 'What would you prefer to be called then? Prostitute? Street walker? Slut? No, I suppose you would think of yourself as something more high class. Hetaera, maybe? The poet, Catullus, refered to them as 'little ladies' and that is exactly what you shall be called!'

'How dare you,' she screamed again, struggling into a sitting position. 'You know nothing about it. Nothing at all.'

'Get dressed. You won't live to ply any trade if you stay in Pompeii at this time.' He was tight-lipped, his voice harsh. 'The quakes are getting stronger and everyone with any sense is getting out into the countryside. It is only a matter of time before the columns fall and the roofs collapse.'

'Do you really think that there is much danger?' Petro asked, calmly wiping a paint brush.

'Of course there is. A thick coating of ash is falling everywhere. While she gets dressed, you will wrap my painting. I do not intend to be in debt to dregs such as you.'

He threw a small pouch of money on the floor which Petro immediately picked up.

'It isn't what you think,' he began.

Gaius Salvius Antoninus took a violent step forward. His fists were clenched by his sides, his arm muscles were braced as if to attack. He stood for a long moment, shaking with anger before he turned abruptly on his heel and began to pace round the small room.

He swirled around to face Marcella. 'What are you waiting for?' He spat the question out ferociously.

'In case you hadn't noticed,' she said tightly, 'I am bound up.'

He took a step towards her and her over-riding emotion was of embarrassment.

The whole room shook from a sudden earth tremor. A couple of pots fell from a shelf and there were increased yells from the street.

'We don't have time for anything! You can come with me as you are. That way you can't get up to any more mischief.'

He picked up a blanket and rapidly wrapped it around her. The building shook once more and a huge crack appeared in the wall as though it were as flimsy as a pastry crust that had been in the oven too long.

He secured the blanket with her tie belt around her waist.

'Make sure I can't escape, won't you?' she shouted savagely. She tried desperately to wriggle out of his grip, fearful for their lives.

'I'll make sure you aren't seen in the street naked, yes,' he responded in an equally brutal tone, bracing himself against another quake and pulling her close to him so she did not fall.

Mortar sprayed down on them and the bricks near the door shook.

'Don't flatter yourself that I find you attractive when you are bound up. Only snivelling inadequates, too lazy to work out how to impress a woman would even consider an unwilling sexual partner. The idea is abhorrent and degrading to men as well as women.'

'Then untie me,' she shrieked.

'Oh, don't get me wrong.' His voice was icy as he manhandled her to the door. 'It doesn't excite my desire to see you bound up. But under these circumstances, I don't find the idea unthinkable, either. You are unfit to be let loose in respectable society. This is a simple matter of keeping a prisoner modestly covered during escort duty.'

His face was drawn with hostility, but his hands were unexpectedly gentle as he pulled her towards the door. She burned with the need for his loving touch. She longed for his mood to change from contempt to appreciation and admiration.

'Be careful with her,' said Petro, shaking dust from his hair. 'A man in a temper can damage a woman by mistake.'

'Worried about your investment are you?'

Gaius' hold tightened on her arm as he paused at the door. His tensed muscles were like iron against her body.

'Worried? Certainly. She is worth money to me.'

Marcella stared at Petro in horror.

'I have escorted more prisoners than you have sketched common trollops.' She felt Gaius tighten his grip further and saw his jaw muscles clench. 'No matter how angry I felt against them and their filthy crimes, no harm has come to any of them. Can you say the same about your models?'

Petronius shrugged and finished wrapping the portrait. 'All life is a risk.'

'I want my bag,' Marcella said fiercely, trying to blot out the horror that his words implied, by thinking of practical matters. 'It contains all my belongings.'

'Your bag! By all means, let us consider something so important!'

Gaius pulled her back from the door so she was thrown hard against him.

'My dear little lady, you have been surprised in this scene of brazen indecency. Our lives are in danger. The entire town is in pandemonium and chaos. And you think of your chalk face powders and your curling irons!'

'You bastard,' she yelled, kicking out at him and bringing her teeth downwards to his arm.

'Don't even think of it.'

He twisted her body round with a swift movement so she was facing away from him. She struggled in vain against iron-hard muscles that were even less yielding than her bonds.

'I can more than match your determination by sheer weight of experience, Marcella. Don't even consider trying to get away. One of the first things I learnt as an adult was how to immobilise a prisoner.'

'I'll bring the bag down for you,' said Petro calmly. 'With the painting.'

Marcella tried to keep her foothold on the uneven wooden boards as Gaius propelled her downstairs in front of him. The steps were creaking and there were new cracks and holes in the walls.

'You evil low-life,' she screamed again, kicking out and trying once more to bite him. The steps were hard on her bare feet and the blanket became caught up between her legs.

He picked her up bodily and carried her the last few yards, muttering, 'Mercury have pity on us.'

A small farm cart was standing by the door to the tenement building, with a rough-looking man holding reins of a terrified horse. People were milling around, some struggling silently with belongings, others shrieking to the gods to protect them.

Marcella saw a woman hurry past with two screaming toddlers clinging to her skirts. Her baby's head lolled dangerously over her arm.

'Ready at last? Got your art work have you? Odd looking statue,' said the carter.

Gaius bundled Marcella into the vehicle and threw a heavy money pouch at the man. 'You can have that back now, as I promised. You don't deserve it after I caught you looting that house. But at least you were greedy enough to wait for us in order to get it back.'

The cart stank of chicken mess and animals and she tried to move to a cleaner part.

'I'm so sorry that this isn't the sort of carriage my lady would prefer, but it was all I could get,' Gaius said as he leapt in next to the carter and took the reins.

Marcella looked up to the mountain. Spurts of fire came from the top and the dark cloud of ash and smoke had spread over the entire town.

Petro tossed her bag and the painting into the vehicle.

'Get Lydia. Run,' she screamed against the sound of the fear and panic of the people around her.

'I'm coming with you,' he replied, holding the side of the wagon. 'Who in Hades cares about Lydia?'

Gaius whipped the horse so it lurched forwards.

'Since you think it is time for painting,' he yelled, 'you go ahead and paint.'

'You should have told me who the boyfriend is,' Petro screeched venomously at Marcella, as his hold was dislodged. 'I'd have painted him something really special.'

The rest of his words were swallowed up by the deafening roar of the mountain as hot ash showered down on them. A cinder fell on the blanket and a small flame flickered. She screamed as she squirmed under the cloth, unable to remove it with her bound hands.

Chapter Nine

'*O*h, lady Fortuna, help me.'

Marcella was thrown roughly against the sides of the cart. The entire street lifted a few inches as if by some unseen hand. She swore out loud and screamed to the gods and goddesses on Olympus to preserve her. The flame on the blanket was taking hold, flickering into life even as the people around her were desperately trying to hold on to theirs. The bonds around her body were still tight, so she rolled over in terror, trapping the fire between her arm and the wooden floor. Pain seared through her and she screamed again.

She lay still for a moment, smelling her own charred skin and feeling the agony of the burn, but afraid to move until she was sure that the flame had been extinguished.

'Mars Ultor, give us strength.' Gaius' voice sounded harsh as the cart careered along the narrow streets and the mountain continued to spit fire and ashes into the thick air.

Without warning, he reined in the frantic horse and leapt to the ground. He picked up the two toddlers that Marcella had seen earlier. Their mother climbed wordlessly into the cart with the baby.

'Let us come too,' cried an old man. 'I beg of you, for I

cannot go any further and my grandson does not deserve to die.'

Gaius lifted him into the cart as though he were a bag of feathers, as the young boy nimbly squeezed in between the toddlers and Marcella.

'He is, or has been, a charioteer,' gasped the old man, trying to fan the filthy air from his face as they continued the perilous journey.

'No. He is an army man – he prays to Mars the Avenger.' Marcella was aware of feeling strangely possessive of the little pieces of information she had about Gaius, as though they were physical belongings to be cherished.

A huge wagon, piled high with household belongings, was rumbling ahead of them at a dangerous speed.

'He is good, but we'd have been better off with a charioteer.' The old man was wheezing badly from the polluted air. 'There is sufficient room for him to overtake – we could gain precious moments, but is he expert enough?'

'Pray that he has Celtic blood in him,' replied the woman in a calm voice, as though she were at home, talking to friends. 'The Celts ran rings around Julius Caesar with their war chariots.'

The air was thickening rapidly with ash and smoke and Marcella coughed into the blanket. The cart drew level with the wagon and a heavy saucepan fell from it, striking the boy who yelled out in pain and surprise.

With a tremendous lurch to the side Gaius swerved the cart into a narrow side-street.

'No,' screamed Marcella. 'This leads straight up to the mountain. Turn round!'

She peered back along the route they had been taking and saw the wagon halt abruptly. Spilt belongings shattered on the flagstones.

'They put a bollard in that street last year, to stop the vehicles using it,' observed the woman, still strangely calm, holding her three children close to her. 'We would have been killed or horribly maimed if he'd taken that route.'

Marcella saw that she had hastily tied around her neck a cheap little effigy of Minerva, patroness of women.

A carved stone architrave fell to the ground and shattered as though made of plaster. The horse reared up in angry challenge.

After a few more sharp twists and turns they passed rapidly through one of the lesser used city gates. The countryside was dark from windblown ash, but the air was clearer than in the town.

Gaius settled into the professional driving position that Marcella had seen so often on the racing circuit, and held the maddened animal to a steady speed along the open, cobbled surface. Gradually the tombstones which lined the road became fewer and more modern and the olive groves and vineyards of the rich villa estates became visible in the clearer air.

'Let me out here, please, lord,' the woman called out, as they reached a small farmstead a few leagues outside the town. 'I have family nearby.'

'We, too, will impose on your kindness no further than the next crossroads,' said the old man very formally.

As Gaius helped him and the young boy out of the cart a few moments later, the old man said, 'May Fortuna and the gods you worship, favour you, lord. I will make offerings to the deities of the Capitoline Hill to give you a prosperous life.'

'May Jupiter, Juno and Minerva go with you, too,' Gaius replied. 'We will all make offerings if we are spared.'

He continued to drive fast and silently for a while. He reined in at a small villa set in lush, well-tended vineyards.

'The horse is tiring. We will need to rest.'

As Gaius strode purposefully to the house, the carter threw the painting and Marcella's bag on to the path and half-pulled and half-lifted her out.

'Untie me!' she demanded, putting cold authority in her voice.

'I wouldn't risk the wrath of the gods or your friend,' he muttered, 'Not after the way he drove. Muscles like an ox and determination to match that of the heroes. I wouldn't bet Hercules against him. I'm off.'

The cart disappeared rapidly. She tried to find a sharp stone or implement with which to sever her bonds, but the paths were so well-swept that any wanted or needed possession had been removed.

'The house is closed up,' Gaius announced as he returned. 'You and I will spend the night here because foot travel is hazardous in the dark. There are no heavy stone pillars to crush us, and, my little lady, we will have to hope that the worst is over.'

'Don't call me that! I am not a prostitute. I am a connoisseur – you said so yourself.'

He pulled her roughly over the wide verandah that fronted the villa, towards the main door.

'If I live through this disaster, my greatest regret will be that I initiated you into sensual matters. You are not fit to be let loose in the world.'

'You have got it all wrong,' she shouted as he put his shoulder to the heavy wooden front door.

He walked over to her, took her roughly by the arms and forced his mouth on hers in a wild, aggressive kiss that had no kindness in it.

'No, I have not got it wrong at all. You are angry with me,' he said harshly, 'because I showed you what a worthless person Petronius was and what a narrow escape you have had. More than that, you hate yourself for the way that you still crave my body.'

The taste of his mouth was ambrosial on her tongue. His touch made her feel as if she were in the fabled land of the Lotus Eaters, from which no traveller ever wished to return. The bluntness of his words could not take away her need and longing.

'You allowed yourself to be tied up in a blatantly erotic pose, and you chose the wrong man. You have to

105

trust someone far more than you obviously did before you can safely play that sort of game.'

He let her go abruptly and returned to the door. The wood began to splinter with the force of his blows.

'I understand the attractions for some women,' he spat out over his shoulder, 'of pretending to be little innocents when they are jaded with the world and its libidinous pleasures.'

As the door came off its hinges he turned to her, his eyes blazing. His face was glistening with sweat.

'You are not one of those women. You haven't the experience to feel jaded. And believe me, if you use your talents properly and chose the right partners, you never will become tired of what are the most beautiful acts in the world – giving and taking pleasure.'

'He wasn't planning to rape me,' she howled, but she faltered as his chest heaved with his anger.

'He might not have been.' His tone held ominous warning. 'But the door was open and anyone might have walked in.'

He took hold of her arm and pulled her inside. He pushed her through the hallway, where the dim daylight fell on a fountain.

'At least the water is still flowing here. When I discovered that many of the wells had dried up, I decided to get out of Pompeii. Wait here while I get a lamp.'

She obeyed him meekly and then followed him into the dining room and sat on a couch while he lit several wall lamps.

'The householders seem to have left in such a hurry that the kitchen fire was hot enough for lighting a taper.' He was still drawn and angry but she was too exhausted to fight him any longer.

She lay back on the comfortable cushions and closed her eyes.

'Feeling seductive, are you?'

'No, bruised and tired after being thrown all over the cart and unable to brace myself at all because you decided not to untie me,' she snapped.

He stood looking at her for a moment, his expression softening.

'There wasn't time to untie you.'

'There was plenty of time,' she retorted. She sensed from the low tone he used that he was feeling less certain of himself. 'You were too busy trying to draw your own wrong conclusions to want me to be comfortable.'

He lifted her arm and saw the burn mark.

'How, in the name of Asclepius, did this happen?'

'A cinder. I had to lie on it to stop the blanket burning.'

'You need a dressing. Wait and I will fetch one.'

'I suppose it is too much to ask you to untie me first? Or, despite your protests, do you in fact prefer your women unwilling?'

He turned and she saw in his expression that she had goaded him too far.

He moved so close that she could feel his angry breath in her open mouth as he pulled her to her feet. His hair smelt of ash, and the strong musk of courage in the face of danger exuded from his skin. He was smeared with ash, dirt and sweat. She adored him. There was no other word strong enough to express how she felt at that moment in time.

'I told you when we first met that I never disappoint a lady if I can help it,' he said harshly, pulling her close. 'You clearly want to believe the worst of me, so I can easily satisfy your desire. You were prepared to bare yourself for that effete little rat. Now it is my turn to enjoy you. Why should I wait any longer?'

He held her firmly and nudged a knee between her legs.

'Bastard,' she said, struggling against him, trying to get her knee free to make contact with his groin. 'You were a liar when you said you would not take an unwilling woman.'

'But you are not unwilling,' he murmured softly into her hair. She could feel the hairs on his strong thigh against her soft crotch as he held her still.

'You may be bound up,' he continued, 'you may have

little choice in the matter, but you are not unwilling! Or are you telling me that if I put a finger inside you, I shall find you are dried up and tight? If I had any evidence whatsoever that you were reluctant, I would stop.'

'You are a thug and an abductor.'

She took a step back. The front of the couch made contact with her knees and he pulled her towards him as if to prevent her from falling backwards.

He pulled his hugely distended penis free of his clothing and slid it with tell-tale ease into her lubricated vagina. She gasped in surprise and felt his hands on her bottom, pulling her tightly towards him.

He pumped into her with a steady rhythm, ignoring her protests as her body responded with profound treachery. Sparks of delight shot through her, starting in her thighs and moving outwards.

He ran his hands down her back and slid a finger into the crack in her bottom, then brought one hand to her breasts. The feel of his nail grazing lightly over her nipples made her feel faint with desire. He held her body close and brought his mouth to hers, possessing her with a firm, arrogant assurance. He seemed to assume that she belonged to him. She was powerless to resist.

'Now tell me no.' His voice was harsh as he stopped his movements.

'No,' she whispered frantically, pushing her hips towards him.

He raised his eyebrows and slid out of her body. She whimpered in an agony of need.

'I meant, no, I can't tell you that. I didn't mean I wanted you to stop.' She no longer cared that she had to grovel.

There was a triumphant gleam in his eye as he pulled her towards him and entered her again. She felt him pound his virility into her with actions that reflected the anger and fear he had suppressed over the past hours.

Over and over they thrust their bodies together in the ultimate expression of passion until they both climaxed in a frenzy. As their shudders of pleasure died down he pushed into her once more with hard insistence, so his pubic bone hit hers in a grinding gesture of physical power.

'Tell me you did not enjoy that.'

He kissed her hard, his teeth clashing against hers, his tongue silky on her lips.

'I did not enjoy that,' she said shakily into his neck as he held her close, his tumescence warm within her. 'I adored it. I didn't want to, but you gave me total pleasures that I shall never forget.'

His kisses instantly changed to being soft and undemanding. They stood for long moments entwined in the aftermath of lust, savouring the smell and taste of each other's bodies.

At last he freed himself from her embrace and pulled gently at the bonds.

'Your painter friend was over-zealous in making sure you wouldn't get away. He has bound you so tightly that the blood has been stopped up. It may hurt a little until you are back to normal.'

'He wanted the painting to look convincing.' He snorted impatiently but his fingers moved delicately as he tried to loosen the tangled knots.

'Had you considered that he was setting you up for one of his unsavoury patrons? He made no attempt to help you when I took you away by force. What makes you think he would have intervened if I had been a pervert or a rapist?'

She shivered, thinking uneasily of Caballius Zoticus.

'Can you swear that Petronius' motives were purely artistic? Can you call to Venus and Juno to be your witnesses that he was on the level?'

'I thought that his strange behaviour was due to the fact that Lydia might arrive,' she said slowly.

'If I hadn't turned up, what other undignified poses would he have put you into? You don't suppose he gets his inspiration out of his head do you?'

'He watches at parties,' she said defensively. 'He says men won't pose for explicit pictures.'

'Some men like to have an audience. Some might even pay to have themselves immortalised with their cocks stuck into some orifice or other.'

'Don't be filthy,' she screamed.

'You have only known him a couple of days. You said that as a lover he was so passive that you were bored. What makes you think this Petro was such a nice fellow?'

He met her gaze with calm, serious eyes as the bonds fell away.

'I suppose it was because he was employed by Lydia's mistress and Lydia is my friend.'

He made a gesture of total exasperation.

'By now you must know that status and money do not necessarily go hand in hand with charm and kindness. Wealth is often obtained by very unacceptable means; the impressive house and the respectable little maid servants are easily bought as a front.'

He left the room abruptly.

She pulled the blanket around her and sat, shocked and afraid of the dangers she hadn't foreseen. She worried that maybe Lydia was being used. Looking back on it, his description of the household in which she worked was only too believable.

The blood was flooding back into her arms with a mild tingle that quickly changed. Tears came to her eyes and she hugged herself to try to remove the sharp, intense pain. As she frantically rubbed the red weals, she was acutely grateful to him for not staying to watch her agony.

She was in control again when he returned with a box of medicines.

'By the grace of Asclepius, these were left behind.'

He sat on the couch next to her and pulled the blanket aside to see her wound.

'The one thing to fault is that although there are many fine wines there is very little for afternoon burglars to eat,' he said lightly. 'We may have to forage in the gardens.'

Her breasts stood out proudly above her flat stomach

110

and she crossed her legs defensively. The weals had almost dispersed and she was aware of wanting him desperately. Their frenzied coupling had sated her immediate superficial desires, but had left her with a deeper need.

'You do not look or sound like a doctor,' she said as he selected an ointment with an air of professional knowledge.

'I have picked up a lot in the army,' he said shortly. 'Soldiers can suffer horrendous wounds. This isn't very serious, though it will hurt you for a few days. You did well to quench the flames as you did. It was brave and it probably saved our lives because at that point we needed every precious moment.'

She sniffed, silently acknowledging that he had moved half-way to apologising for abducting her.

He was tenderly considerate when he placed the bandage over the soothing creams. When he had finished he held her hands and drew her to her feet. The blanket fell to the floor and he looked into her eyes seriously.

'You made me angrier than I remember for years. I think I might have beaten that painter to a pulp if the mountain had not intervened. You have made me see another side to my nature. I knew I could be angry with the ways of men at war, I never knew a woman could make me that enraged.'

'It wasn't what you think,' she said gently. 'He was painting me. I don't think there was anything else involved. He does love Lydia. It was obvious when I saw them together.'

He raised his eyebrows.

'I do see that it was folly to take the chance.' She conceded the point reluctantly.

'Then why in Hades did you do so?'

'I needed the money.'

He stared at her.

'That is ludicrous! You could have applied to me. Like every other man of my rank in society, I have hundreds of dependants. When I am in Rome, the clients queue up

111

every morning to petition for this or that amount of ready cash or funding for new business ventures.'

'It is easy for you to say that now, isn't it?' she shouted, out of control. 'I am not one of the fortunate few who have a rich patron. I am freeborn, but I have to earn my living the hard way.'

'By the same token, you don't have any large over-heads. And you don't owe anybody the traditional right to patronage and financial backing. Why could you possibly want money that much?'

'I wanted to find you again,' she screamed. 'I see now I was mistaken – you are nothing but a hot-headed, arrogant and ill-tempered bastard with more anger than compassion in you. I thought you were different.'

He let her go abruptly and she stood there simply, arms by her sides, looking at him, feeling betrayed.

He brought his hand to her face and softly stroked her cheek.

'I did not even stop to consider that I might have been partly the cause of that terrible scene. I saw you lying wantonly on the couch and my first thought was of lust. I wanted you Marcella, really wanted you then.'

She caught her breath as the force of his passions hit her. She realised once more that his anger and antagonism were born of his strong physical desires for her. The thought once again made her feel powerful.

'In that small moment I imagined walking over to you, tasting your beauty, ravaging the plump, ripe spheres of your breasts, plundering the softness of your mouth with mine. In my mind's eye, I had worked at your body with my own till you had cried out in exquisite bliss, your body shuddering even as my own erupted into you. It was an instantaneous vision of Olympian delight. That was what you gave me. And then it was shattered.'

He gripped her nude body and stared into her eyes with fervour.

'Can you imagine the desperate desolation that follows if hope of such bliss is offered and then destroyed? It

112

would be better never to taste the food of the gods if dry bread is to be the only diet on offer for ever more.'

'Yes,' she said softly, 'I do know that desolate misery.'

'Then I saw that you were not alone, and worse still, you were bound tightly. Not lightly as a model for a painter might be, but firmly. And that self-loving dauber was watching you as though you were a lump of meat or a bowl of fruit to be sketched. My baser nature took over and I wanted to kill him.'

He held her arms again, his body shaking as he pulled her close to him. She could feel his breath on her cheek and the slight rasp of his chin.

'I was thinking of you,' she murmured. 'Didn't you see that I was ready?'

'I could see you were swollen and available for love but I also knew that I was not the focus of your desire.'

'But you were,' she whispered softly, her lips against his neck. 'You have never stopped being that.'

'And now you are here I want you with such an explosive need that I can hardly keep myself from picking you up, throwing you to the floor and ravishing you.'

'I would prefer a bed,' she said boldly.

He shouted with laughter in a sudden release of tension.

'We have all night ahead of us,' he grinned, 'and this time I will not allow my immediate male urges to take over from the more sensual pleasures.'

The cold plunge bath was a delicious agony. Her nipples stood out in hard little peaks and she hesitantly opened her legs to let the water swirl around her crotch. The shock was exquisite – a rare experience, delicate and sensual. She dipped her hair into the water to wash away the ash and felt clumsy because in the past there had always been a slave to help.

'It is a pity that the furnaces have gone out so there is no hot air, but we will soon adjust to the cold and use water instead of oil to cleanse our bodies. The barbarians

113

seem to manage,' he said as he waded towards her. He was erect, and his movements were unhurried and precise, as though he were savouring every moment that they had together.

'I suppose you have lots of experience on the northern frontiers, if you don't mind this.' She was avid for information about his life.

'Britannia and Gaul you mean? Subduing the Druids and the fierce Caledonians?'

His laugh echoed around the austere little room.

'I have been to Cisalpine Gaul once or twice – they have snow there all the year round on the mountain tops. It is so cold that it almost burns your fingers! You wouldn't believe it possible until you had felt it.'

'You fought on the Danube frontier then?'

He kissed her mouth softly, the warmth a delightful contrast to her cold body.

'I am not nearly brave enough,' he said lightly. 'I arranged life so I was posted further south. I like the lush land and the easy living: heat that shimmers over the land, and sunsets that blaze like fire for a few moments before night falls. I have a little place in Tripolitania where I like to rest up.'

He reached over to a pile of towels that she had found and placed on the black and white tiled floor.

'Do you want to talk about my military career all evening?'

He rubbed the cloth briskly over her body until she warmed up and then threw it aside and touched her body with his hands, as if for the first time, looking intently at her curves. She forgot what she had been saying and gave herself up to the sensuality, running her hands over his torso.

'You look just like the statue of Apollo in the town Forum,' she said. 'The shape of your body is the perfect Greek ideal – wide at the shoulder tapering to narrow hips.'

'You are very knowledgeable.' He smiled.

She brought her hands down to his long legs and

114

swirled the water across his shapely calf and thigh muscles.

'I am educated,' she said indignantly. 'I am not like the average tavern maid, even though that is how I have to earn my keep. When I was thirteen, my parents were killed in a freak storm at sea and all their money was lost. I was about to be married, but the boy's parents backed out when they discovered that I no longer had a dowry. I was lucky that my uncle and aunt took me in.'

She ran her hands from his shoulders along the line of his backside and then round to the front to his inner thighs.

'You know how to enflame a man, my darling,' he murmured, his cock pulsating visibly against the gentle lapping of the cold water.

He put his hands to her breasts and her senses leapt with desire.

He spent time drying her breasts and between her legs, a blissfully slow experience that made her throw back her head and clutch him with her arms outstretched.

When they were both dry, they walked hand in hand to a bedroom and he stood facing her for a long moment.

'Lie down and spread your legs for me, Marcella. I have been consumed with the memory of your enchanting womanhood, open and inviting with its warmth and softness.'

She backed away from him, unable to take her eyes off his erect penis, wanting him inside her. She needed to feel the force of his naked body on hers and to know that he was using his formidable strength for her pleasure.

She lay back and parted her legs, almost shyly, and heard him breathe in sharply.

'You are even more beautiful than you were then. This time you are smiling at me and you are not afraid or ashamed. And you are ready. Your feminine folds are swollen and hot.'

He knelt on the bed in front of her, his knees keeping her legs apart, his shoulders wide and enveloping.

Supporting himself on his arms he began to kiss her mouth with short movements that left her breathless. She opened her mouth, their bodies hardly touching and he entered her with his tongue, gently and slowly. He took her lower lip in his mouth and sucked for a moment, then transferred his attention to the upper lip. She brought her legs up around him, tightened her hold on his torso and pulled. He was like a rock, refusing to move down to her.

'My darling, you will seduce me and ravish me, and I refuse to be drawn into unthinking passion a second time today. I want you to remember this night for the rest of your life. And I want the memory to be sweet – not something that is over in a few moments.'

He sat across her thighs, his manhood high and hard above her stomach, and she put her hands to it and felt the smooth, dark strength. She ran her fingers round the bulbous tip and gently teased him.

She sat up and pushed him roughly away from her till she could put her mouth over his masculine hardness. It felt as though she were coming home. It was bliss to caress the gleaming bulb and lick the tiny bead of moisture from the tip. Prolonging the delight, she licked her lips and gently sucked the top, wanting more of the delicious liquid. She needed to savour every delight his body had to offer.

His hands moved to her nipples, teasing them till they were erect with her desire. The gentle rolling movement of his fingers and thumbs made her writhe until she lay back with her legs apart in silent entreaty. He grasped her legs and placed them over his shoulders.

'I like to look at you close up, open and ready. It is a delightful sight. The best in the world, Marcella.'

The feel of his gaze on her made her flex her internal muscles in anticipation. He smiled and put a gentle finger on her labia. He slid it along the length, then back up again. She pushed her lower body towards him but he was immovable.

He brought his mouth down to a nipple so her legs

were spread wide over his shoulders. He flicked his tongue against the tip with a fast, insistent movement that made her moan with rapture. Transferring his mouth to the other nipple he continued the gentle rolling movement with his fingers.

She tightened her legs each side of his neck and felt the hairs on his chest against her velvety, vulval folds.

He continued to work at her breasts and she felt the fire of desire move through her. She instinctively pointed her toes, tensed her leg muscles and pushed her stomach and pelvis towards him. The marvellous sensuousness of his touch enflamed all her senses and his voice, murmuring into her ear, was like a thousand pipes of Pan on the wind. Without warning, she reached a peak and was suddenly still.

He smiled down at her and kissed her lips gently.

'As I said, you are a real connoisseur. Not all women can be given the ultimate pleasure in that way. You are wonderful, Marcella, wonderful.'

'I've never climaxed like that before.' She felt at once exhilarated and humbled. 'It took me by surprise.'

He ran his tongue between her breasts and down to her stomach. Roughly, he pushed her legs off his shoulders and rested his hands on her hips.

'And now you shall be pleasured like this, my dearest lover.'

The fast flicking movements of his tongue on the soft little gem of her clitoris made her moan with delight. She was being wafted on to Olympus, taken on silken wings into a sphere of delight that she had never before reached.

He gently kissed her clitoris with closed lips and then ran his tongue along the lengths of her glistening folds. He fingered her little bud of desire and took her labia in his mouth. She could feel his tongue inside her as his finger continued to strum on her clit. Her tension increased and she groaned out her pleasures, holding his hair and forcing his head down on her pleasures.

The sensation of release as she shuddered under his

117

tongue came slowly, in great waves of bliss. As the ripples died away, she drifted into blissful relaxation.

After long moments she moved on top of him. She could feel her crotch damp against his legs as she slid down his body.

'Now I shall ravish you,' she said with her hands on his hard, potent, virile stem.

He laughed. 'You have already done so. I am already captivated by your beauty and the natural way you respond to my appetites. You are the most exciting woman I have ever known, Marcella.'

She took him in her hands and then enveloped the silken manhood in her mouth. His fingers were entwined in her hair as she worked at him, plunging her mouth on his erection so he penetrated deeply. Then she slid off and swirled her tongue around the tip. The taste of his passion made her greedy for more, much more.

Abruptly, he pulled her head away.

'That is too much, my love.'

He moved to lie on top of her. 'I want you to climax over and over,' he whispered as he peacefully entered her. 'It will be no good if I have spent. I want to come inside you and feel your body shake and shudder with rapture under me.'

He kissed her mouth, plunging his tongue into her and captivating her body and her soul.

The rhythm of their mutual enchantment was hypnotic and she forgot the present. She moved again into a state of unthinking bliss. The waves of passion gradually built up into a crescendo of unspent power. She lay quietly under his motionless body as he gently stroked her cheek and whispered lovingly in her ear.

He suddenly jolted her awake with a series of urgent movements. She opened her eyes and smiled, straining against his body with ever-increasing power. The sheer hardness of his penis deep within her was exhilarating. She tightened herself and felt the exquisitely subtle internal friction as his body pulled on the muscles that gave her most pleasure.

An intense shudder of partial release pulsed through her. She lay back limply and he fingered her breast and pressed the nipple between his thumb and forefinger. Instantly, the movement triggered her need for further movement inside her.

'Darling, Gaius, I need you. I really need you,' she cried out. 'Hard, really hard.'

Time and time again she matched the strength of his ardour. His firm erection rubbed and massaged the soft velvety depths of her womanhood, pounding along the smooth passage of love, backward and forward in waves of continuous pleasure. The sensation made her lose all sense of time and she was aware of nothing except a total feeling of completeness with his manhood inside her.

Twice she indicated with a mere flutter of her hands that she most craved his fast and hard penetration to achieve a peak. Twice he obliged with a gentle kiss on her mouth and a vigorous thrusting.

She lost count of the times she climaxed and then lay without moving, waiting for the next bout of wild gyrations. She was content simply to savour skin and breath and pulsating nerves.

Finally, he began to move inside her with a fast, intense rhythm he had never used before. His own excitement was mounting and she sensed that he was now relinquishing his self-control. It was like running up a mountain knowing that there would be the other side to come down soon. She strained against his heaving body, matching the strength of his body in her hips, his pubic bone stimulating her externally with each deep thrust. He was glistening with exertion as his body shuddered with uncontrollable and uncontrolled desire.

'Marcella, you betwitch me, like the Sirens. I can't control myself any longer, I have to take my own pleasures with you, with your body.'

He shook long and hard as he reached his climax and she was awed by the majestic strength, the incredible dignity of his moment of release.

119

After a few moments he moved carefully to lie beside her, tumescent and comforting within her body, his hand on her bottom to keep her close.

'You bewitch me, my love, you really do. I haven't met a woman like you and I never will again. I want you near me for all my life.'

The words were like a balm and she lay quietly in his arms till the last vestiges of their passion had quietened down and they could move apart without feeling pain or loss.

Chapter Ten

'Greetings. I have found food. The food of the Gods,' she announced laughingly, as she stumbled over the uneven step of the veranda next morning. A few plump, ripe grapes fell to the tiled floor.

She did not tell him what else she had found whilst exploring the villa and its grounds. She wanted to keep some secrets from him and asking advice would be a sign of weakness.

He was sitting on a low bench, looking very serious. She was conscious that the clothes she was wearing were plain and sensible. The heavy outdoor shoes made her ankles look thick and made her feel like the prim and proper Roman matron whose storage chest she had raided. The brightening look on his face showed her that he was not taken in by exterior appearances and she smiled.

She bent to touch his brow with her lips. Her breasts rubbed tantalisingly against the harsh linen of the other woman's dress. He put his arm around her thigh in a poignantly possessive gesture.

'And I have found some very dry cakes and some eggs in a wooden box. We will have to make do with those.'

'The eggs may not be fresh, but we won't know till we try them.'

She found some olive oil and looked dubiously at the food.

'I think we should be moving on. I feel there are more earth tremors on their way,' he said. 'The earth was heaving all last night and the wind is blowing stronger.'

She smiled at the memory of the quakes. She had lain in his arms feeling safe but at the same time she had been aware that society would frown on what they had been doing. They had pleasured one another many times, waking and taking their physical delights after they had replenished their energy. She felt that there was not an inch of his body that that she did not know intimately.

Half-way through the night they had found some wine and a few stale pieces of bread that were as hard as rock. Dipped in the alcohol they had tasted like a banquet.

'I hoped that we would be safe here in the country, but it is no longer possible to see the mountain for the cloud of ash and we are too close to it for safety. The air here is much thicker than last night. I fear the worst for the town itself.'

'The garden is covered with a fine layer of ash. I didn't know these things could happen,' she said helplessly. 'I thought Terentius was making stories up for effect.'

'I have heard of such disasters, but have never experienced them. The eminent geographer, Strabo, considered it to be volcanic, because of its shape. When Spartacus and his renegade slaves climbed into the crater all those years ago, they managed to get behind the legionary lines simply because nobody imagined that they would be so reckless or determined!'

'I have heard that story,' she said. 'But most people thought the mountain was safe now.'

His hands were moving sensuously over her hips

'Perhaps the Pompeians were made complacent because Spartacus got away with it, coupled with the fact that the quakes seventeen years ago were fairly minor. Talking of coupling . . .'

He wiggled his thumbs towards her mound of love and then lifted her dress and pulled away her muslin

122

loincloth with sharply impatient movements. Her womanhood was exposed to his intimate gaze.

'I may be over-cautious to insist on leaving now, when we are alone in a comfortable villa,' he said gruffly, 'but I want to live to give you many pleasures again. And again.'

He raised his eyes from her with a glint in his smile that made her loins churn with anticipation.

She placed one foot on the bench beside him. He touched her clitoris with his finger before dipping inside her as though testing a new confection. He withdrew his finger and sucked it.

'You taste as good as nectar. Better. I imagine that even the gods would not turn away from such a feast.'

She straddled over his body so she was sitting facing him. His silky fingers stroked her secret places. She pulled at his tunic and held his firm cock in her hands, rolling it tenderly between her palms.

Lifting her bodily, he gently placed her over his rigid erection so her body weight forced it inside her. She fell towards him with the pleasure and nuzzled his neck. He tasted of sweat and passion, manhood and eroticism.

'I like to have my meals in comfort,' he said, grinning. He looked carefree and young, the harsh facial lines receding as he relaxed. He handed her a grape from the table. 'Particularly before a long journey.'

'We haven't any transport,' she said prosaically, elegantly catching some escaped juice with a finger on her chin. She moved her hips from side to side. The effect made him grimace with pleasure and she smoothed his brow with her fingers. He put a hand on her breast and held it gently through the dress, as though it were a precious artwork.

'We will have to walk.'

He closed his eyes as she put a grape in her mouth and kissed him, transferring the fruit to his mouth. She tasted the juice as he bit into it.

She took half the grape and rolled it round her tongue before swallowing and he laughed. His face crinkled into

123

pure delight and his eyes sparkled with uncomplicated appreciation.

'The road was in good condition and we can reach the sea by noon if we hurry,' he said unevenly as she moved her hips rhythmically. 'From there we must hope to find a fisherman who will take us along the coast to safety.'

She continued to move her hips gently as they ate. He held the beaker to her mouth as she drank diluted wine and he laughed as he lapped up the spillages from her neck.

'Have you had enough?' he asked as the floor trembled underneath them, rattling pots and pans and vibrating his body deep within hers.

'No, I haven't had enough,' she whispered. 'This was meant to be. Even the gods want us to enjoy each other. They are doing all the work for us. I don't need to move and nor do you – the gods are sending vibrations of pleasure to us through the earth.'

He put his hands on her thighs and pulled her body towards his with an almost violent insistence that shook her with its intensity. Her inner muscles responded to his movements with deep primeval spasms and she erupted with a force she hadn't known could be possible. His body answered immediately, bursting its inner reservoirs into her, to release the last of the tension and emotion he had withheld from the previous day.

His musky scent mingled with hers and she held him tight. They sat still for a long time, their bodies sated as they silently enjoyed the quiescent closeness of lovers who had known each other a long time, but who also knew that this was only the beginning.

'The mountain has begun to spit fire again.'

Several hours later, they were standing at the roadside looking back towards the town but seeing only a thick pall of smoke. Gaius' eyes were sombre and tired.

She felt the last vestiges of his passion between her legs and tightened her muscles. She wanted to keep the memories and sensations he had given her so willingly, inside her for all time.

The quakes were very potent and they had been constantly thrown off balance as though they were on board a ship in a storm. She was feeling sick from the indigestible meal and the growing fear. She was bruised in a hundred places from the hard, cobbled road.

'What has happened in the town?' Gaius called to a man who was trudging steadily towards them, carrying a small satchel over his shoulders.

'It was a vision of Hades last night. We thought we could escape this morning but the chaos was terrible,' he replied without changing his pace and they fell into step with him. 'Hundreds have been killed by falling bricks and stone and the air is thick. Old people and children are falling like flies, unable to breathe. I saw several completely crushed by fallen capitals.'

'We were lucky to get out yesterday,' said Gaius. 'We should have gone the day before.'

'I got away with this bag,' the man replied bitterly. 'There wasn't time to take more of my belongings. I am ruined. If the town isn't destroyed by the time I get back, everything I own will have been looted. There are people out there with no sense.'

'Don't we know it!' said Gaius harshly.

'They are raiding the houses of the rich, piling the abandoned treasures on any vehicles they can find. Thick, molten rock is pouring over the crater's lip and over the houses near the top. I saw people and animals overcome by it as though they were flies in boiling syrup. I only escaped because I used to be an athlete and I can still sustain short bursts of sprinting. In places the lava was flowing faster than a horse can gallop.'

'Mars Ultor and Vulcan preserve us,' muttered Gaius. 'We should have moved out last night despite the dangers of travelling by night.'

'Mars Ultor and Vulcan are the right gods to appeal to,' called a second man as he strode determinedly past them. 'If I live through this day, I will make a huge donation to Vulcan – I will work until I have enough to

125

commission a statue. Then I will have it placed in a temple in Rome, no less. This, I solemnly vow.'

Marcella pulled the cloak tighter around her. She watched the strong muscles flex, and noted the scars of terrible leg wounds that had been sustained in the long-distant past.

'He's a charioteer,' she whispered to Gaius. He nodded.

'I saw some appalling sights,' the man said as they hurried to catch up with him. 'Even I was shocked, and I thought I'd seen all there was to see on the racing circuit. There are often crashes and deaths, and even more often, horrible injuries, but nothing like this!'

'I thought I'd seen it all in the field of battle,' replied Gaius tersely. 'The gods notice when we become arrogant and think we know it all, and they send us signs of their power.'

'There was this man standing there, cool as you please, making charcoal sketches of the dead and dying. He had their expressions perfectly – real terror and pain. He wasn't ignoring them because he was saving his own skin or those of his loved ones. He simply drew them on planks of wood so he could make money out of them later. He doesn't deserve to live.'

Petro: greedy for the last denarius to be gained from a situation. Could it have been him?

She shivered. 'I wonder what happened to Lydia – and my aunt and uncle. And Petro.'

'Save your worries for yourself, Marcella, not him.'

Gaius' tone was fierce as he quickened his speed, leaving the charioteer behind. 'That painter was the sort of filth that deserves whatever happens to him. You still can't believe that, can you? You were on the road to degradation. Don't think a freeborn woman can't sink into slavery.'

'All those beautiful houses and the art works,' she cried, stumbling after him, unwilling to believe she had been so deceived.

She had wanted so much for herself. Gaius had introduced her to a way of life that was a dream: servants, beautiful clothes, fountains playing in the heat of summer, marvellous colours in the decor and, more importantly, sensual fulfilment. Petro had offered the means to buy her way into such society. Now, it seemed, she would be lucky to get away with her life.

'Beautiful houses are nothing compared to lives.'

His face was tense and set, like a general in a battle, she thought. Suddenly he was the man in command. The lover who had been so delightfully out of control in her arms only a few hours ago had disappeared.

She looked in awe at his determination and strength. Her body was tired and unwilling to walk or run, though her mind was alert to the new sensations he had awakened in her. She wanted only to lie sleepily in his arms and dream. Instead, she had to stumble over the road surface that was treacherously uneven where the quakes had loosened the cobbles.

'I have to rest a while, Gaius,' she said wearily. 'These shoes are sturdy enough but they are too small. Their owner suffers dreadfully from bunions and the leather is hard and has moulded itself to her feet. They cut into my feet and are giving me blisters.'

'You should try carrying your own luggage – I never knew women's make-up could weigh so much,' he replied dryly.

She sat down on the bag and put her head in her hands despairingly.

A massive explosion shook the earth with overwhelming ferocity. She was thrown to the ground as ash and cinders rained on them. The hard surface of the road bruised her knees and elbows and the bandage twisted painfully over her burn.

Gaius threw his thick cloak over her protectively and they huddled together until the worst was over. She felt his breath on her face and smelt his musky skin. She put her lips on him in a gentle caress.

'We have to move on. Now. Or you will have worse

127

pains than a couple of blisters,' he shouted above the noise of the sudden, howling wind.

She rose to her feet and they ran hand in hand down the road in the half-light from the falling debris.

Burning hot cinders occasionally fell on her but the cloak she had taken from the villa was thick enough to withstand the budding flames.

A scream of anguish from the side of the road caught their attention.

'Juno and Hestia, Diana and Minerva, preserve me!'

Three men were bending over an aged woman. One kicked her with hard, gladiatorial-style boots; another was pulling at a small bag she was holding.

'That is all I have in the world,' she screamed.

Dropping Marcella's bag, Gaius shouted, 'Run. I will catch you up.'

He leapt at the tallest thug, felling him with a blow in the small of the back.

'No,' screamed Marcella. 'I won't leave.'

'Go now. Run!'

He kicked the second thug in the face with a mighty blow that sent him hurtling over the woman's body. Blood spurted from the robber's nose and he bent double, but Gaius was already facing the third man who was ready to spring. The first began to stagger to his feet. A knife glinted as he began to move with the precision of a gladiator whose life depended on the outcome of the fight.

She screamed, 'Gaius!'

He was tough, she knew that, but he was used to exercising in the gymnasium, not fighting in the street. Because he was army-trained, she guessed that he would fight according to the rules. He could never prevail against three professional street fighters, intent on murder and theft.

She knew in that instant that she not only lusted after him, revelling in the delights their bodies could create together, but she felt something more, something that would endure for ever.

128

'Ganma, ganma.'

The plaintive voice of a tiny child cut through the noise of the fight and the fury of the natural elements.

He was about two years old and scarcely able to talk plainly. Marcella bent down and picked him up, holding the frail body close to her. He was passive and collected, too young to understand the dangers from either the volcano or the attack.

'It's all right,' she said, her heart beating wildly as she stroked his short dark curls.

Once more the earth shook and she fell heavily on her elbow in an attempt to protect the infant. A cloud of debris enveloped them and he began to cry for his grandmother.

'Hush, she will return soon. You have to be a good boy and play this new game. Can you breathe through this material?'

She held the cloak over the child's face and her own.

'Keep this over your face. This is a game,' she told him determinedly when she dared to open her eyes.

Clasping the cloth to her own mouth and nose, she looked to the place where she had last seen Gaius.

There was nothing but a cloud of ash.

The people had vanished.

Nothing alive was visible.

Shrieking with fear, she staggered blindly to her feet. The child gave a cry so she picked him up and took the road at a dead run, the heavy bag of belongings banging awkwardly against her legs. She held on tightly as fear gave her super-human strength. Molten rock rained down around her. Some hit her and bruised her shoulders and head.

She stumbled on blindly, coughing out the smoke-filled air, tears of fear streaming down her face, blurring her surroundings to an outline.

She had found her lover only to lose him again within hours.

She stumbled on into the semi-darkness of a world

that had turned to chaos. The gods had turned their attentions to destruction, not harmony.

'Oh Vulcan, god of fire,' she prayed, 'Have mercy on us.'

There was no hope in her voice or her heart. The gods were at war with one another, and with the human race.

Chapter Eleven

She was holding the side of a medium-sized cargo
boat, and the child was clinging to her with pathetically frail limbs. She had no recollection of how she had
got there.

All around her, people were shouting. Some screamed
abuse at each other, others shrieked anguished pleas to
the gods. They offered sacrifices, gifts, major art-works
or even architectural wonders, to honour the deities if
they were spared. The water was very turbulent as the
volcano continued to pour out its molten contents over
the land and into the sea. She could see several boats
nearby having difficulty as they struggled to take sur-
vivors to safety. Floating bodies further impeded the
rowers. The air was still thickly laden with ash and the
shore-line was completely concealed as though in a sea-
mist.

She became aware of strong muscles and a harsh face
she dimly recognised. The man beside her was quietly
offering prayers to the gods who watched over fighters
and soldiers. Their names reminded her of Gaius and then
she was aware of the numbness in her soul: he was dead.

'They've brought out the war-ships.'

She focussed her eyes in the semi-darkness and could
make out the shape of a huge ship ploughing strongly

through the water towards the shore, the oars moving in perfect, professional unison. The silent power was terrifying and she realised that she was witnessing a scene that civilians never normally experienced. On the occasions in the past when the war-ships had passed the bay, they had been merely drifting, maintaining a presence in peaceful waters, and not displaying a fraction of their full capacities.

'The worst is nearly over for us,' the man next to her continued. 'We have only to reach those rocks for calmer water.'

He pointed to some still, dark shapes in the distance.

'We met you on our way from the town,' she said, dazed. 'You are a charioteer.'

'My name is Virius. You were with the hero-type. He called you Marcella. He hadn't a chance.'

'You saw?'

'I didn't have time to help. The debris must have covered them completely.'

The matter-of-fact way he spoke seemed as unreal as the entire scene and she clung tightly to the child and stared through the filthy air. It felt like an age before they reached the rocks where the water was calmer in the shelter of a promontory. The passengers and crew suddenly fell silent as a huge torch of fire spurted through the dark clouds of debris above the distant volcano. The full horrors of the situation they had escaped were made graphically clear. She felt disorientated, unable to think further than her loss. Gaius was dead. He would never return and she would have to lead her life without him.

'Back to normality,' said Virius and she prayed to the Olympians that he was speaking the truth.

A gull circled overhead before swooping to pick up a scrap.

Hours later, the boat drifted northwards across green seas under a blue, cloudless sky.

'I half-carried you the last few hundred paces,' Virius told her.

132

The pandemonium on deck had frightened the child and made Marcella dazed so he had taken them into the deserted cargo hold to rest on the sacks of corn.

'You were nearly unconscious, and the child was clinging on to you so tightly that I had an arm free for both our bags. I thought he was yours.'

The crooned harmonies of the rowers, as they rested on their oars, were lulling the little boy to sleep in Marcella's arms.

'You race on the circuit,' she said dully, aware that he had saved her life and that she owed him at least politeness.

'In Gaul most of the year, and Rome during the September Games. I was in Pompeii to study their training methods.'

He laughed, and his light-heartedness seemed strange after the tension.

His dark curly hair and the flashing white smile against his swarthy complexion would, she thought bleakly, give him instant appeal on the race-track. He would be attractive even from a distance and women would drool over him.

'How many races have you won?'

The social enquiry was torn from her. She wanted to scream and destroy things, to rid herself of her anger and fear, but instead she had to nurse an innocent child in her arms and make conversation with a stranger whose way of life was totally different from anything she had experienced.

His deep laugh rumbled through his thickset body as he lay a few feet away from her, sprawled out and at ease.

'I have lost count, but I shall retire after the next Games in Rome. I will go back to Syria, where I was born, and return to my family's glass-making business. Or maybe I shall manufacture pottery statuettes of Mars or Vulcan. After this tragedy, people all over the Roman world will be keen to buy.'

'Over the years, I have watched many races and seen

many accidents,' she said slowly. She felt humbled by the calm, unassuming way he was dealing with the tragedy, when they had been surrounded by near-hysteria for hours and she had totally collapsed. 'Somehow, from the safety of the stands, the dangers of the circuit seem less real.'

'Charioteers risk their lives in every race for the enjoyment of the crowd and are expected to perform with courage every time,' he agreed.

The little boy sighed deeply and gave himself up to sleep.

'You need sleep too,' Virius said. 'You are not used to danger and physical exercise.'

Hours later, she was still listening to the noises from deck, the tension in her mind and body refusing to leave. She could hear a few people laughing and exchanging stories of their escape. The child was fast asleep and Marcella became aware that Virius was intermittently thowing her half-hidden glances as she lay back, willing the memories to leave her in peace.

After a while, her body began to shake uncontrollably and tears fell. He took her gently in his arms and she sobbed against his hard, muscular chest. She could still smell the ash and smoke on their clothes, a terrible reminder of all they had escaped.

He held her tight, and twined his legs around hers as she lay on top of him, clinging on fast. She knew that he made his living by challenging the gods to destroy him, daring them to spill his chariot or make his horses lame at the wrong moment. He had survived.

Under the strong masculine odour of his skin, she also detected the feral strength and determination.

As she shook in his arms and the sobs gradually subsided, she felt as though his physical and mental powers were being transmitted to her. She craved his reassurance and the life-force he represented. As if he sensed the change in her, he put a hand on her chin and kissed her deeply. Her body responded with gratitude.

The potency of his physical power overwhelmed her senses. The image he presented was immensely strong and comforting as he silently moved on top of her and she parted her legs slightly to accommodate him. The great weight of his body felt secure and right, close to her. He pulled at her dress and she sighed as his hard manhood penetrated her feminine softness.

The effect was tenderly euphoric and secure. Now that Gaius was gone, there wasn't any other place in the world she would rather have been. She desperately needed the reassuring sensation of Virius' thick, hard penis inside her. She tightened her inner muscles and felt him move into erotic spasm. The ripples of released tension pulsed through her as she tightly squeezed him with her internal muscles. She pushed upwards so her clitoral muscles were stretched taut.

He immediately began a frantic series of thrusts that she countered with urgency. The tragedy and the horror made her fight the elements through his strong, resilient body.

They hurled their bodies together as though they were back in mortal danger and there was no other way out. He ran his teeth along her neck, grazing her skin and she dug her fingernails into his back and then beat against him with her fists. His mouth plundered hers in a fierce, possessive kiss. She bucked against him as if she wanted to possess his innermost desires. He was like a creature owned by a spirit of the woods and she matched his wildness as though she were Diana, goddess of the hunt. In their frenetic coupling gentleness, tenderness and softness were irrelevant. She wanted to tear from him the secret to her future happiness and keep it for ever.

She screamed out two sharp, fast, pulsating releases of tension and lay back, exhausted.

He grunted in satisfaction and lay still, on top of her, for a few moments. She could taste the sweat and smell the musk of his efforts.

Slowly, he began a repetitive action with his loins. Now that her first spasms of need were over, she felt

135

secure enough to think about him. His prick was enormous, but the sweet, familiar tightness she felt with Gaius was absent.

In. Out. In. Out. The act suddenly took on a lack of urgency and did not even seem to have anything to do with her, except as a pleasant, comforting way to spend time.

She watched the top of his head as he grunted and groaned. She flexed her muscles experimentally, but the urge to gain further satisfaction from him was absent. She felt that he had already given her the strength she needed. To take more would be greedy. She consciously calmed herself down and began to concentrate on the man whose strength lay within her. His needs were now the most important thing.

After a while she became aware that the rowers were once more active and the instructions were being shouted out loud: in, out, in, out, in, out.

Virius closed his eyes and unconsciously adjusted his coital strokes to theirs.

After the tense hours of danger, she tried to concentrate, but the bubbles of laughter threatened to overflow. As her body shook, a small spasm of lust ran through her and that in turn made her laugh all the harder. She pushed her fist into her mouth so he would think she was once more in the throes of passion. In. Out. In. Out. She felt hysterical giggles welling up.

He erupted in his climax long before she had expected and she cried out an instant later. She deliberately shook her body as if with the fever of orgasm and shrieked out the last of her pent-up energy and fears.

'That was good. In the dark. No contrived stimulation. No competition. Superb.' He pulled himself out and adjusted his tunic and her dress.

'Nobody would know we had done it. I'll go and get us some food – there must be a crust of bread on board somewhere.'

She lay still in the darkness feeling calm and more

136

optimistic. She silently gave thanks to Juno for saving her life.

'What did you mean when you said there was no competition?' she asked later, as they ate some pastries that he bought from the crew.

'The racing circuit is a notoriously dangerous way of life,' he replied. 'And there are many compensations. Money is one. And women like charioteers! Some of them very rich and well-born.'

His grin was frankly lascivious.

She smiled, still bemused.

'When they visit us,' he continued, 'Our colleagues and trainers are aware of this. They make wagers and try to watch. We have to put on a performance in bed as well as on the racing circuit. The athletes and boxers say the same. After a day risking your life or your future health, you feel like something quiet and relaxing, not another feat of endurance. I enjoyed being with you without any of that.'

When the boat neared the port of Ostia, the refugees began to crowd the side, anxious to disembark.

The little boy began to cry, so she gave him food, but he pushed it away and screamed louder.

'You want your granma. I want my lover,' she whispered sadly as she held him tight, trying to recapture in her imagination the feel of Gaius's body.

'We will be in Rome before the day is out,' muttered Virius into her ear. 'Then we can relax.'

'The passage was free. Disembarking will cost you,' shouted the captain as the ropes were secured.

The passengers swore and cursed, but the sailors lined the side near the dock and there was no other way off. Ahead of them, a showy girl simpered and flounced until the seaman nearest her gave her a wink and pulled her behind some bales.

'Women and girls can pay in the usual way for stowaways if they haven't the coins. Men – either you pay or the slave masters will pick you up.'

The captain pointed to a group of tough-looking men on the quayside.

Marcella thought furiously that if she had to open her bag, they would see how much she had and would take the lot. She had earned the money the hard way and wasn't prepared to lose it.

'I will not gratify some disgusting, disease-ridden sailor,' she said challengingly.

'The lady is with me,' said Virius. 'And the child.'

The captain glanced at him as though about to argue and a flicker of disbelief crossed his face.

'Virius. The one they call Invictus,' he said flatly.

Virius nodded. He looked like a rock, even next to the heavily built seamen.

'I saw you race in the September Games, the year you won that title.'

'I remember that year.'

'You careened round the corner of the circuit like a madman! One wheel off the ground and the crowd screaming. I had a large pouch of silver on you to win and I thought I'd lost it.'

'I took a chance. The only thing that team of horses had in their favour was that they were nimble. Their speed was miserable. Everyone else was going for a wide corner sweep and expecting to make up the time on the straight.'

'It seemed like a mad fool decision. You turned them on the inside, going far too fast. I thought the horses were going to break in half to get round the end of the central spine of the course. I'll never forget it.'

The nearest seamen were looking on with expressions ranging from open admiration to unease.

'I'll never forget it either,' Virius Invictus agreed dryly. 'I was lucky. Be lucky yourself.'

It was a veiled threat, thought Marcella, but the man decided to interpret it as a good wish. He stood aside as they stepped to the firm ground unharmed and free.

The little boy suddenly struggled vigorously in her arms.

'Mama!'

A youngish woman slid out of the crowd and the child melted into her arms.

'He has been spending a few weeks with his grannie,' the woman explained, hardly looking at Marcella as she stroked her baby. 'It is a miracle that I have found him again after the eruption! My mother-in-law will be around somewhere, I expect.'

They clung together and Marcella turned away, unable to find words to explain that the grandmother would never return.

'The gods favour us. We owe it to them to keep our minds open to all possibilities,' said Virius as they began to search for a lift into Rome.

'Gaius must be dead,' she replied with sorrow. 'The gods sent him into my life for a short period of passion and sensuality. Through him they introduced me to a new way of life where sensual matters are to be enjoyed, not suppressed. There must have been a reason for that.'

Virius looked confidently down at her, his dark good looks beginning to glow as the danger and the black memories slowly receded.

'I have long-standing invitations to stay with several friends in Rome. Many of them will be out of town at the moment, escaping the heat, so we won't lack a bed for the night. We need a few parties to cheer us up. Even at this time of year there should be a few worth going to.'

Virius took her to a modest house on the outskirts of Rome where they slept undisturbed well into the next day. She awoke in a comfortable bed and found him fumbling at her breasts under the cover. She turned towards him sleepily and kissed him before allowing her hands to stray downwards. His penis was huge as she stroked it gently and moved to straddle his body.

'No,' he said, 'I am too tired for all that. Something quiet and easy.'

He lay beside her so his mouth was near her mound

of love, his loins by her head. She could smell his intimate musk as he began to lick her clit, holding his arm under her thighs in a close embrace. She pushed towards him and felt his tongue slide up to her vulva in gentle caress.

She reached for his penis and sucked the tip, her hands stroking its length.

His insistent tongue was enflaming her, forcing her to flex her leg muscles and push herself to a climax. She quickly took her mouth from his manhood for fear of hurting him involuntarily as she reached the zenith of her pleasure. It came fast and sweetly as he expertly rolled his tongue around her clit and held her tightly.

She sighed and lay still, his face resting on her thigh so that his breath fanned her secret places.

She took his prick in her hand once more and almost immediately he erupted, the spend spraying her breasts. She felt as if it were a healing balm, giving her strength and vitality.

'Nice and quiet. Nice and gentle. Exactly how I like it,' he muttered.

Much later in the day, newly bathed and wearing one of the gowns she had been given in Pompeii, Marcella stepped out of a litter in front of a superb town house.

Virius took her arm and walked by her side into the hallway.

'The party is already underway,' she remarked as they reached a large ante-room which contained no furniture. She watched the guests closely, eager for a taste of Roman sophistication.

A woman called out in a low, slightly husky voice. A girl in a blue dress turned and smiled, elegantly poised on whisper-light slippers.

She was slender as a nereid, and swathed in a gown of white silk that had been embroidered with silver to complement the white blonde colour of her hair. The older woman was a stunning contast. She was dark-skinned and sultry with long tresses that were parted in the centre and caught up in a gold-embroidered ribbon. Her dress was shorter than was the fashion, showing her calves as though she were a man.

They embraced warmly, like friends. The dark woman put her mouth on the girl's lips and tongued her vigorously. The girl put her hands up to her own breasts and began to knead them as the woman touched her between the legs.

Marcella stared.

'Hetaerae. I've fucked enough of them to know they often don't much like men,' said Virius disparagingly. 'They make a good living, but they are all show and no real feeling. They are often too intellectual to be truly carnal, but they can put on a good performance, I grant them that!'

'They are lovely.' Marcella was captivated by the girl's ethereal looks. 'I never thought to see such beautiful people. They are unashamed to show their needs and passions in public. Wonderful!'

She was wearing one of the gowns she had been given in Pompeii. It was blue, embellished with silver braid. She had tied the belt above her waist so that her breasts were caressed by the soft material. Her arms were bare except for the matching silver jewellery and she wore the jet ring.

'You are beautiful, too. You look like the wife of a lesser senator or the mistress of a very important man indeed.'

'You wouldn't have brought me to such a high-class house if I had possessed only my plain travelling clothes,' she suggested boldly, still watching the two women as they gracefully parted and walked off side by side. Their hips swayed alluringly so that the material of their gowns swirled and accentuated their curves.

'Wasn't it lucky that I was able to bring some of my clothes with me from Pompeii?'

'Fortuna has been with us. I will bet you haven't tasted anything like this before.'

He gestured to a dish of a whitish substance that a slave presented to him.

'Go ahead, taste!

She dipped a finger in and shrieked. 'It is hot! But it isn't steaming!'

He roared with laughter. 'It is not hot. It is cold. Try again.'

She remembered Gaius telling her that the snow in Cisalpine Gaul had been so cold it felt hot. She took the silver spoon and plunged it in, putting some of the substance in her mouth.

'It is cold – very cold. You are right. Where does this come from?'

Some of the delicious food began to melt and she licked it from around her mouth.

'It takes practice to eat this,' she said with a laugh.

'It starts out as a huge lump of ice and fleet-footed teams of horses haul it from the mountains. By the time it gets here there is very little left. The Emperor Nero started the craze and now it is here to stay. It is good, isn't it?

'Is this what snow tastes like? It is like honey and eggs and . . .'

He chuckled. 'No, this is not what snow tastes like. It is what it tastes like when it has been mixed with honey and eggs and so on.'

She spooned it up quickly as he watched indulgently.

'The heat of the room is causing it to melt quickly. Hurry up so we can go to where the action is. I am tired of being the centre of attention. I want to see the others sweat for my pleasure this time. There's an interesting contest about to start. I have put two sestertii on number eight.'

Licking her fingers, she followed him through the throng of gorgeously dressed people.

The rooms were sumptuously decorated with intricate floor mosaics and richly encrusted plaster ceilings.

'I knew a painter,' she said. 'I once thought he was the

most talented artist one could imagine, but these gilded ceilings are well beyond his capabilities.'

Had Petronius lived?

Had Gaius survived?

Her heart was heavy as she followed Virius into a room, luxuriously embellished with rich colours. The painter had created open vistas of olive groves in the latest, elaborate fashions, but nobody was admiring the decor.

People jostled each other in the small space so she had to crane her neck and stand on tiptoe.

'Ladies and lords, freedmen, slaves. You are all welcome if you have the coins to make a wager. Those who do not wish to stay may leave now. I warn you that Epicurians and Stoics, philosophers, prudes, educators and aesthetes will not find this show appealing.'

'What is the show?' asked a tall, withdrawn-looking man.

'It is fucking good, master, and I don't use the word lightly! But if you have to ask it's probably not for you!'

The Master of Ceremonies was a small but forceful freedman. The gold chains around his neck proved that he had put his freedom to good use and was now very prosperous.

A number of people began to leave, some with rueful smiles to indicate that they were too poor to stay. Others had contemptuous looks on their faces. Marcella noted that they were generally respectable-looking matrons and their repressed-looking spouses.

'How much do we need?' she whispered.

'That is all taken care of. I told you, I have contacts in Rome. Which of the men do you think will stay the course longest?'

She looked at the line-up of manhood standing about five yards from a board on which a series of circles had been drawn in charcoal.

'I don't know – what do they have to do?'

'The first contest, ladies and lords, is the long-distance throw.'

She bit her lip with disappointment.

'The man to hit the target or get nearest to it takes the prize.'

The line of men lifted their tunics and showed their erect cocks. Marcella gasped.

'Which of these will hit the board first?'

Late bets were being taken. People, especially the women, were inspecting the contestants, occasionally prodding their cocks with speculative fingers. A man at the end of the line lost his erection completely and retired. There were gales of laughter. Another started to wilt but a woman from the crowd bent and sucked him for a moment or two until he leapt into readiness again. He grinned his thanks and blew a kiss.

'Who have you wagered on?' Marcella asked Virius.

'The man near the end – number eight. He is taller and his prick is big, so he is likely to hit the target whatever happens. The others may have greater force, but he has the advantage of height.'

'Let the contest begin.'

The Master of Ceremonies clapped his hands and the men began to get themselves ready. Two of them used their hands in long up and down strokes. One had brought a male slave to help. Three had brought female attendants to blow and squeeze alternately. The tall man stood there without stimulus.

'He is useless,' she whispered.

A number of other people agreed with her.

'Our money back. You fraud, you wastrel. Our money back!'

'Wait,' said Virius. 'This is just his way. I have seen him before, in Africa Proconsularis. He was invincible. He takes a time to build up – but if he makes it, the effect is outstanding!'

Number eight glanced at the contestant next to him who was being helped by a female slave. She was kneeling on the floor between her master's legs, sucking him hard and using her hands around the base of his prick and his balls.

'Yes, nearly there, nearly there!' somebody shouted.

Number eight continued to watch them, his prick still huge and hard. It began to pulsate as the woman worked with enthusiasm on her man.

'Yes!'

The man pulled himself from the woman and pointed his stem towards the board.

The tall man erupted with force. The spend flew across the room as a cheer rose from the crowd. It spurted in a fountain, high into the air, the lights catching it and exaggerating the arc.

Marcella caught her breath as the dark decor behind showed up the spend in great clarity.

'They chose the right venue for the greatest effect!' she cried in astonishment as the spend splattered the board fractionally before the other man's. The victor laughed and dropped his tunic to collect his earnings.

'I have won a handful of coins on that. Look – he's beaten them all,' replied Virius with satisfaction.

The losers looked frustrated and Marcella tried not to giggle as they unsuccessfully attempted to walk with dignity from the room, their tunics distorted.

'And now – the next context.'

The two hetaerae that Marcella had noticed earlier stood at the improvised stage, hand in hand and totally naked except for voluminous muslin scarves.

'They look magnificent!' she murmured in awe.

'The first couple will use only what the gods gave them!' announced the Master of Ceremonies. 'The second couple will use an artificial device which was invented in the east.'

'There isn't a way they could prove who had won if women compete,' said Marcella to Virius.

'This contest is won on points – it is an act of artistic merit, because, as you say, women can fake it.'

As the couple got into position she glanced across the room and saw, in horror, her tormentor from Pompeii – Caballius Zoticus.

Chapter Twelve

The nude woman moved gracefully across the stage. Ankles flexed, she thrust her breasts forward so that her back was arched. Her transparent scarf billowed out and caught on her shapely calves and neat little buttocks.

'That material must have cost a fortune,' said Marcella, keeping one anxious eye on Caballius Zoticus.

The dancer's blonde partner reclined on the floor and writhed with a matching elegance. She beckoned with her arms and flexed her long slim legs in open invitation. She ran her hands along her body to emphasise its curves. As the crowd began to sigh in appreciation, she threw one leg in the air with toes pointed. She brought her legs modestly together, with her knees bent at the knee to shield her body.

The dancer pirouetted and turned her back, strutting purposefully away, tossing her dark hair voluptuously. The young woman on the floor sank down dejectedly, her arms gracefully folded along her legs. Her hair concealed her face and cascaded almost to the floor like a silver-gilt curtain.

The audience moaned in sympathy and the dancer turned, looked around her with exaggerated surprise and then, finally, with theatrical dismay, noticed her partner's gloom. She flicked the blonde hair carelessly

146

with her toes and kicked her leg high above the reclining woman's head. The gilt on her showy ankle chain caught the light.

The woman on the floor sat up and caught hold of her partner's leg. She ran her fingers along her calf and licked the arch of her foot as if she were starving.

The audience hooted their approval as the dancer once more made a high kick over her partner's head. Marcella saw the hard look on Caballius' face as he caught sight of the woman's crotch. She shivered.

'This will be hard to beat,' muttered Virius. 'It makes a change, I can tell you, watching women working for their own pleasures instead of expecting me to do it for them. Lazy cows, most of them.'

She put her hand under his tunic and felt his tumescent cock. 'Is that a challenge?'

'Be silent and watch. This isn't the time to sulk and try to prove your expertise.'

He pushed her hand away.

The girl on the floor began to moan. She shook her breasts, put a hand on her nipples and stroked them delicately in her palms. She tried to reach them with her tongue. The women in the audience shouted encouragement. One nipple began to peak as she tweaked herself, coaxing the little circle as though it had a life of its own.

Opposite Marcella, a woman was staring avidly at the show. She pulled a breast from her dress and the man standing behind her took it in his hand and began massaging. Her breast was soft and voluptuous, though not comparable in beauty to those of the dancers. The woman threw her head back, felt behind her for his cock and the two stood watching the show, their hands working in unison.

The girl on the floor moaned and beckoned. The dark woman strode towards her, kicked a leg in the air and did the splits. The blonde reached up, stopped her partner's legs as they slid towards the floor and held her above her face, in a graceful pose.

The audience began to scream in frenzied approval as

147

the woman on top began to manipulate her own breasts, her head thrown back.

'How does she manage that?' asked Marcella 'She must be so supple!'

'They start training when they are young. Usually they are the daughters of successful courtesans. It takes more than one generation to make a really good intimate dancer,' Virius replied.

The watching woman with her hand on the man's penis began to moan and a second woman knelt in front of her, and plunged her head under her skirt. Marcella could see the draperies move as she sucked and licked.

Caballius was watching the two on the floor, his eyes fixed between the dark woman's legs. When the audience began to chant, the girl on the floor began to lick her partner's vulva and the audience shouted with each rhythmic shake of her breasts. Caballius began to talk to the Master of Ceremonies.

The second pair of contestants walked to the stage – a brunette and a redhead. The first wore a leather thong around her loins and two triangular pieces of leather over her breasts. The redhead was completely naked.

The crowd went wild.

'Maybe I was wrong. Perhaps there is something better,' muttered Virius in Marcella's ear. She could feel his breath on her neck and his hard body against her back. He lifted her skirt at the back and slid his fingers around to her mons so she was still modestly covered. She parted her legs a little and he bent close to her and pushed a finger inside her. She rocked gently in response to the delicious feeling as the heel of his hand pressed against her clitoris.

'She has an exquisite figure – perfect,' she whispered.

'She is like a wood nymph,' he agreed.

The henna'd girl strutted to the centre of the stage, her little breasts pushed high. Her labia were prominent as she arched her back and thrust her legs wide apart, almost like a sailor on board ship. She appeared oblivious to the other couple.

She wriggled her hips and her breasts, eyeing the watchers boldly, deliberately taking the attention from the couple on the floor.

'What is she going to do?'

Marcella rested her weight against Virius and parted her legs further to encourage him.

'This is a new show to me – don't ask me,' he said hoarsely.

The darker woman brandished a long implement, showing it to the crowd as though it were a trophy.

She walked straight up to the redhead and lifted one of her legs unceremoniously so the crowd could enjoy a further glimpse of her soft pink cleft.

Marcella glanced around and saw that Caballius had disappeared. She sighed with relief. Virius' strong hand gently massaging her most intimate areas felt warm, secure and comforting.

The redheaded performer turned to look at her audience and slowly smiled as the phallus was inserted into her. With each twist she convulsed her body theatrically and closed her eyes. Her partner continued to pump the implement into her and she threw her body back, arching it until her long hair touched the ground behind her and the taller woman's arm was straining with the effort of supporting her.

The blonde and the dark-haired beauty on the floor finished their gyrations and stepped apart gracefully, but it was the team that was still engrossed who had the crowd's approval.

'You may now stop,' cried the Master of Ceremonies.

The brunette continued to pump the phallus into her partner who moaned loudly.

'This isn't faked,' whispered Marcella as the ripples of desire pulsed through her own body.

'I don't think so either,' he muttered.

The redhead closed her eyes and her partner pulled her up so their two bodies were pressed together. The brunette's thong fell unheeded to the ground as they kissed with depth and passion. Her hand began to rub against her own clitoris each time she pulled the phallus out, using a grace and elegance that surprised Marcella. The crowd gradually became hushed.

'You win – you can stop now,' announced the Master of Ceremonies.

The redhead brought her hand to the other woman's mound and began to vibrate her clitoral bud. The crowd fell silent and then someone began to clap slowly.

They moved in unison, with the rhythm of the clapping. At last, with a cry from the redhead, closely followed by a strangled little sound of pleasure from the darker woman, they fell apart.

Virius held Marcella tightly, rocking her body against his and she felt his body shudder in ejaculation. He withdrew his hand from her body and straightened up.

The brunette gently withdrew the phallus and showed it triumphantly to the audience. The applause was tumultuous. They both smiled and hugged one another, dimpling with their success.

'And another time!' shouted a woman. 'One more.'

They glanced at each other and smiled knowingly. Each put one hand to her own crotch and one to her partner's breast.

The crowd whistled and called out lewd slogans. The women shook as if in climax, fell apart, pirouetted gracefully and swaggered off to collect their prize money.

'We have an unusual additional item tonight for your delight, lords and ladies,' announced the Master of Cememonies. 'An auction of a very fine painting that will be of interest to all lovers of great art.'

To Marcella's horror, a slave held up Petronius' board painting of her private charms, that she had last seen in Pompeii. Virius chuckled into her ear.

'The girl in the painting looks a bit like you.'

Marcella stood with her arms clasped round him, hugging him close to distract his attention. He kissed her hard on the mouth.

'Give generously, ladies and lords, because the vendor

has recently escaped from the disaster in Pompeii. We heard today that our illustrious and generous Emperor Titus is sending aid to the town. Here is your chance to help a refugee who got out with only the clothes he stood up in and this fine picture.'

As the bids began, she felt herself going scarlet with disgust and shame. She moved closer to Virius.

The bidding rose very rapidly and the painting was bought for a vast sum by a thin, mean-looking man with bad teeth. Marcella shook with anger at the small amount that Petronius had paid her.

'By Jupiter you are full of lust, aren't you,' observed Virius. 'You'll be ready for love tonight if you are this excited now.'

She smiled wanly.

'And now,' shouted the auctioneer. 'The contest you have all been waiting for – the fucking. Ten of the best, most throbbing cunts in Rome and ten lusty contestants. Who can thrust into all ten at least five times and not lose his stamina?'

As her tension lessened, Marcella looked at Virius in amazement.

'The man who fills the bowl at the end of the line of girls gets a bonus prize,' he explained. 'There will be several of these line-ups but I've seen enough – haven't you? The air is getting too smokey. It's always a mistake to put too many oil-lamps in one room.'

'I expect they want us to see the show more clearly.'

'It is self-defeating. We see better at the beginning but when things hot up our eyes water and everything is hazy. Come on, let's find a board game. I have a few coins I want to wager.'

'But I've never seen anything like this,' protested Marcella.

'It becomes dull,' he said dismissively. 'This sort of thing is exciting at first, but there is more to life.'

'But you have seen it before.'

'You mean I am selfish by not letting you watch?'

'Just a little. Please, may I watch just one or two of the contestants?'

He smiled indulgently and stood her in front of him once more, his arms protectively around her body.

A line of ten girls marched out, their figures totally obscured by wildly coloured dresses and togas. They smiled and simpered under thick make-up and then turned to face away from the audience.

'Let the first contestant begin,' cried the Master of Ceremonies.

A huge man walked forward and stripped off his loincloth so that his magnificent penis was visible. It stood ram-rod straight and looked even bigger than it was because it had been oiled. The glans was a deep purple and Marcella wondered if it had been dyed with vegetable juice. She was glad of Virius' hands on her breasts, because the thought of such a vast manhood penetrating her inner secrets stirred her deepest womanly senses.

The girls lifted their skirts in unison and, shuffling their legs slightly apart, bent down to present their bottoms to the watchers. Their labia were just visible, rouged so that the audience could see them more clearly.

The man ran his fingers up and down his cock and grinned at the audience, inviting their admiration. Amid the cheers, he turned and immediately pushed into the first girl.

'One, two, three, four five. Out. Next. One, two, three, four, five . . . .'

The crowd chanted as he thrust into each girl in turn. He ejaculated over the floor before he could get inside the sixth.

Disappointed, he picked up his loincloth.

'Next contestant. Any whore already entered may retire now if she wishes. Let the replacements be brought,' shouted the Master of Ceremonies.

'I've seen enough,' said Virius. 'Caballius Zoticus was here earlier – that means he will be competing. He always wins because he can keep an erection going as long as he wishes. I don't think he's normal. Certainly he must have been blessed by Priapus himself. I want to make a few bets.'

They edged their way out and she glanced around the hallway for Caballius Zoticus, but it was empty except for a line of patient harlots, waiting their turn.

'I will meet you in about an hour, Virius,' said Marcella. 'Gambling holds no interest for me because I have no money. I am hungry – I need to store up some energy for later!'

He grinned.

The view of the room was distorted as she looked at Caballius Zoticus through her own splayed legs. She had managed to beg and bribe the row of harlots into helping her. When she explained her intentions, they had giggled as they dressed her and rouged her outer folds with wine dregs.

'Let the contest begin,' announced the Master of Ceremonies. He sounded weary.

'Hurry, hurry. Come on Caballius, you bastard, come on,' she hissed under her breath.

Caballius grasped her hips roughly and pulled back his pelvis ready for a mighty thrust between her legs. She realised that she had a mere fraction of a moment to act or she would simply be rutted for the count of five by the man she loathed more than anyone.

She saw his legs flex. She brought her hands between her legs as he thrust himself towards her.

He roared with the surprise and discomfort as she tightened her grip on the muslin bag she had filled with honeyed ice. She crushed the slivers around his rapidly wilting dick and could not resist squeezing really tight for the count of five. She hoped that it felt like glass.

He ripped himself away from her and she shunted the bag sideways to the girl next to her. The prostitutes passed it rapidly along the line, hidden by the long skirts and togas.

The crowd was roaring with laughter at his flaccidity

and he kicked out at her, but she was ready for his viciousness and turned quickly to evade him. She grinned triumphantly at the watchers, confident that under the cheap, thick, make-up nobody could recognise her.

'Leave her alone. She beat you fair and square,' shouted a man.

The crowd roared its delight. The bag of ice now safely removed, the painted whores stood up and cheered. The prostitute next to her hugged her and a woman from the audience threw her a small bag of coins.

'She's frigid. Cold as the winter in Ultima Thule!' Caballius roared. 'I demand an enquiry and a fresh line-up.'

'Bah!'

'You are just a bad loser!'

'You've lost the knack!'

'Go and practise. You are finished in this kind of sport.'

'He'll never live this down. Never. Serves the bastard right.'

Marcella basked in her success and smiled at the cheering audience, twisting and turning so her voluminous skirts floated away from her body. She pirouetted as she had seen the dancer do, and strutted from the room in triumph.

Outside, the line of prostitutes were agog for the gossip. She quickly filled them in on the details until they were convulsed in giggles.

'You have a customer,' the girl nearest her said, looking over her shoulder, still laughing.

'Congratulations.' His voice was cold.

She turned to look at him and saw that his face was set and harsh.

'Yes,' he said, his eyes hard and glinting, like polished jet. 'I too escaped the volcano.'

'Gaius.'

He pulled her roughly across the hall, out of ear-shot of the whores.

'What a waste! You eluded the wrath of the gods. Then you threw away a magnificent talent to become a common harlot and take part in these vulgar games. I had thought you had more pride and discrimination than that, Marcella!'

Chapter Thirteen

'*G*aius! I am so pleased to see you!'
    She was shaking with the shocked delight of seeing him again. Delight because he was alive and well. Shock because he had seen her dressed as a whore.

'I thought you were dead. Don't be angry. I had to run – there was nothing left in the place where you had been standing.'

'I don't blame you for running. I told you to do so.' His voice was cold. 'You have my contempt because of what you have done with the life the gods so generously allowed you to continue.'

'Don't let this uniform fool you – I am not a harlot!'

'That,' he said scornfully, 'is what they all say. They are courtesans or hetaerae, ladies of the night or any phrase that suggests they are cultured and educated. No high-class courtesan would be seen dead dressed as you are!'

His body was shaking slightly with the shimmering intensity of deliberately shackled emotions and desire.

'Look at yourself! In the degrading clothes of the most common prostitute, for whom sexual favours are no more than a method of getting money. I thought that you were the rare kind of freeborn woman who has an insatiable need which she channels into an art form.

Where, in the name of the Olympians themselves, did you get this toga, if not from the kind of whore whose idea of hard work is to kneel down for a few moments behind the Colosseum with a handful of dupondii in her hand and a stranger's cock in her mouth?'

She turned away from him, blinking at the violence of his crudely expressed feelings, but he spun her around and kissed her roughly.

'How many men have savoured your pleasures for money, since I last saw you?'

He forced her behind a pillar and held her shoulders with a hard grip.

'If I want you again, I realise that I shall have to be quick, or your price will far too high for me to afford!'

He groped around under the toga, his face dark with anger. His fingers made contact with her feminine creases. She wrenched herself free and slapped him so hard that he shook his head and grunted with the pain. He grabbed hold of her again. 'If you don't like the image you are presenting, why use it? Have you taken a good long look at yourself, Marcella? Have you seen how far you have sunk in a matter of days?'

His grip was like a vice as he propelled her towards the bedrooms that lined the hallway near the courtyard. She hoped, desperately hoped, that he intended to ravish her there, in the privacy of the darkness. He was filled with the kind of pent-up energies that had overtaken her and Virius on the boat. She longed to be the one who would bear the force of his emotions and urgent drives. She wanted to feel his hard body pumping into hers till their mutual passions abated. She knew that, once his lust and anger had been assuaged, he would be able to see things clearly and forgive her.

He opened a door and threw her inside so she fell to the bed. He sat down and pulled her towards him. Her breath came faster in anticipation of the delights that would follow.

He threw her over his knees and pulled the harlot's clothes up so her lower body was exposed. The sting of his hand on her backside was so sharp she cried out in surprise.

'You say you are not a wanton, so you must be a naughty child. As such you need to be spanked, to teach you to behave,' he said harshly.

His hand came down once more on her soft flesh. It stung. She wriggled frantically to escape, but he held her still. Over and over, his palm came down. Her clitoris was touching his bare leg and with each stinging slap it was stimulated by the hard muscles of his thigh. Her bottom became hot as he continued punishing her. The fragrant oils of her femininity began to flow as she was pounded against him.

She was breathing very fast. She clenched her bottom before each rhythmic slap in order to minimise the acute discomfort, but her actions merely intensified her sexual arousal.

She was draped over his legs so her head lay close to his calf. The light slaps kept coming so fast that the smarting was gradually replaced by a delightful warmth. His palm seemed to caress her skin and she felt his fingers deliberately lingering in the cleft between her buttocks before he lifted his hand for another stroke. She licked the salty skin of his leg and held on tight, willing the orgasm to come soon.

'Gaius, please.'

She was so close to the maximum pleasure that she hardly knew she was saying the words.

Abruptly, he stopped and pushed her to the floor. She turned in a swirl of skirts and stared at him, her desire instantly changing to anger.

'Was it all too much for you? Can't you restrain yourself?' she asked spitefully.

'It was evidently too much for you,' he replied shortly.

She sat cross-legged, knowing that she was exposing her most intimate parts to his gaze and tantalising him. She could see that he was becoming erect as he glanced down at her.

'Is your pride so great that you won't acknowledge that you want me?' she demanded.

'My pride is too great to allow me to engage in the act of lust with a harlot. You should take a look at yourself and ask yourself how any decent man could find you attractive!'

He pulled her to her feet and dragged her out into the corridor where a young slave girl sat outside one of the adjacent rooms.

'Fetch me a mirror,' he said silkily as she stared at him with wide eyes.

His grip on Marcella was hard, his body shaking with the force of his anger.

'You are frightening her, Gaius. She looks barely twelve years old. Is that what you like to do, frighten children? Would you like to spank her too?'

'Don't be such a bitch.' His tone instantly reverted to harsh contempt.

'I know what I look like, and I know the reason. You don't! And you don't know how terrifying you can be when you are angry. She is only a child.'

'You always have an excuse ready for your disgraceful behaviour, don't you? Well this time you have gone too far,' he retorted savagely. His hands hurt her arms as he shook her.

'Go and get a mirror,' he repeated gently as he turned to look at the little girl. 'You aren't in any trouble. You are clearly a very modest and pretty maiden who knows how to behave like a respectable woman.'

He winked and smiled at the child, his anger totally controlled and focussed only on Marcella. Incensed, she tried to shake herself free of his grasp as the maid dimpled at him and disappeared into the room.

'You bastard, Gaius! You are prepared to flatter the poor little thing just to get what you want. Is that the secret of your success with women? You never listen to what I have to say, do you? You go thundering off without stopping to think. Is that how you run your century?'

His bark of laughter echoed across the marbled hallway.

'My century?'

'I know that you are an army man!'

'I've never been a centurion in my life!'

'You spoke of your army career. Are you a liar too?'

She lunged at him, trying to hit his jaw, but he caught her hand and held it to her shoulder.

He let go of her abruptly as the maid returned, holding a huge polished bronze mirror, its back decorated with an intricate pattern.

She stood before them with neat dignity, and held the mirror up, looking enquiringly at Gaius.

'Let her see her face. She went too far with the make-up,' he said in a deliberately soft tone.

The girl's eyes shone as she looked up at him.

Marcella kicked him hard on the shin.

'Look at yourself!' he snapped. 'And the clothes you are wearing! Where are the pretty dresses and the respectable gowns you had when you left the villa outside Pompeii? I do not believe you left your bag behind, heavy though it was. You were ready to risk death rather than be parted from your belongings!'

'If you will let me explain!' she screamed at him as she saw herself in the mirror.

Her face looked like a theatrical mask in the soft sheen of the polished metal. Her features were distorted with anger and the gash of her red mouth across the white lead powder made her look terrifying.

'Exactly! You look totally disreputable. It is you who are frightening this poor little girl, not I!'

'I had a reason for doing it,' she said staunchly. 'But I don't look good, I admit that. I want to change now. I left my dress with the harlots.'

'Hah! And you expect to get it back?'

His derision cut through the air around them.

'I hadn't thought. I didn't think,' she began, her self-confidence waning. 'Yes, of course they will give it back to me! They helped me.'

'Clean her up and give her one of the cast-off dresses your mistress keeps for when her guests have accidents. Then burn those clothes.'

He gave the child a handful of coins that made her gasp in surprise.

'Put it towards buying your freedom.'

He turned and walked swiftly away through the house.

Marcella took her time in letting the girl dress her and fix her hair. She wanted to make Gaius sweat, and to regain her composure before she confronted him again. With some subtle make-up and a charmingly under-stated dress that had been mended twice in the past, she wandered through the party searching for him. Her buttocks were still warm from the stinging slaps and the unsatisfied ache inside her was as insistent as real pain. As Gaius had prophesied, the harlots had taken her beautiful dress and the jewellery that matched it. She realised with distress, that he too, had left.

She saw Caballius Zoticus with a dark, hard-looking woman and knew that he had recognised her in her respectable clothes and make-up. She made no attempt to evade him, knowing that the only way to deal with bullies was to stand up to them.

'Whore,' he said unpleasantly, as the woman looked on, with a slight smirk. 'I thought I saw you earlier but I was too busy selling the picture of your charms to make sure.'

'You are nothing but a bully. Get out of my life.'

'Wouldn't you just like that? You ran out on me in Pompeii and you won't get away again. You will come into my life and do exactly what I want.'

Caballius gripped her arms painfully and she wriggled in disgust.

'I shall publicly denounce you, I told you, if you do not do exactly what I say.'

After his own, highly advertised defeat she knew he

would need some very special consolations to restore his self-esteem. She felt weak with fear.

'I will not give in to your filthy threats,' she said venomously. 'I have nothing to lose – I do not know any of these people, so why do I need to fear what you say about me?'

He stared hard at her for a moment as she pulled against his iron grasp. He began to hurt her seriously and she bit back the pain.

'Caballius, I am getting bored,' the hard-faced woman said in a strongly Gaulish accent. 'We are on our way to collect your money from the auctioneer, in case you have forgotten. And if you don't pay me in advance, and soon, I won't be able to get you the women you want tonight. The kind you need, who are willing to work together and have the right kind of experience, are always booked up early. And I have no intention of catering for your tastes alone.'

Distracted, Caballius loosened his grip.

'Stop nagging, you stupid bitch.'

Marcella wrenched herself free and fled. She realised, too late, that she was not dealing with a mere bully who would back down if challenged: Zoticus was in a different league altogether.

She found Virius in one of the gaming rooms. He looked strong and calm, with a marvellously straightforward expression that renewed her confidence – he might be single-minded and selfish, but at least he wasn't warped.

'Marcella!' he exclaimed happily. 'Where did you get to? I thought you had run out on me!'

'I met up with some people I knew.'

It sounded so inoffensive that she began to giggle with relief.

'Come back to my friend's house now. You will enjoy this, I promise you. Our evening is only just beginning.'

Meekly, she accompanied him to a litter in the street and he walked beside it, pointing out features of interest as the slaves bore her easily through the streets of Rome.

She saw the temple of the Heavenly twins – Castor and Pollux; the Temple of Vesta, where the eternal fire was tended by the Vestal Virgins, and the remnants of the Golden House built by the mad Emperor Nero and now half-demolished because of adverse popular opinion. She was aware that his enthusiasm for architectural details – pediments and architraves, columns and capitals – would normally have bored her, but tonight his words lulled her tumultuous emotions.

There were three men in the courtyard. Their bulging muscles and easy way of moving, showed Marcella that they were athletes. They were smiling, and looked like large puppies about to be given a meal, she thought as her spirits rose slightly.

'I want you to meet my colleagues – Dulcitius is the one with half an ear missing – he is a boxer, as if you couldn't guess. Ulpius is the one built like an ox. He is a wrestler. The puny runt is Rufus,' announced Virius, beaming.

'Greetings!'

The smallest man smiled. He was an immensely tough, wiry individual of barely medium height.

'Puny?' she said faintly. 'You look as though you could knock a house down single-handedly.'

'I make up for my size with my agility, and these slow-moving lumps of tallow know that! I am a sprinter.'

'Greetings, Rufus,' she replied, unable to resist grinning back at them. All four shared an air of gauche innocence which overlay their obviously energetic personalities.

Intrigued, she allowed herself to be led into a side room and made herself comfortable on a heavily cushioned couch.

'Let us drink to Venus and Cupid, and more especially to Bacchus and his maenads,' cried Virius ebuliently. 'I won a good pouch of silver this evening. The gods are smiling on me and I want to thank them in the only way possible – with a true bacchanalian celebration!'

She sipped a goblet of exquisite wine and ate tiny honey cakes, and patties filled with spiced peacock meat that were served to her by silent, well-dressed slaves. She felt pampered and alluring as she basked in the frank admiration of the four desirable men.

'I agree,' she said slightly recklessly. 'There are things that the gods want to happen and things they do not. We mortals must accept what is sent to us. Tonight we are fortunate. Tonight we have comfort and pleasures. We must enjoy them to the full.'

Ulpius whooped and kissed her on her cheek before collapsing near her couch. He had huge shoulders and his upper arms were as thick as her waist. She could not help wondering about his cock and let her eyes wander to the skirt of his tunic. His muscular thighs were visible where it had risen up and she put her hand on his knee and saw a bulge appear and continue growing under the material.

'Take your eyes off him and try these oysters,' Rufus said, sliding one into her mouth. 'Don't chew – just let them slip down easily.'

'They taste delicious – soft and slippery,' she murmured.

'Twenty-four hours ago they were in Camulodunum, in Britannia,' observed Dulcitius watching her from the couch opposite.

'The food in Rome is mouth-watering – it seems to come from all over the world!' she marvelled as she sipped more wine and savoured the familiar tang of the Tuscan grapes.

Dulcitius came to sit down on the floor near her feet. He removed one of her slippers. He was drinking steadily from a silver goblet that was decorated with a bacchanalian scene. His hand slipped up her calf to her knee and then higher, sending delicious tingling sensations to her loins. She wriggled, wishing his fingers would move even higher.

She finished her wine and a slave moved forwards to

replenish it. The hazy feeling in her head was delightful and she smiled happily.

Virius clapped his hands and the slaves withdrew.

'Now we will all drink this special potion and toast each other's health and pleasures,' he announced, slightly blearily.

Ulpius produced a small phial of white liquid and carefully poured a few drops into the five full goblets. They drank deeply and she lay back lazily, as they lolled on the couch or the floor beside her.

Her breasts suddenly seemed ultra-sensitive as Virius idly slid his hand under her neckline and tweaked her nipple. She licked his hand and sucked one of his fingers into her mouth.

Dulcitius crept up her body and kissed the inside of her elbow. The effect was thrillingly powerful and her body tingled. Rufus' head was suddenly in her lap. He pulled up her skirt and exposed her private parts. She writhed with delight as his fingers made contact with her hot feminine folds. She was enflamed further by the thought of the four men looking at her womanhood with desire.

'You will have four orgasms tonight,' explained Virius, his speech slightly blurred. 'I can only manage to give you one.'

'One would be nice,' she said, her head lolling. She was beginning to feel delightfully hazy and uninhibited from the aphrodisiac.

'No.' He put a finger to her lips and kissed her on the side of her mouth. 'You don't understand.'

His speech was indistinct and she smiled.

'They have the same problem as me. They don't like long sessions. I made arrangements to make you happy.'

The world began to swim around her in the most delightful manner and she could hear someone humming a tune. People were laughing and drinking, but they all seemed a long distance away.

She drank more wine and her head swam again in wonderful liberation. She felt as though she were flying into the air, then swooping down again. The feeling reminded her of how she had felt when Gaius' hard manhood was inside her.

'He has rejected me, again,' she confided hazily. 'He wanted to believe that I have become a common harlot who sells her favours for a couple of dupondii.'

Virius laughed, somewhere near her left ear.

'I don't understand a word you are saying.'

She could feel his tongue on her breast. She wasn't wearing any clothes, but she didn't remember taking them off.

'I don't remember what I was saying,' she said vaguely. 'And that pig humiliated me. He won't leave me alone, I know that one day I will have to stand up to him. It was pure luck that he does not know that I gave him the ice-pack.'

She felt hot between her legs and when Virius put a hand on her mound she moaned loudly and arched towards him.

'I want to suck you,' she slurred sleepily. 'All of you. Nobody else matters, except you.'

'You want to be fucked, sweetheart,' someone said in the distance.

'That would be nice,' she said foggily, lying back and letting Virius part her legs. It felt wickedly enjoyable and utterly forbidden and she adored the feeling that they were all there, ready to give her bodily pleasures. Someone, somewhere in the mistily distant past, had humiliated her, but these men were all admiring her most intimate places. They were not humiliating her.

She felt wonderful – as though her body were light as a feather. The four big men stood in a row, their faces a blur from the love potion. She began to giggle. They were fully dressed and she wanted to see how long they would last if she sucked them.

'Put out the lights,' cried a voice and someone else took the lamp snuffer and the room became pitch dark. 'No one is to watch this and make wagers. This is a private affair between friends, to honour Bacchus.'

166

A pair of strong hands felt for her breasts. Another fumbled at her crotch.

She could feel kisses in her mouth.

'Virius?' she said hoarsely.

The fingers that touched her clitoris were hard and calloused – but they did not belong to Virius. A tongue began to lap at her folds with the eagerness of a child in a peach grove on a hot day. Was it the same person? A finger was inserted into her secret, female place, and then withdrawn. In the darkness she could feel the heat of male bodies, but was unable to distinguish who was who. She tried to guess.

Two mouths began to suck at her breasts and she almost cried out at the sharp sensation.

'Rufus?' she called softly.

There was a grunt and a third person began to kiss her brow and mouth from the side.

Her loins were suddenly free, the air felt cool with the damp saliva of her unknown admirer. She groaned.

The men continued what they were doing and she put her hands each side and found, as she had expected, two hard penises.

She squeezed and pressed the softly cushioned tops. She heard the sharp intakes of breath, and then, as she continued to manipulate them, faint cries of pleasure. She calculated that Ulpius was the one kissing her, and Dulcitius and Rufus were working on her breasts.

Where was Virius?

Her clitoris was throbbing and she could feel the oils of her desire, cool against the air.

Hands moved to the sides of her neck, and a mouth caressed her earlobe, her nipples were raw from the hard sucking.

She cried out, 'Virius, have pity. I need a man's hardness inside me.'

A strong pair of male hands that she recognised as his, grasped her thighs and roughly parted her legs. She felt a blissful sense of release as his long, hard stem of manhood was pushed inside her.

167

Time and time again the familiar thrusts came. Her entire body shook with the force of his passions. She gasped and grunted her intense satisfaction as the deep internal massage wiped out the bad memories of the past. She gripped the sides of the couch with her hands and flexed her body towards his movements, meeting each with her own, feminine force. The strength of the orgasm shook her and she sobbed uncontrollably when her final wave of climax came.

He withdrew and another pair of hands held her tightly. Her body welcomed the new experience.

'Dulcitius. Now – push now,' she cried hoarsely.

This time the rigid rod that entered her did so with agonising sluggishness. It seemed to take an age to become fully embedded. Once inside, its movements were slow and she felt she would die as the interval between them became longer and longer. Dulcitius withdrew his penis till only the tip was inside her, moved it side to side a few times and then very slowly moved deep inside again.

She was boiling with desire for a second physical liberation, and yet the man kept her waiting. She tried to push against him, but his weight crushed her into immobility. She was panting out her needs, unable to climax, yet equally incapable of finding the strength to throw him off.

'Oh, please.' She whispered the words into his ear.

He kissed her mouth and continued his slow almost ponderous movements.

'You like to tease and tantalise,' she whispered, guessing. 'That is your way.'

'You will come when I want you to and not before,' he said firmly. 'I don't play games with women, or jump to their every whim, but they are never unsatisfied, I can promise you.'

He lay totally still. There was nothing else for her to do but concentrate on the magnificent sensation of his huge, hard, virile stem, deep within her. She could hear his deep, regular breath in her ear and knew that he was deliberately savouring the marvellous warmth of their fused bodies. She writhed against him, but he lay inert in the darkness, leaving her body in torment with the need for frantic movement. She flexed her inner muscles and the tension became unbearable. She pushed with her hips, but his weight kept him deeply, immovably, within her. She began to squeeze him, unable to assuage her needs in any other way.

'You are getting the idea at last,' he whispered and the sound of his voice and the feel of his breath against her neck freed her inner strengths.

When she was frantic with need, he quietly and unexpectedly began to move inside her. She erupted into life. Her inner muscles churned over his stiff cock as it pounded in and out of her with massive energy and strength. A thousand flames flared up inside her and burned intensely. Release came quickly for them both.

'That was good,' he said quietly. 'Minimum effort for maximum effect in bed and maximum effort for minimum risk on the circuit: that is my philosophy.'

He slid out as she sighed her pleasure into the darkness.

A third man held her hips: Rufus. He pushed her knees high and thumbed her clitoral flower in a practised manner. He ran his fingers down to her bottom and silkily caressed her, moving his hand from one cheek to the other with a light, dusting movement.

She groaned and in response he pushed a finger inside her.

She bit her lip with the pleasure as she thrust her hips towards him. She was afraid that he would leave matters there and, like Dulcitius, would make her follow his own pattern.

She wanted more than the simple manual stimulation that was rekindling her senses.

As she had almost given up hope, he lay between her open legs and pushed inside her. She gripped his strong torso with her thighs to force him deeper inside and rubbed her soles on his backside in blissful sensuality.

His penis was much smaller than the others she had experienced, but he moved with confidence and her inner muscles were able to grip him tighter than ever before, creating a deeply satisfying friction. The sensation was exquisite and she involuntarily adjusted herself to his movements, rocking her body towards his, her pelvis fitting his perfectly.

As if able to keep up the movement for ever, he settled into an easy rhythm that took her in ever increasing waves of pleasure nearer and nearer release. He gauged her needs with precision and moved faster as her excitement grew until, at last, the end came. It was a quiet sensation of warmth inside her and it spread out from the centre of her pleasures until it enveloped every part of her body. They lay still together for long moments, savouring the aftermath of bliss.

'Thank you,' she said softly into his ear.

'My pleasure,' he said with a low chuckle.

When he had rolled away from her, she lay in the darkness with only the sighs and pantings of the sated men audible. She felt content, and yet not totally fulfilled. She would have liked Rufus to continue, and bring her to the heights many times, as Gaius had done so effortlessly.

'Ulpius?' she whispered. 'Where are you?'

The big man carefully lay down on top of her, supporting his bulk, and immediately entered her with smooth decisiveness. She gasped at the immense proportions of his stiff manhood and the delicious friction it produced.

As he pushed into her, her entire body shook and she grasped his shoulders, pulling him close. She lightly grazed his neck with her teeth, in her desperate need for one final climactic spasm. She knew that they had planned it so the largest man should go last and she also knew that this would be her most exhausting orgasm.

He repeatedly pushed into her, gently, deliberately, as if he were afraid he might hurt her, yet still confident that he could give her the ultimate satisfaction. Here, she knew, was the stamina of the truly heroic wrestler, the man who depended on his strength and will-power to win. Almost like Hercules himself, it seemed as if his muscles were built for super-human deeds.

Her body strained as she pulled him closer. She could taste the sweat, and pulled his face towards her, demanding that he should kiss her and confront her as a person.

The size of his huge cock inside her made her feel complete. As she became used to him, he gradually increased the speed and force of his thrusts and her body responded joyously. He reached his climax before her, but only tiny moments before. The feeling of his huge body, convulsed with passion as his penis was deeply embedded within her, instantly produced a major climactic reaction. The waves of desire rolled away to be replaced by undulations of sweet release. They rippled through her breasts, across her shoulders and down her arms. They moved slowly across her stomach and to her loins, leaving a delightful relaxation in their place. She rubbed her legs along his as her need turned to satiety.

He moved away from her and she felt someone kiss her gently on the lips.

As she lay quietly in the room, half-asleep and totally sated with sensuous pleasures, she heard them moving around and a few muttered words. The door opened and shut and she fell asleep as her mind blurred over and the effects of the aphrodisiac took control.

In the darkness she felt dazed and lost all sense of time and place. The sensual feelings had repeatedly rolled over and through her with the force of an earthquake. Alone in the silence, she relived those last few hours in Pompeii.

Gaius was alive and in Rome: tomorrow she would find his house and go there. She would not let him walk out as though he were the victor in a battle – their passion was reciprocal and should be confronted by them both, as equals.

171

Chapter Fourteen

Gaius' home was a huge, old-fashioned townhouse in a very high-class area of the city. It was the embodiment of class and old, senatorial, money. The walls were decorated in the plain, sombre style that had been fashionable a century before. The dark greens and reds added to the feeling of harsh austerity. There seemed no signs of the man who had laughed and loved with her in the shadow of the volcano.

The most senior house slave sat aloof and motionless on a wicker chair, his dark skin lustrous in the bright sunlight of the open fountain room. Busts of Gaius' illustrious ancestors and a number of important Greek writers stood in specially fashioned niches, giving an air of extreme formality despite the trailing plants and trellis work.

'My master left for North Africa before dawn.' He scrutinised Marcella with a speculative, almost wary, expression.

She put down her heavy bag and stared at him in disbelief. 'But he was here, in Rome, last night and I cannot have spent more than a couple of hours finding the right house this morning!'

He shrugged. 'There is trouble with the border tribesmen. Most army personnel have been recalled as a matter of urgency.'

She felt totally defeated and sank, unbidden, to a wooden chair.

'You look tired – take some refreshment with me and we will try to find a way to help you,' he said suddenly, rising and clapping his hands. Immediately a serving girl entered the room.

'May I bring something for you, Imilico?' she asked.

Even the youngest slave girl in Gaius' household, speaks with an educated, patrician accent and has impeccable, reserved manners, thought Marcella.

Imilico was not at all unfriendly, but under his polished hospitality was an aloofness that daunted her. As Marcella talked about the escape from the volcano, she felt he was making mental calculations.

'I met Gaius in the chaos of the eruption at Pompeii,' she explained evasively. 'I have some unfinished business with him.'

There was a short silence before he began to chat about inconsequential matters. She knew that he expected her to outline the type of business. It was clear from what he was saying that most practical or financial matters could be dealt with by Gaius' many personal servants. He made it evident that he could not see how she fitted into Gaius' neat, traditional life-style and was delicately fishing for clues about how to treat her.

'What did you do for a living before the disaster?' he said at last, and she was grateful that his good manners forbade him from interrogating her further.

'I worked in my uncle's tavern.'

He smiled. Instantly, he was less offputting.

'Over the next few weeks,' he said unexpectedly, 'I am bidden to distribute gifts to a number of Gaius Salvius Antoninus' friends in the coastal towns and villas in North Africa.'

She raised her eyebrows in surprise.

'Like all men of his class,' he explained, 'my master borrows the villas and houses of friends instead of using the posting stations or taverns on private journeys. He repays the favours in kind and with gifts, so this is an

173

important part of my duties. I was to travel with him, but he has gone ahead by fast, travelling carriage. By now he will be on board ship, probably well into the sea journey.'

'So there is no chance of my catching up with him,' she said, feeling totally defeated.

'The military posting system is highly efficient – he will change horses frequently and arrive exhausted having driven through the desert night. Knowing him, he will then start work.' He rose to offer her some food. 'You shall accompany me as far as the last villa on my list. I will enjoy the company. Then you must make your own way to the fortress of Theveste.'

Two days later Marcella was beginning to regret taking up Imilico's offer. She could hear the voice of the driver urging his tired oxen on to the next stopping place. With every jolt of the wagon she felt more dispirited and disoriented.

Imilico was watching her. He had finely formed limbs and perfectly white, even teeth. He was a superb specimen of manhood, healthy and beautifully groomed, but she sensed some barrier between them, or even a hidden motive.

She smiled at him uneasily.

'You are afraid that Gaius Salvius Antoninus will have left again when you finally reach Theveste?' he asked astutely.

'He has eluded me so many times before, I am beginning to wonder if the gods mean us to meet up. He will have moved on with his life and will have no good thoughts about me.'

He smiled strangely and she was further perturbed.

'Not necessarily,' he said with a speculative look. 'He was in a foul mood when he arrived home on his last night in Rome. That is very unusual for him. I presume he was upset over something. He was short with us all, barking out his orders and then shutting himself up in his room.'

She decided to gloss over the party and her last meeting with Gaius, though it was obvious to her that Imilico was determined to discover the details of her relationship with his master. She too changed the subject.

'My uncle always takes out his problems on Terentius. Gaius didn't punish you, did he? Was I the cause of that?'

He smiled as though she had said something preposterous.

'He never punishes anyone without reason.'

She thought back angrily to the speed and efficiency with which he had administered a stinging punishment on her buttocks, for no good reason.

'Even if someone in his household does wrong,' continued Imilico, 'he is willing to listen and to compromise over repairing the damage. He conceals his emotions well. When he is angry about some political set-back, for example, he is careful that his household does not suffer.'

He never listens to my side of the story, she thought furiously.

'I am glad to have company on the journey,' said Imilico, once more smoothly changing the topic. 'These gifts are beautiful but they cannot converse.'

He waved a hand to indicate the cushions of red and purple wool, bales of brocade and silks, luxurious tableware of silver and gilt, a table with ornate griffin's claw feet and several heavily wrapped packages that, she guessed, contained breakables.

'I am being a tedious companion. I will try to be less anxious,' she replied. She tried to find a more comfortable position on the bales of material.

In the distance she could hear a soft, rhythmic noise. It had had been growing louder for the past hour and sounded like heavy rain, or even distant earth tremors. The hair on the back of her neck stood on end at the terrifying memories.

'What is that sound?'

'Probably marching troops.'

He sounded unconcerned as he sat motionless, his legs crossed under his body, his back very straight.

'Africa has been under Roman rule for over two centuries, surely the borders are secure?'

'All border areas are vulnerable. My master recently had several audiences with the Emperor over security. Titus thinks highly of him. Like the Emperor himself, my master is one of those rare people who have personal charm and ability, combined with inherited wealth.'

'I knew that he was an army man, but I didn't know that he was so influential,' she said with sinking spirits. The more she found out about Gaius, the less they had in common.

'Lady,' he said, smiling, 'Gaius Salvius Antoninus is legate to one of the top legions – the Third Augusta. As its commander, naturally, he is a senator and knows the Emperor. It is a double-strength force of about twelve thousand men and the defence of the African provinces depends on it.'

'He didn't even hint at such responsibility.' She felt even more unsure of herself – the man she was following belonged to a totally different world from the one she knew. She looked at Imilico enquiringly, avid for information.

'He has a campaigning career as long as your pretty little arm. He is unusual in thinking that a legionary commander should go to the front line personally to see the situation for himself and encourage the lower ranks. He campaigned in Britannia for a while, until his skills were needed in more challenging environments.'

'That isn't the way he told it to me,' she said slowly.

'I detect that you have a tender spot for him. You won't be the first, and you won't be the last.'

He saw her wince.

'I can make you feel more relaxed,' he said, 'I am trained in the arts of massage and perfumery – skills which have been handed down to me from those used in the court of Cleopatra herself. It is also part of my duties to ensure that guests are comfortable in every possible way.'

'Not the female ones. There must be a masseuse for that!' She smiled slightly. 'Besides, what is wrong with me cannot be put right with a few drops of oil and a bracing rub down.'

'There is more to my art that you might think from a routine trip to the public baths. You should not hastily refuse your own pleasures.'

He looked like a statue carved by a court sculptor who wanted to flatter his subject. There was a still calmness about him that hinted at an oriental ancestor – maybe a Nubian from Upper Egypt she thought idly.

'Your problems cannot be put right by anything I might do to you,' he agreed, rising to his feet and swaying slightly with the movement of the wagon. 'But your view of the world can be made more optimistic. If your body is relaxed and healthy, your mind will function better and you will be more positive about everything you do. Then you will find a way to deal with your problems.'

He knelt by her and put his hands on her shoulders.

'Lie face down on the cushions.'

'I don't want to. There is no need,' she began, but he started to rub her shoulders, moving swiftly over her muscles. She cried out with the pain as he hit the most tense.

'That proves my point,' he said dryly. 'You need some delicate attention from an expert. You must never neglect the body's needs. Some old Republican-style families still favour austerity, but they end up unproductive and embittered.'

He opened a small bag and brought out two or three tiny jars of oil. The movement of the wagon on the uneven road surface began to lull her and she watched his economical movements with lazy interest.

He spread a thick white cloth on the cushions in the centre of the wagon, carefully smoothing out the wrinkles as though preparing a banquet for an emperor. His hands were like those of a dancer, moving with grace and elegance as though somehow slightly separated from his body.

'Take off your dress and lie on this so the oils do not mark the cushions.'

'I will not! So that was why you invited me along! You wanted repayment in kind!'

'You need not fear for your virtue.'

'Why not? What makes you different from every other man I meet?'

She thought wearily that she could not be bothered to fight off his advances – much less did she feel like responding to them. Despite his obvious physical beauty, she could not imagine being anything but passive if he tried to take her, though his air of gentle sensitivity and refinement suggested that he would be a considerate lover.

'Different from some of them, not all of them,' he replied with a slight smile. 'I don't find girls attractive in a physical way. I prefer men. One particular man, as it happens. That means I am quite safe around the women of any household.'

She stared.

'I have studied the effects of particular oils and scents on the human mind and body,' he continued smoothly. 'I learnt in the east. Now, take off your dress and let me show you some of the delights you can accept from a man without having to exhaust yourself with libidinous matters.'

Slowly, she removed her clothes and sat in front of him, her legs hunched up, her arms defensively around her knees. She felt shy, realising why she had, at first, found him aloof.

'Once or twice I have paid for a masseuse at the baths, but the girls were in a hurry and their hands were too brisk to be of any benefit. I felt worse after they had done their job than I did before.'

'That will not happen this time, I promise. Lie down and let us begin. Some fragrant oil first.'

He poured some liquid into his palms and put his palms to her shoulders, working round in a circular movement with a light but firm touch. The misty fragrance entranced her senses and she began to feel sleepy.

He brought his hands down to her buttocks in long sweeping movements and dug his thumbs into her spine. She sighed as the rhythm took over.

He worked over her entire body, teasing even her feet, her ankles and her arms, until she was relaxed and lethargic.

Time and time again, he replenished the oil on his palms. He turned her over gently and she closed her eyes as he sat astride her legs, working the oil into her shoulders. He brought his hands down to her breasts, gently lifting them and passing each one from one palm to the other.

He moved down her body and massaged her stomach with a circular movement and then probed her pelvic muscles.

'I didn't know I had so much tension there,' she murmured in surprise. 'I was aware only of the tension in my shoulders.'

'You were tense all over, but the worst muscle knots are in your hips and pubic area. Even if I did not already know, I would be aware that your worries concern a man. This problem is common amongst women of your age.'

He brought his hands to her thighs and massaged strongly up and down the long muscles before concentrating on her knees and calves.

She felt almost totally relaxed. The only ache left was between her legs. Inside, she felt a physical pain with the need and longing for Gaius close to her.

'You need something more than this, I think,' Imilico said at last, as he ran his hand over her forehead and round the hair line. Her scalp tingled with the unaccustomed delights.

'What more could there be?'

She lay back comfortably, knowing that nothing except the hard penetration of a virile man could satisfy her needs.

'I will show you.'

He brought a leather baton out of his bag. It was nearly as long as her lower arm and she saw in astonishment that it was a phallus. The leather had been formed carefully to resemble an erect penis, with a handle at the other end for ease of use.

'I have never seen such a lifelike object before,' she said in amazement. She was jolted out of her languour and fascinated by the ridge around the tip and the deep crevice. Her labia began to become engorged and her feminine juices flowed at the thought of this implement deep inside her giving her new pleasures.

'It is the only way to massage the internal muscles properly if a man is not available. I appreciate your body from an aesthetic point of view, but I cannot become aroused at the sight of a woman. So I am unable to oblige you. Besides, even if I were able, I would get into trouble for having such a close relationship with a lady.'

'I wouldn't tell anyone,' she said, smiling at him.

'There could be all sorts of reasons why I might be found out, as you know,' he said laughingly. 'Besides, the act of love and lust with a man is usually strenuous for a woman if she is to gain any real pleasure. This way you will be relaxed and happy, but with hardly any effort.'

'I can't believe that,' she said, sleepy once more, 'but I can believe that I am too tired and relaxed to wish to take any hard exercise.'

'There are hundreds of the Empire's finest fighting men about a thousand paces behind us down the road, so we will be able to discover how well I can satisfy you. If you lust after them as they march past us in an hour or two, I will know I have failed.'

She laughed and watched him oil the phallus with long, smooth fingers, moving them sensuously over the leather as he worked the oil into the wrinkles of the material as though he were caressing a lover.

'Now you feel it.'

She put out her hands and grasped the implement of pleasure. It had more resistance than a man's erect penis, but was excitingly, almost frighteningly rigid.

'This can never wilt,' she said, running her fingers around the tip. 'I want it inside me, but I feel it is wrong to take pleasure in this way.'

He smiled as he rubbed her nipples with the implement, circling each one, slowly.

'A lot of people might think it was wrong if they watched us. Think about the elders of the Town Council – what would their wives think if they knew you were showing your private areas to a male slave?'

He parted her legs with his long elegant fingers. She was quivering with the need to be touched and caressed. He massaged her upper thighs and then gently parted her inner folds with his thumbs.

'Think of the most disapproving people you know and then imagine them watching you now. Think of them as tied up so they have to watch and are unable to intervene. Think of how jealous they would be even though they pretended to be angry.'

His touch was gossamer soft.

'Bend your knees,' he ordered and she obliged. Her body opened for him. 'This shall be a secret. Nobody else shall ever know what passed between us in this wagon. I shall give you divine pleasures that would be forbidden by society!'

'You are not supposed to know about this sort of thing if you prefer men,' she said, her breath coming fast. 'I know lots of people who would be shocked just to know that you are so knowledgeable about the female body.'

He took the phallus and gently placed it at the edge of her feminine creases.

The size stimulated her intimate juices. It was even bigger than Ulpius' stem, but she was confident that she now had the experience to accommodate it and derive immense pleasure from it. Internally, she was more than ready to welcome this deliciously new source of bliss.

He eased the implement inside her.

'Remember,' he said, 'this is our secret, a totally forbidden experience which we will share and never speak of.'

The movement and the soft words made her involuntarily open herself and she felt relaxed and at ease as the leather finally penetrated deeply.

He knelt between her open legs and left the baton in place as he massaged her thighs again, bringing them gently down to lie flat. The firmness of the phallus inside her was wonderfully soothing, but her inner muscles began to flicker in wild response.

She straightened her legs fully and put a hand on the phallus.

'I will do that for you,' he said gently. 'I want us to share the moment of your ultimate, most personal, pleasure. I want to be the cause of it. Put your hands on your breasts.'

He began to move the dildo gently from side to side and round and round, her internal muscles still tight around it. He increased the vibrations till the leather fired her body with delight. The speed of the vibrations increased, the phallus moving in and out a fraction as well as in circles.

'Oh, this is agony. A lovely agony.'

She rubbed and tweaked her nipples in a frenzy. He held one of her breasts in his hand, continuing the vibrations with the phallus. He gently kneaded as she lightly pinched the nipple and the sensations were sweet and sharp, plunging sparks of fire down to her loins.

He began to vibrate the instrument fast with infinitesimal delicate backward and forward movements. As her muscles tensed further he moved it as she craved – in and out, with a strong but gently rhythmic movement. She closed her eyes and imagined she was with Gaius. She clenched her legs and pelvis muscles, as if against some physical shock.

He poured some more oil on her chest so it trickled down beside her breasts. Still keeping up the movement on the phallus, he massaged the oils over her nipples. He put his finger lightly on her clitoris and rubbed it with a circulatory movement.

Inside her, the phallus moved even deeper and faster with a gentle insistence.

'Our secret, Marcella, remember that,' he said quietly.

Her inner muscles contracted fiercely. The phallus was firm but yielding, instantly responsive to the urgency with which she squeezed it. The need for physical release grew in her and she began to push hard and fast. Her breath came faster and stertorously as she threw back her head and pushed her body upwards amidst sparks of sensual delight. Her excitement rose to ever increasing peaks until her senses erupted in paradisiac explosions. Her inner muscles contracted over the leather dildo and her thighs burned as the tension fled from first her bottom, then her legs. Intense satisfaction undulated through her pubic mound and finally reached the depths of her womanhood, wringing the muscles of all tautness and leaving her both depleted and envigorated.

She lay still, unable to move or think.

He gently withdrew the phallus and the deliciously soft friction finished her sensual enjoyment with long, rapturous ripples of pleasure. He was smiling at her when she opened her eyes.

'You see, there is a way of being pleasured that means you can do almost no work at all. You didn't believe me, did you?'

She shook her head.

'It was so quick, at the end. I just exploded.'

'To watch a person's face as they reach the peak of their sensual gratification is a privilege that is rarely possible. You gave me much pleasure too. Because I was not concerned about gaining my own satisfaction, I was able to concentrate entirely on your needs.'

She closed her eyes and allowed herself to drift into sleep, her body totally sated, her mind at peace.

* * *

When she woke up, Imilico was peering under the wagon covering and she could see that he was aroused. The sound of marching feet on the cobbles was deafening.

'They have caught up with us?' she asked sleepily.

He nodded, still watching.

'I heard them talking. They are on their way to Syria, eventually – definitely nothing to do with my master, may the gods be praised. I don't think I could stand the tension with all these legionaries around for days on end. The first three centuries have gone past. Aren't you going to watch?'

She raised herself from the cloth and used it to wipe her body free of the last vestiges of oil.

'I feel wonderful. You were right, even the thought of thousands of the finest men in the world doesn't excite me. Give me a few hours and I may feel differently!'

'You are lucky,' he replied, steadfastly looking out of the wagon.

She crept up to the tear in the cover and peered out. Burnished breast plates, helmets and swords glinted in the sun. Bronzed legs and arms strained with the marching. The faces were attractively harsh and reminded her of Virius.

'These are the Empire's finest fighters, on whom the safety and prosperity of the provinces depends,' she whispered in awe.

A centurion glanced at them, his attention caught by the movement of her hand.

'Juno,' she said under her breath. 'That is a superb-looking man.'

'I had noticed,' said Imlico, dryly.

'Are you going to meet some of them for a drink at the next tavern?'

'That would be more than my position in Antoninus' household is worth. That sort of behaviour would be a huge breach of trust to my partner as well as my master.'

'You are very moral and loyal.'

'I also have a strong sense of self-preservation. As a

rich man's slave, I lead a life of luxury and privilege. When I have saved enough to buy my freedom, I plan to remain in Antoninus' household because he will finance a business for me, for a cut in the profits. Besides, if I left, I would break up my most intimate relationship.'

She nodded. 'That is the tradition. My uncle was simply not rich enough to give Terentius enough bonuses for him to buy his freedom. He certainly could not afford to finance a business for him.'

'Exactly. I do not intend to jeopardise my position for a quick, unsatisfactory fumble in a tavern! I can control myself until I get back to my permanent partner. In the meantime, I will simply have to burn up with the strain. Why do you suppose I understood how you felt?'

She put her hand under his tunic and felt for his stem. It was long and slim, with a neat glans.

'I don't find girls attractive,' he said helplessly.

She began to work at him with her hands.

'I don't seem to have discouraged you,' she said after a short while. 'Let me give you back some of the pleasure and relief you gave me.'

She tucked the tunic into his belt so his penis was free.

'You are very elegant, even here,' she observed, running her hands along his slim hips and down his long and graceful thighs. His skin was very dark brown, with a subtle, black sheen.

She tightened her grip on the base of his stem and then smoothly brought her hands to the tip and back down. He began to breathe faster, still watching through the tear in the wagon cover.

'You are enchanting. Very kind,' he said.

He began to move, pushing his penis into her hands. It felt warm and comforting and he erupted with a gentle sigh as the legionaries slowly passed them on the hot dusty road.

They crossed the Mediterranean to Carthage where Imilico distributed gifts. During the following weeks, Marcella saw several magnificent, cosmopolitan towns in

North Africa. They stayed for several nights in Thabraca before moving along the coast to Hippo Regius and Cuicul, where she was able to do some shopping and become accustomed to the different manners and customs. With the money she had been thrown from the audience when she had humiliated Caballius, she bought a little bronze statue of Juno and dedicated it in a shrine as thanks for her safe deliverance.

She learnt the names of many perfumes and their uses and was instructed in the gentle art of massage for men and women.

'I can't remember the technical terms for the parts of the body and I haven't more than a fragment of your knowledge, but I am confident that I can give anyone a relaxing and pleasurable hour or two,' she told Imilico.

The heat was intense as they rested supine in the cushions during the final stretch of their journey together. She whiled away the time watching the olive groves and vineyards.

As they turned into a long farm lane, west of Sitifis, Imilico stirred and said, 'This is our final destination.'

Sleek horses grazed in neatly fenced paddocks, tended by a few, unhurried workers.

'I'm impressed,' she said.

As they stepped from the wagon a short, stocky man of about sixty walked out of the villa.

'Greetings!' he said. His hair was grey, with tight curls and he spoke Latin with the accent which all the North African Romans shared.

'Greetings! Marcella, Hasdrubal is the steward of the villa,' said Imilico. 'You two will get along fine.'

The old man smiled at her easily, his expression welcoming, his dark skin heavily lined from the hot, dry climate.

As she changed into one of the plain dresses she had purchased in Hippo, she reflected that there was something odd about Imilico's manner, and her unease returned.

She joined the rest of the staff for a light meal in an

open, columned courtyard that was surrounded by climbing plants.

'We are short-staffed at present and my master's son will soon arrive with his friends. I made a double offering to the household gods when I received Imilico's message that you were arriving with him and had experience with serving food,' observed Hasdrubal.

She stared at him, perplexed.

'We will need all the help we can get for the next month or two.'

She hid her surprise and anger by fiddling with the unfamiliar fruit on her plate.

'It is pointless buying slaves for a short period only,' he confided. 'It is always necessary to sell at a loss because the buyers think they must have some hidden weakness. You will not be disappointed with the rates of pay, I assure you!'

'But I am not here to –'

'She isn't here entirely for the money, Hasdrubal,' interrupted Imilico. He gave her a hard stare. 'She wants to reach Theveste. Eventually. This arrangement is particularly convenient for her.'

'Working here would seem like pleasure rather than work,' she replied non-commitally, thinking hard.

Imilico grinned. 'You will never wish to leave.'

'This place is a paradise on earth,' she replied carefully. 'The superb mosaic floors and painted walls, the upholstered benches, this delightful garden and these high quality beakers and platters! I am not used to such luxury.'

'If you think this is sumptuous, wait till you see the other rooms,' said Hasdrubal dryly. 'These are only the staff quarters.'

'I knew you had an ulterior motive but I couldn't imagine what it was!' she accused Imilico when they were alone. 'Why should I stay? More to the point, why did you deceive me?'

'By helping them out, I build up goodwill which will

come in useful when I am in business. You, on the other hand, will gain some money and repay me for the favour of the free, safe and comfortable journey here.'

'You are very devious,' she replied uncertainly. 'But I do not like being manipulated. It seems to me that I will lose valuable time in tracking Gaius. He will have moved on by the time I reach Theveste. Every day that passes means one more when he is believing the wrong thing about me.'

'There is too much unrest on the desert borderlands to allow him to leave.' He smiled slightly.

'Was it your purpose to hold me up?' she cried as suspicion flooded her mind. 'Are you telling me the truth? Is he in Africa? Or is he still in Rome? Is this nothing more than a convenient way of abandoning me in the middle of nowhere, so I will never find him again? How do I know that you are telling me the truth?'

Her mind was jumbled up with a fear that had been slowly growing in her mind. Was Gaius Imilico's special male friend? Had Imilico misled her because he wanted to keep Gaius for himself? Was her lover unable to face up to his passion for her because Imilico was not simply his slave, but his high-class catamite, too?

'As you make such wild accusations,' replied Imilico calmly, 'I see that your feelings are as strong as his were! No, I have my moments, but I am not quite so unscrupulous.'

'Then what lies behind all this?' she asked heatedly.

'Until the army has quelled the rebellions of the Garamantes tribe, civilians are expected to keep out of potential danger. Besides, my master will be in the remote desert borderlands, many hours' travel even from the fortress. I was simply using the situation to all our advantages.'

She thought for a while and then conceded reluctantly, 'I do see that. But I don't want to waste time before explaining things to Gaius.'

She no longer cared if he guessed that her business was extremely personal. She wanted to watch his reactions, to challenge any passion he might feel for Gaius.

'Even if you reached him he would not thank you for turning up in the middle of a military crisis,' he said smoothly, giving away no emotions. 'If he does not handle the situation successfully there could be a major war that might last for years. The Garamantes control the caravan route through the desert, so the effects could be far-reaching.'

She looked at him thoughtfully.

'I see that I must wait, but the thought that he will be risking his life is frightening.'

'Everyone is attracted to the way he acts in crises and is so modest later.'

'He told me that he wasn't brave enough to fight in the north, but chose the easy life in the south,' she said, in anguish. It hurt to know that Imilico knew Gaius so much better than she did. She passionately wanted to have secrets about her lover that were hers alone.

'He always says that sort of thing. He hates people to fuss over him.'

'I suppose that explains the fierce, suppressed intensity of his nature,' she said. 'He grasps the pleasures of the moment as they are offered. That is understandable if he constantly risks his life and that of his men.'

There was a strange expression on Imilico's face.

'Have I said something odd?' she asked.

He smiled. 'I have simply never seen my master in that light. He is never one to grasp the pleasures of the moment. He enjoys the good life, but he is frighteningly able to walk past temptation without any inner conflict at all.'

She stared.

'It is clear that you have touched a part of my master's personality that has long been hidden,' he said gently. He kissed her lightly on the brow. 'I have to start my return journey tomorrow, so I cannot even offer you some physical relief, but I am sure you will find a method of keeping yourself from burning up.'

* * *

189

The staff at the villa were well trained and efficient. There were about thirty house slaves and a few freedmen and women. A comparable number of people worked in the gardens and the stables. During the next few days Marcella learnt her way around the sumptuous mansion and got to know some of her colleagues. Few of the house servants, and none of the outdoor staff, spoke Latin fluently, so her progress was slow.

'You will be expected to turn your hand to whatever is needed in the house, though serving in the dining room will be a priority,' Hasdrubal explained as he showed her where the silverware and glassware was stored.

He explained how the routine of the household would change when the young people arrived.

'You will have to be up early and work late into the evening. If the young men want it, we have to stay up all night serving wine and food. However, the villa generally shuts down in the middle of the day due to the heat. Working in a tavern, you will be used to set hours,' he pointed out. 'Here, like all of us, you will be on duty at all times.'

During the second week, he found her sitting depressedly in the sun.

'You must relax. You will need all the strength you have when the young men arrive.'

She lifted her head and determinedly wiped the despair from her expression.

'The traumatic events of the past few weeks must have taken their toll on your vitality. You have lost your home, your friends and your family.'

She was thinking, I have also lost my lover.

'It is strange that for years I resented the restrictions my family placed on me,' she said. 'Now, I miss them all dreadfully.'

'That is only natural.'

'I felt so optimistic during the journey from Rome, but I have begun to have doubts. I am out of place here.'

'I went to Greece once with my master. I understand how you feel. It was strange.'

She smiled sadly. 'The food, the climate, even the air is different. It smells thick and sweet.'

'In time, you will learn to love the land and understand the language. You are being too hard on yourself.'

Deep down, she was acutely aware that she had not tried to find her family and friends. Instead, she had followed a man whose interest in her did not extend as far as listening to her side of the story. She pushed the thoughts to the back of her mind and smiled at Hasdrubal.

'Tell me about the young people who are coming to stay.'

'While my master and mistress are away, their son, Julius, usually lives with his uncle in Italy. He sent word that he and three friends intend to spend some time here. They can all be rather boisterous. It may be that his uncle has been imposing rules and they calculate that they will be freer here, without supervision. If they are intent on hell-raising, I'm afraid our life will be difficult.'

'Maybe they will take my mind off my problems and jerk me out of this negative way of thinking,' she said hopefully.

Hasdrubal laughed and ruffled her hair as he left the room.

Chapter Fifteen

'Come on in! There is to be no stupid prudery here,' cried Julius merrily as he stood, totally naked, in front of Marcella. 'Mixed bathing isn't allowed in Rome or the public baths but here it is quite the fashion! Particularly since my father is away.'

His light, youthful voice echoed around the luxurious suite of baths. The stone walls and ceilings were beautifully decorated with blue and white mosaics and no outside sounds penetrated.

She was holding a pile of towels in her arms.

'I have work to do,' she mumbled, trying to keep her eyes off his body. He was slightly built but muscular, with beautiful half-golden curls cut into the latest Roman fashion that she had observed in the party. His pubic hair was the same colour. It framed his tumescent penis like the leafy fronds of a water plant, protecting the long, delicate stem of a budding flower. As she watched, his erection rose higher and its semi-softness made her hungry for sensual gratification.

She tore her eyes away, reminding herself that she was here to serve and work, not to experiment with libidinous matters or seek physical release.

'I've sweated in the hot room and I've been pummelled and oiled for hours. Now I want some entertainment. My father is very keen for me to go though the full rigours of the Spartan room followed by the cold plunge bath – he fears I will get too soft. I'm definitely not too soft.'

Julius winked. She saw that his rod was unflinchingly standing upright.

'You would like a massage, lord? I am skilled in the art.'

'Take your dress off so it doesn't get wet, and join me. That is an order,' he said, his eyes twinkling.

'Hasdrubal will be angry,' she replied without conviction.

Looking round, she saw that the slaves had disappeared and they were alone.

She wanted a man's touch on her body, longed to relish the thrust of a real prick inside her. She wanted to work at her own pleasures and those of someone else.

'Hasdrubal works for my father. Since my father is away, I am the head of the household.'

She wondered how far she could respond without risking her job.

'Hurry up,' he cried impatiently. His face fell slightly. 'Don't you want to?'

His prick began to droop and she felt a surge of feminine power. He wasn't ordering her, so much as begging: his exhuberant manner concealed a profound lack of self-confidence.

'I can't resist,' she said softly. 'I have to take the opportunities the goddesses are giving me. I cannot live for ever on hopes and dreams.'

She dumped the towels unceremoniously on a mosaic of the mythical lovers, Dido and Aeneas. Slowly, she untied the long belt of her dress and watched his eyes following her every movement. She moved sensuously and allowed her gaze to wander openly to his groin as she ran her tongue lightly over her lips and slid her hands down over her hips. The curls of hair framed his tight little balls and his rod began to grow again. She could hardly wait for it to be inside her. Her body clamoured for his slender young body to pump into her with the same infectious enthusiasm he displayed in his conversation.

She placed her discarded clothes on the towels, knowing that the line of her hips and the gentle swellings of her breasts were accentuating her slim waist. She saw him gawping at the soft creases between her legs.

'Hurry up – I am burning up,' he shouted with gusto.

'So am I, lord.' She grinned an invitation.

The sight of his lithe body, all primed up for pleasure, made her moist and ready. She shook her body so her breasts bounced up and down, then side to side.

He waded through the thigh-deep water and put his hands on his penis, fondling it suggestively. It leapt under his touch and she felt the old, familiar longing. She could imagine holding it, stroking it, tasting it.

She bent her knees and lowered her bottom slightly, shaking her hips and breasts at the same time.

He yelled, 'I want you now, woman.'

'You have to catch me,' she shrieked into the reverberating echo. Turning, she wiggled her neat little bottom at him.

He leapt out of the water and ran towards her but she eluded him and jumped into the pool, taunting him with laughing eyes.

He splashed back in as she was climbing out of the other side. She turned and shook her breasts at him once more, trying to evade him. He caught her and pulled her around to face him, his hands slipping on her wet body. She giggled and put her hands between his legs, feeling the soft sacks and the silky-wet hair. She ran her fingers lightly up and down his delectable, totally desirable stem and smiled when he laughed with delight.

'I want you, now. In the water.' He fumbled for her but missed his footing.

She was on him before he could fully recover his balance. She plunged her mouth over his cock and sucked, rolling her tongue around it with slow, thirsty movements. He tasted wholesome and full of youthful spirit. His penis was thinner than any other she had experienced. She knelt on the pool floor and felt the water lap around her breasts as she pulled his body towards her, with her hands on his buttocks. With deep satisfaction, she kneaded the cheeks and relished the tight, neat muscles.

He roared at her in a frenzy of anticipation. His penis was pulsating in her mouth so she pulled away quickly and threw water over it before splashing his whole body. They laughed and screamed at each other, splashing the water in ever-increasing waves. Her hair was dripping wet, her crotch throbbing. She couldn't take the image of his prick out of her mind: having it inside her seemed to be the most important aim in life.

She climbed out of the pool, knowing that she was presenting her bottom to him. The cheeks were parted and she guessed he could glimpse her labia. Deliberately, she bent over nearly double and allowed him a good look at her most intimate areas. She had seen how this position had incited the men in the competition and it excited her own lust to know how he was likely to react.

He splashed after her, shouting for her to return. She turned with a grin and ran to the nearest archway.

She paused, realising her mistake.

'Going into the the hot room means a dead-end and almost unbearable, dry heat,' he shouted. 'There's no way you can escape that way. I will have my wicked way with you, woman.'

The very naivety of his words further enflamed her. He might be only half-man, half-child, but she could teach him so much and his enthusiasm was invigorating.

Ignoring the entrance to the gymnasium, she flung open the only other exit and ran outside into the bright sun. The heat beat down on her shoulders and bottom, and the path to the house was hot underfoot.

Naked and shouting with glee, he sprinted after her. Two gardeners stopped pruning the flowers and stared in their direction.

Looking back for a moment, she saw that Julius was

gaining on her. She redoubled her efforts on the hard, dirt path.

She could hear his breath and imagined she could feel the heat of his body. She rounded the corner of the villa and saw the rows of stables ahead.

A groom placidly moved a superbly bred horse out of her path and stood back to watch, his eyes screwed up against the sun.

Julius managed to touch her shoulder with a finger and she wriggled and shrieked with laughter. The horse whinnied and threw up its head, but she had no time to notice any other reaction as she fled into the deserted stable. Rows of stalls, filled with clean straw, offered no escape.

She turned around to face her pursuer, breathing very fast. His penis was now huge – seemingly larger than normal because of the slight build of his body.

'Lie down!'

'Make me,' she challenged.

He lunged at her, taking her off balance, so they both collapsed into the deep straw of the nearest compartment.

The hard stalks bit into her backside like a thousand needles. He had almost no body hair and was silky to the touch. She moaned her delight at the exquisite contrast between the straw and his soft skin on hers.

'Open your legs, you Siren,' he muttered, his face hidden in her hair as he nuzzled her ears and his hand inexpertly fumbled for her labia.

'Say please,' she ordered and he laughed.

'Please.'

'Say please, lady. Please, please open your legs. And mean it.'

'Please, lady. Please, please, please, please, please open you legs and let me into your temple of delights.'

She laughed, holding his face in both her hands and kissing him.

'You don't need to go that far.'

'I need to go much further than that. Much, much

further. Further than I have ever been before. Do you know that? You are my first woman. And I want you. I want you now!'

His kiss was deep and wet. She felt for his tongue with her own. He began to laugh and held her hands above her head, pinioning her body under his.

'Reluctant are you? You won't be able to resist me. Once I'm inside, my animal magnetism will entrance you. Open your legs. How can I get inside with them tightly clamped?'

'You need to be taught a lesson,' she said severely. She pulled her arms away and rolled from under him. 'You have to learn that a woman needs to be ready before you enter her. If you can't impress her before then, you will be doomed to failure in love all your life.'

His expression changed to chagrin and she saw his erection begin to wilt.

She bent her upper body towards him and took his prick in her mouth. Immediately it sprang into action.

'Jupiter! Ulysses!'

She laughed, pulling herself away. 'Lie back. As I said, you need to be taught a lesson. Or two or three lessons. In physical love.'

She straddled him and allowed him to feel her open folds on his penis. The heat felt wonderful and she longed for the rod to be inside her, but she knew she would have no satisfaction if she allowed him to enter her too early.

'You did not misread the signals,' she assured him. 'I want this as much as you do. More, possibly, because I know what delights there are in store for us. I have intimate knowledge of a man's body and I really want to feel your cock inside me.'

'Then let me inside,' he groaned.

'I will. I want you to know that not all women would like to be chased and ordered about. An innocent young girl might be afraid of you and all other men for ever if you chase her as you have chased me. You don't want that, do you?'

'I want women to fall at my feet, offering themselves not just willingly, but with ardent cravings.'

She rubbed her labia along the length of his penis and then pulled his hands to her breasts, showing him how to manipulate them.

'Jupiter!' he exclaimed again.

As she moved up his body to squat over his face, he gave a loud moan of amazement. His fingers flew to her and he avidly examined her folds and the deep crevice between them.

'I've never seen inside a woman before.'

He pushed a tentative finger inside her and she groaned her encouragement.

When he moved to her clit, she almost leapt with the pleasure that Fate had withheld for so many days.

Julius began to vibrate the delicate place immediately above the bud of pleasure, with his finger.

'You may have limited experience with women, but you certainly know what to do,' she panted appreciatively, falling forwards and supporting herself on her hands.

'The maids sometimes take pity on me, in secret, but they won't let me inside their bodies in case they get pregnant and my father finds out. My father only lets me fondle the male slaves – he is such a conventional old stick! Just because that was the fashion when he was young, he won't let me do anything else. You are going to let me in, aren't you, Marcella?' he asked with an anxious frown.

'Of course I will, if you will give me the release that I want. At the same time you will learn how to secure the gratitude of any willing woman so she will be begging for more.'

'Oh please, show me. I want to know, now.'

He was still manipulating her clit, with one finger inexpertly fumbling inside her.

'You don't have to use your hands alone.'

She lowered herself to his mouth.

His slightly slack, full lips felt wet and warm on her

petalled folds. He licked her clitoris and began to vibrate it with his tongue. She moaned with delight.

'You are a natural,' she gasped, rocking herself against the force of his lips.

He grasped her thighs and held her tight as she quivered with a partial orgasm.

'That was so sweet,' she told him as she lay down with her cheek against his chest.

'Now I want what you promised,' he said, and she turned over and spread her legs with eagerness.

His penis bumped against her mound of love and then against her buttocks so she gently took it in her hands and guided it inside. Gently, she kissed his lips and he sighed and moved his hips towards her, twice. He climaxed inside her with huge shudders that lasted for long moments.

He rolled off and lay beside her with his eyes closed and a deep grin on his face.

She stroked him and reflected that what Imilico had said was correct: it would be wonderful to watch a person taking the ultimate pleasure.

She felt uncomfortable and unsatisfied, because the weak orgasm had simply reminded her of what she had been missing for weeks. Her body ached for real satisfaction, deep within. She closed her eyes and drifted into a light sleep.

'I am getting bored. In fact, we are all getting bored,' said a cool voice.

Julius sat up abruptly and surveyed the group of young men at the door, silhouetted against the bright sunshine.

'Greetings, my friends!'

'Quintus ejaculated, merely watching her backside over your face,' the young man drawled, indicating a tall lanky youth.

'You came when I did, Publius, so you can't scoff! It was a heroic coupling. The best thing I've ever seen.'

'I'd like her to do that for me,' said the third, a quiet

looking boy with startlingly blue eyes. 'Would you be willing?' he asked Marcella.

She looked away, unsure of the situation. Her bodily needs were gnawingly insistent. She desperately craved the physical fulfilment that she had not achieved with Julius.

'You would think of that, Felicius!' Publius sounded languid and world-weary. 'I bet Julius can't do it again.'

'Give me a quarter of an hour or so and I will,' sighed Julius.

'You've had more than half an hour to recover already. You were snoring, you lazy good-for-nothing. We became bored, so we went away and when we came back you were still flat out. You said, "Come and spend a few weeks at the villa while my parents are in Syria," and all we have received for entertainment so far is watching you sleep!'

'Yes – it's a poor show and you are well on the way to being a poor host!' smiled Felicius. Marcella thought he looked deliciously desirable.

'I'll need longer then – she has exhausted me!' As Julius started to get up, Publius moved forward.

'I'll wager you two denarii that I can get you to ejaculation within a count of five hundred.'

Transfixed, Marcella watched as his friend lay down next to Julius, his hand on the now flaccid penis. Their tongues slid familiarly into their open mouths.

'I'm off – this is too tame and I've seen the show before,' said Quintus. 'How about a game of dice, Felicius?'

Felicius didn't take his eyes off Marcella.

'I'll be along in a while. I want to watch them. I find it calming as well as informative.'

Marcella got up and stood in the straw, embarrassed by her nakedness.

'Put this around yourself,' Felicius suggested, holding out a thick horse blanket. 'We can get your clothes from the bath building later.'

'How do you know where they are?' she asked.

'You are the talk of the villa – the gardeners and grooms told everybody about your chase. That was why we came to watch.' He chuckled. 'Let us get to know one another. Where do you come from? You have an unusual accent – not Roman, but not Tripolitanian either.'

Felicius held her breasts gently, as if afraid they would break. He smelled fresh and wholesome and his kisses were softly enticing.

The couple on the straw were still rapt, but their arousal had been slow and Marcella and Felicius had tired of exchanging stories about their childhoods.

'I want a real, deep orgasm with a hard male rod inside me,' she whispered.

'I know,' he whispered back. 'That episode with Julius merely served as an appetizer didn't it? Now you are on fire with need. I may be young, but I can quench that fire. Unlike Julius, I have had a woman before. I know what women want.'

'You remind me of someone,' she said.

The stables were dark and quiet and the horse blanket felt rough on her skin.

'I think he has lost his wager, it must be nearly an hour since they began!'

Marcella rolled to one side to observe them.

'I, too, like watching them,' admitted the boy kissing her neck. 'It makes me feel good. They obviously enjoy it so much, but I don't feel the need to join in. Julius is lucky – he will be able to take his pleasures wherever he finds them for the rest of his life. We will be confined to members of the opposite gender.'

He moved gently on top of her and pushed himself inside her willing and ready womanhood.

'You have done this before,' she said admiringly. 'How old did you say you were?'

'Sixteen. And two weeks. My father and uncle share a slave girl. She is about twenty-four years old and they have taught her well. Neither of them mind if I occasionally experiment with her. She is willing and so long as I don't leave her too tired, they are pleased for me to keep her happy if they are away, for example. I guess that my mother and aunt know about her, but they turn a blind eye.'

'How civilised! The rich really do know how to live, don't they?'

He began to move inside her with a casual precision.

'I will hold back until you have climaxed. How many times would you like to do that before I end it?' he asked.

She giggled. 'You sound like a shopkeeper taking an order. One sounds fine.'

She pushed her loins towards him and found the delicious resistance of his thighs on hers.

'That is not nearly enough for a woman like you,' he said with certainty. 'We will start with two and then see how we feel. I find you so exciting, I may not be able to last any longer, though sometimes I can go on while Candida climaxes over and over. Our record was twelve, spread over a long summer hour. We timed it on the water-clock.'

The picture of long, drawn-out bliss brought on an intense internal spasm and she moved her body so her breasts were rubbing against his soft chest, the nipples hard with anticipation.

The couple on the straw suddenly groaned and changed position.

'For Priapus' sake Julius, suck me quickly,' muttered Publius.

The two lay beside one another, a cock in each hot mouth. Their tongues were working fast as their hands kneaded each other's buttocks.

Marcella was entranced by the beauty of their enjoyment. She could see Julius's face: his eyes were closed, his brow smooth.

'Oh, Juno, it is beautiful to see someone else's pleasure . . .'

Her body took over in a fierce orgasmic convulsion

that rocked her. She shuddered and shook under Felicius for a moment.

'Personally, I like to do these things together,' he panted.

She looked towards the young lovers.

'Concentrate on me, Marcella,' he said sharply and he pushed so hard she gasped.

She heard the couple on the straw begin to grunt rhythmically. She found herself responding with moans and finally, as the two boys erupted in each other's mouths, she climaxed with force.

The ripples of pleasure ran through her, starting from the top of her head, down her arms to the tips of her fingers, along her legs to her toes. She arched her feet and rubbed the soles of her feet against his legs to prolong the intense pleasure.

She lay still for a moment or two and then opened her eyes and smiled.

'Now for the best time,' he whispered laughingly in her ear. 'Concentrate. Push hard. I can't control myself any longer. But you will not be allowed to go free until I have brought you to one more climax, this time with me.'

'You definitely remind me of someone,' she said, and the thought of Gaius made her erupt for a final time. She lay exhausted and totally surfeited, her entire body completely relaxed from sheer pleasure, freely and happily given.

'Gaius Salvius Antoninus will have a problem getting the tribes to agree to a peace this time,' observed Publius.

Startled by the familiar, much cherished name, Marcella nearly dropped the platter of small roasted birds that she was carrying. She was enjoying their admiring looks and the occasional surreptitious fumble as she helped the slaves serve wine and food. Quintus threw a grape in the air and she managed to catch it as she passed. She expertly tossed it into his mouth. Laughingly, he patted her bottom.

'He's got out of tighter spots than this,' replied Felicius. 'The Third Legion was honoured by the Emperor Augustus and have remained a crack force. They will manage.'

'The tribes are definitely in a nasty mood,' observed Quintus. He washed his hands in the perfumed water bowl beside him and dried them on his towel. 'I suppose they have finally realised that the desert will always be patrolled. When they built the fortress at Theveste four years ago, the Third Augusta showed that Rome meant business.'

'You will inherit that spread near the coast, if he is killed, won't you, Felicius?' said Publius reflectively. 'I hear it is nearly a palace – even bigger and more sumptuous than this!'

'I believe it is bequeathed to me. But frankly I'd rather have my cousin, Gaius, alive. I have enough money as it is.'

Marcella stared in astonishment – Gaius was Felicius' cousin! No wonder he had reminded her of him.

The rest of the dinner was torture for her. The conversation kept returning to Gaius Salvius Antoninus, but she was unable to join in or ask any questions. The 'little place in Tripolitania' that he had spoken of so modestly was mentioned frequently as the ultimate in rich, luxurious living.

Had Gaius misled her about other matters to? Matters such as his relationship with Imilico?

She stamped into the kitchens towards the end of the meal and threw a cloth on the table, unable to suppress her impatience and frustration.

'Tired? You've had a strenuous day,' smiled Hasdrubal sympathetically. 'I hear you have been able to keep Julius out of mischief.'

'Racing naked through the gardens?' She grimaced.

'I only saw the part where Felicius brought you in under the horse blanket. I missed the athletic episode. You have given the staff enough to gossip about for months. You would hardly believe it to judge from

Julius' behaviour, but his parents are particularly strait-laced and intellectually minded. We haven't witnessed such sights before. And I doubt we will again!' He chuckled.

'You did tell me to keep him happy at all costs,' she pointed out defensively.

'And I want you to keep up the good work. Don't take the gossip as adverse criticism. You know that we often find him a handful. He has too much energy for his own good and the horses benefit from being ridden carefully. Their mouths are ruined by the way he punishes them by chasing game all over the countryside at breakneck speeds.'

'He does seem a little wild,' she admitted, smilingly, thinking of his enthusiasm for her body and his own pleasures.

'We dread him coming, to be frank. But now he has discovered women, perhaps things will be better. His problem lies with his father – an aesthete of the old school. He is a good man and a fair master, but it doesn't always do to repress youthful energies,' he replied. 'Felicius' father is the same.'

'They will want to play games later – I can hear them working up to it,' she said wearily, slumping against the wall. 'They are talking about all the men they know who are really tough. It is only a matter of time before they get on to the mythical heroes – Theseus, Hercules, Perseus.'

'Once they have convinced themselves they too are grown men, you fear that they will think their appetites must be relieved on a heroic scale?'

'Exactly. I can't face it again! It was fun this afternoon – but now I am tired.'

'Go to bed. I will take in the last courses and you can simply disappear,' he suggested. 'You have already made our work load lighter. It won't do us any good if you fall ill with exhaustion on the third day.'

* * *

She heard them calling for her in the cool of the night. She lay in her bedroom, revelling in the comfort of the soft bed and perfumed cushions.

When everything had quietened down, around the fifth hour of the night, she rose and walked into the garden.

The moon illuminated the plant-clad columns with an unearthly blue light. She sniffed the silent air. Somewhere far to the east, on the edge of the desert wastelands, under the same moon, surrounded by hostile tribes, was Gaius Salvius Antoninus. Although the fortress itself was well behind the area of danger, Imilico had been certain that Gaius would be with the men under his command. He would be living rough in the army tents behind temporary pallisading, constantly on the alert for attack.

He had introduced her to sensual delights and no other man had even remotely approached the level of bliss she had experienced with him.

Had he any thoughts for her? Or was her memory so bitter that he wanted to obliterate it for ever? Was his need to control the situation so great that he would avoid anything – including the pleasures she could offer him – that upset his sense of power or challenged his household arrangements?

Chapter Sixteen

'**Y**ou are looking better this morning.'

Hasdrubal dipped a piece of cotton material into some water and then into a bowl of fine sand. He rubbed hard at a huge silver dish.

'I slept well,' she lied, selecting some bread and filling a beaker with goat's milk. 'That is a beautiful object.'

'My wife died a few months after this was given to my master – it always reminds me of her because she used to love to clean it.'

'I'm sorry,' she said. 'You must miss her.'

'We were married for nearly forty years. She was born in Gaul – where this was made.'

He held up the massive platter to inspect his work.

'What a marvellous gift!' she said, as she ran a finger over the gleaming metal.

'Gaius Salvius Antoninus sent it with Imilico. It is solid silver.'

Gaius again. She tried to shake off the memories as she watched Hasdrubal delicately burnishing the chubby figure of a child.

'The young Hercules, wrestling the serpents in his cradle,' she observed.

'The rest of the dish shows the twelve labours of Hercules.'

They examined it.

'Here he is slaying the Nemean lion, and over there, the nine-headed Hydra of Lerna.'

'This shows him capturing the stag of Arcadia, and the wild boar of Erymanthus. And here,' she said, running her finger over a scene thoughtfully, 'He is cleaning out the Augean stables.'

She stood up and paced the kitchen, picking up a second piece of newly-baked bread and crunching into it absently.

'Those young men have far too much energy. They want to be heroes. I shall give them a challenge!'

He gave the dish a final burnish and picked up a goblet decorated in the same florid style.

'Then of course,' she continued, 'I shall instruct the victor in the gentle art of physical love. After all, if we women don't tell men what we like, how can they possibly know?'

'Besides, you are missing your lover.' He looked at the silver plate, with a faint smile. 'He must be attached to the Third Augusta if you are going to Theveste.'

'You are jumping to conclusions!' She glared at him, but he looked unperturbed.

'A woman like you will burn up if you can't be with him soon. Spending your time with four lusty youths will focus your mind on sensual matters, whether you like it or not, so giving instruction to the victor will serve all purposes.'

'The winner will have two hours of my individual and undivided attention, in the place of his choice,' she told the young men later that day.

'So, what impresses you? My father owns half of Tuscany and a chunk of Rome,' drawled Publius.

'That is certainly not fair – everyone knows your family is the richest amongst us,' cried Julius.

'What about our relations? My sister is married to –'

'I'm not impressed by who your families are – they are all more illustrious than mine. I don't think you understand,' she said patiently, aware of Hasdrubal laughing quietly in the background. 'I genuinely mean that you have to do a series of Herculean tasks yourselves.'

The youths looked at each other uneasily.

'We are patricians – we never carry out physical work,' said Quintus, faltering slightly.

'It is not beneath a patrician to attempt to join the ranks of the Heroes, is it? You want to be like Theseus, Hector, Hercules and Lysander don't you?'

'But they are Heroes from the myths – there aren't any modern monsters to fight,' said Felicius uncertainly.

'Every woman wants a hero, made pure by the effects of hard, maybe impossible tasks, bravely attempted. Many mortal men attract women. Mostly, they aren't lazy, effete weaklings. You know yourselves, that people like, well, like your cousin Gaius, Felicius, are very attractive to women.'

She saw Hasdrubal looking at her curiously. She avoided his eye, aware that there had been no reason for her to bring Gaius Salvius Antoninus into the conversation.

'In the event of a tie, I will set other tasks until there is a clear winner.'

She pretended not to notice their loud groans of protest and placed a wax tablet in front of them.

'This is a list of your tasks.'

They crowded around the table and read the scratched words.

'First day – muck out the stables,' read Publius, sounding enthusiastic. 'Just like Hercules!'

'Second day, dig over the field behind the villa ready for planting.'

'Now that is a challenge. It may take longer than a day.'

'Today's task will be easy, my friends,' muttered Julius as they left the kitchen. 'The grooms have always finished their chores by midday, so there will be nothing to do at all if we take our time in the baths.'

'What a shame that the grooms haven't got around to

mucking out today,' Marcella remarked innocently to Hasdrubal.

His eyes were twinkling, though he retained an air of speculation.

'It was a pity that I had to send them into the countryside to search for the master's dog. I doubt if he will be found before tonight.'

'Certainly not, since we locked him in one of the barns,' she replied, laughing.

The stables housed many fine horses, fit from the lush land that bordered the desert.

The four young men toiled all day, moving manure and Marcella sauntered past at intervals to call encouragement. She allowed her hips to sway seductively. Occasionally, she bent down to pick up a piece of straw in such a way that one of them could catch a glimpse of a firm breast or her slim ankles.

They stripped off to under-tunics and sweated in the hot sun. Their muscles were undeveloped compared to the men she had known intimately, but they were healthy and well formed, fit from long exercise in the gymnasium and good food. Quintus was the most muscular – she could see that his chest was already well-covered in hair.

She felt alive and desirable.

'It is so pleasant here, Hasdrubal,' she remarked as she tidied up the dining room. 'You have no idea how marvellous it is to be amongst people who are dedicated to the higher things in life.'

'We do our best.'

'Here, even the slaves live well and strive to create an orderly, harmonious environment. When the young men get drunk and disorderly, they aren't as loud and coarse as the men in my uncle's tavern used to be.'

'The rich do not tolerate disorder of any kind. I was born into this family, and my father before me, so I know nothing of the life you describe. I would hate it.'

'I love Africa. I am learning a few words of your

dialect and everyone I speak to is courteous and friendly.'

'We always have room for people who fit in and work hard.'

She looked at him, feeling emotional.

'I should love to remain here, Hasdrubal. It seems so safe and I have to put the past behind me.'

'Then you must stay,' he said. 'That is settled.'

The young men completed six tasks and Marcella felt unsettled and impatient for the end of the work, when she could welcome one of them between her legs. In the still of the night she put her hand to herself and thought of Virius and his friends, trying to blot out the memory of Gaius.

One afternoon, as the youths toiled on the seventh labour, she wandered into the deserted bath house. The furnaces had been stoked up so the hot room was up to its full capacity and the warm room was comfortable. The tile-lined suite of rooms was decorated in a fashion that had been out-of-date in Pompeii and looked old-fashioned to her.

Her thighs ached with the need to embrace a strong male body and her feminine folds and creases were throbbing with need.

To ease her craving for sensuality, she bathed, sweating for a punishing period in the hot room and then leaping straight into the water in the cold plunge. Exhausted from the rigours, but still aflame with loneliness and physical desire, she wandered into the small gymnasium. The rest of the villa was so sumptuously appointed that she was certain it would contain some fine sculptures, and after her adventure with Petronius she was interested.

She wandered round, trailing a towel casually behind her. A few marble busts stood in niches. She recognised Julius Caesar and the writer and politician, Cicero. Both were symbols of the austere character of the old Republic when frivolity and luxury had been regarded as un-

211

Roman. She recalled Hasdrubal saying that his master admired such attitudes. The first Emperor – Augustus – stood apart in a larger niche, and next to him was the present emperor, Titus.

Her heart turned over: in a niche by itself stood a bust of Gaius Salvius Antoninus.

The desolation of her life without him was unexpectedly drawn into poignant perspective. She knew that she had been deluding herself in thinking she could be happy in this place.

Her despair was made unbearable by the knowledge that if he was thinking about her at all, it would not be in a kindly way. She felt weak at the knees and in her loins as the memories flooded back. She collapsed on the stone floor and subconsciously felt for her breasts, as he had done, manipulating them with a feverish need. She put her other hand on her clitoris and rubbed, remembering his silken touch. But she felt numb rather than relieved. She opened her labia with both hands, ran her fingers up and down the glistening petals of her womanhood and moaned gently, her head moving from side to side in her agony. She wanted Gaius, not some young boy whose body was only three quarters of the way to manhood and whose mind was still trapped in childish attitudes.

She opened her eyes and looked at the white, still face. She rose and put her arms around the statue's neck. Passionately she kissed the cold lips, running her tongue over them, sucking and nuzzling in vain.

Lying on the towel, on the hard stone floor, she began to masturbate in earnest, one hand to a nipple, the other over her clit. She thought of his face, his arms around her, his firm manhood that was so silky smooth and so potently able to give pleasure. She flexed her legs and pushed towards her need. In desperation, she crossed her legs and pushed her hips upwards. She rubbed her thighs and calves together furiously, as her hand moved ever more vigorously. She urged herself to her climax, but her mind refused to instruct her muscles to go into the spasm of bliss she so desired.

In her frenzy of need, she could feel his tongue on her, and his arms around her.

A strong, hairy torso pressed down on her – or was it her imagination? Muscular arms grasped her in a close embrace and she involuntarily parted her legs without opening her eyes, afraid that the moment would pass into a mere dream. She moved her hands to his groin, gently stroking. His balls were tight with readiness.

She touched the rock hard stem and ran her fingers along its length. She slid further up his body and placed her arms around his neck in desperate entreaty, sighing with a deep sense of relief and gratitude as he pushed deeply into her.

They moved together smoothly, their bodies in complete unison, his ability proving long years of experience and patience. She felt completely safe and at peace as their breath came first slowly, then with increasing speed. She began to moan and make little cries and he grunted with her. She rubbed his buttocks and pulled him closer, liking the feel of his hair on her breasts. Her nipples, hard and erect, caught on the curls with a tender-sharp sensation. His profuse pubic hair brushed hard against her clit as they pushed towards their mutual release.

She erupted into a thousand sparks of light. Her mind shattered with fragments of delight and need. Her body was wet with exertion from the expertly performed act of lust, friendship and gentle passion.

She opened her eyes and smiled as he shuddered in response and lay still.

'Hasdrubal,' she said, 'You should be ashamed of yourself, at your age! You have the stamina of a man forty years younger.'

He grinned, rolled her over so she was lying on top of him and kissed her on the mouth.

'I had a wife for a long time – a man gets to know his limitations and his advantages. The moment I set eyes on you, as you pulled that absurdly heavy bag out of the wagon, I knew I could give you real pleasure. Even if I can't be the one you really want.'

He kissed her again.

The four young men were exhausted after their Herculean-style labours. Bathed and dressed, they reclined in the dining room in postures of discomfort.

'I expect,' Marcella said, 'That you will want to go to bed early tonight. Tomorrow you are to flatten the lane to the main road – it has a large number of potholes.'

'That is totally stupid,' said Julius. 'No patrician would do such a thing.'

'You want to command a legion and perhaps be carried through the streets of Rome in a Triumph after a great battle?'

'Of course – but a legate doesn't have to labour physically.'

'The army builds roads and the commander should know what to expect of his men,' she argued.

'You sound like my father.'

'And my cousin, Gaius,' said Felicius.

She shook away the warmth his name brought to the dark, secret place between her legs.

The young men groaned and Publius threw a piece of bread at her.

'We have nearly completed the tasks. You can dance for us,' he said. 'I don't see why that would break the pact – come on, dance. Something provocative.'

She thought for a moment.

'No touching – just a show. You deserve a small reward tonight.'

Felicius laughed and she saw a fleeting glimpse of Gaius Salvius Antoninus, the man she felt she would never stop craving.

She left them to eat their sweetmeats while she changed into her elegant saffron coloured dress and the amber and jet jewels. Around her shoulders she draped a diaphanous scarf that she had bought in Hippo Regius.

She wore her dainty gold-impressed slippers and pinned scented flowers from the garden in her hair.

As she went into the kitchens, Hasdrubal turned from his chores.

'You look incredibly beautiful,' he said in a husky voice, his eyes very serious.

'I am going to dance for them,' she smiled. 'You will be glad to know – as I am – that they are so tired out that they haven't the energy to get up to any mischief. They will definitely not stay up late tonight. Can anyone play the pipes or the lute?'

Hasdrubal translated what she had said and immediately two slaves scrambled up.

'They can play the flute and the cymbals.'

She strutted slowly around the room, sticking her breasts and her bottom out like the hetaerae in Rome. She flung her arms above her head so that the scarf was suspended above her in an arc, copying the pictures of Venus in her hometown.

The rhythm started slowly as the two musicians felt their way into her mood. Then they began to perform like professionals. She stamped on the mosaic floor, whirled and kicked, swirled her dress around and shook her hair over her head as the tempo increased. The young men began to clap and the serving staff joined in.

She threw the scarf to Julius, who caught it deftly and drank deeply from his goblet. She took off a slipper and discarded it with graceful insouciance, under a chair.

The flautist changed the tempo to a haunting little melody that she did not recognise. The tune summed up the loneliness of the desert, the shimmering danger of living in an environment where a person could die in the cold of the night or the heat of the day.

She discarded her other slipper and her belt as the youths began to shout slurred instructions.

She lifted her skirt delicately and allowed them a fleeting glimpse of her ankles.

'More than that!'

'Take your dress off – don't be a coward,' Publius cried.

She whirled around the dining room twice more and then bowed low.

'Goodnight, lords,' she murmured gently. 'Goodnight.'

The musicians continued to play their evocative tune as she walked down the long corridors to her bedroom. The high notes of the flute pierced the silence of the great house with eerie echoes, as she finally closed the door and lay down in the darkness thinking of her lover. Gaius.

'I have worked like a slave for weeks. Your slave, Marcella. I have completed the tasks,' shouted Quintus breathlessly, as he ran the last few steps to the villa. The other youths were plodding over the fields behind him.

'Then I pronounce you the victor.' She laughed as she placed a wreath on his head. 'We didn't have any laurel, so I've used leaves from the kitchen.'

'I was more motivated than the others,' he said as he leant against one of the veranda pillars.

He already sounded more adult, she thought in surprise.

'You are too slow! Kneel before the lady and make your apologies for not living up to heroic standards,' he shouted to his friends who jeered in return.

'You haven't named the place yet,' cried Publius.

'I do not intend to – that is between Marcella and me. I'm not having you ogling bunch of perverts watching!'

An hour later, he held her tightly around the waist as though he was afraid she might run away.

'Julius' mother usually uses this carriage on her shopping expeditions,' he said, controlling the two ponies with one hand.

The air was cooling and the fields were deserted. He found a quiet spot where the grass was lush and a few trees afforded some privacy. In the far distance, the trembling heat of the desert distorted the hills.

216

He poured some wine from a container which he produced from a wooden box.

'Stop stuffing food into your mouth,' she said at last, gently taking his hand. 'There is nothing to be nervous about.'

Hours later, he lay back, relaxed and content with his achievements and she smiled.

'We have to go home in a week's time. Will you stay in Africa, so we can visit you every summer?' he asked quietly.

She rolled over and watched the incandescent colours of the hills in the late afternoon heat.

'There is something I have to do. Some business that is unfinished,' she said slowly. 'I want to stay, but a part of me calls to another place.'

'I hope I shall see you again, Marcella. Soon. When I am a man, I shall hope to know you then.'

'I will look forward to knowing you for a long time,' she said, smiling. She kissed him.

Chapter Seventeen

'It is now safe for you to leave for Theveste,' said Hasdrubal when Marcella and Quintus returned to the villa. 'The uprisings have been quelled and there has been no trouble for long enough to believe that the peace will last. It is time for you to meet Gaius Salvius Antoninus again.'

He smiled sadly at her. Her heart leapt with satisfaction mixed with apprehension.

'A contingent of the Third Augusta is due to pass here soon. I have arranged for you to travel south with them.'

'How do you know they are on their way?' She felt totally disorientated.

'An official with a military dispatch passed through on his way to the southern outposts.'

'More trouble?'

She felt cold.

'It it was fresh trouble we'd see the messengers riding like Mercury northwards to Rome!'

'You get to know so much about politics in the depths of the country,' she said in surprise.

'Italy is far from the Empire's borders, so you were shielded from the harsher realities in Pompeii. Here, and in the towns there is rarely any danger, but we are kept aware of any developments.'

'I had no idea things would be so hazardous when I started out from Pompeii,' she said sadly. 'It all seemed like an adventure and I had so many hopes and dreams.'

'You may well be able to fulfil some of them.' He smiled, his eyes very serious. 'I will take you to the main thoroughfare. They will be expecting you because I sent a message back along the road with one of the local merchants. The troops will be on foot, of course, but they have supply wagons with them and you can no doubt squeeze into one of them.'

The journey was hot and uncomfortable and the legionaries made it clear that her presence was not wanted. She missed Hasdrubal's kindly protection and the organised, carefree life she had enjoyed at the villa. Instead she had to endure heat and discomfort and dirt.

'You all seem very ill-tempered, Brutus,' she said apprehensively to the senior centurion as he inspected the wagon in which she was travelling. He was a dashingly handsome man of about thirty with medium brown hair and piercingly blue eyes.

'Six months ago we were detailed to man a tiny outpost in what turned out to be a safe area,' he said forbiddingly as he pulled a loose rope taut. 'We've had nothing to do but watch the lizards and count sanddunes.'

She didn't dare offer any platitudes in the face of his anger.

'Then, after the action was over,' he went on, 'We were ordered to bring supplies to the gallant fighters. They might have let us stay put like all the other outlying troops. But no! We had to be the ones to fetch and carry fruit and vegetables, like matrons at the market. We'll never live it down!'

'Your colleagues will understand, surely,' she said helplessly.

'Our only hope is to arrive earlier than expected with the luxury items they are missing the most,' he replied tersely. 'On top of all that, we have to take a detour further south than we should need, to drop off some supplies at an outpost. The whole exercise is difficult and uncomfortable. Of course we are all angry.'

The legionaries marched by night and pitched camp during the day, allowing her to sleep in a wagon. Forty-eight hours later, the terrain was becoming increasingly less fertile, with fewer olive groves and vineyards. During the silence of the day, when they were trying to rest, the men became increasingly nervous, waiting for attack.

As dawn broke on the fourth day, she saw that the countryside was more fertile again, with mountains close by. As they were about to pitch camp, Brutus decided to change policy.

'We won't stop – we will continue marching through the heat of the day, with frequent rests. That way we will arrive before midnight,' he ordered, looking grimly into the distance.

She was totally exhausted when they reached the fortress and they could see the walls rising above the shanty town near the gates. In the thin moonlight they were dark and forbidding, and the torches on the wall-walks shone like communications beacons.

She felt very apprehensive as a grey-haired centurion came out of the HQ to meet the convoy.

'Greetings, Nicomedes! I hope we didn't disturb your beauty sleep.'

'You never did have any consideration, Brutus.'

'We heard you were all dying of malnutrition and were in urgent need of such necessities as vintage wines, dormice for roasting, truffles and pomegranates to pep up your strength.'

'We are,' said Nicomedes dryly. He spoke with a strong Greek accent that Marcella found difficult to understand. 'All we get is bloody women complaining about the plumbing and the architecture. The legion built an aqueduct to get the water here, but suddenly that isn't enough and we should have decorated the damned baths with flowers. We've built ruddy great stone walls and a fine HQ in stone, but the legate's wooden house isn't quite up to scratch because it is still the temporary wooden structure.'

'Who is complaining?' asked Brutus. 'These things take time – that is quite normal.'

'Some of the civilian visitors who arrived to witness the peace negotiations. They won't even touch the local liquor to mellow them. Pitched battle would be a softer option.'

The two men laughed. 'Tell me about it over some Falernian,' said Brutus, suddenly looking far less forbidding as he conversed with his friend. 'They'll never miss a couple of jugs.'

Marcella felt totally out of place as the troops disappeared with well-trained speed to their quarters. A few men from the permanent garrison looked at her and made comments in a language she did not understand. She shivered with foreboding.

'What language are they speaking?' she asked Nicomedes.

'They are Gauls,' he replied tersely. 'There are men from all over the Roman world here, but don't worry, we are all citizens here, so we all speak Latin.'

'What are they saying?' she asked uneasily.

'They are surprised to see you. There are very few females here and all of them are the wives of civilian officials or some of the higher ranks,' Nicomedes replied as he lifted her bag down from the wagon. 'Jupiter Maximus, what do you women find to carry around, that weighs so much?'

'I have come a long way,' she said inadequately. 'And I went shopping in the towns.'

'We'll have to put you in the commander's house. We haven't the facilities anywhere else.'

'I have business with Gaius Salvius Antoninus.'

Nicomedes raised his eyebrow, his expression speculative. 'It will have to wait until tomorrow because he is exhausted from the campaigns. He has been over-working as usual and now he has to entertain VIPs on top of the official records that have to be made up-to-date. I do not intend to wake him now for anything less than a full-scale tribal attack.'

She crept into the house, nervous and ill-at-ease. She refused some food and retired to a small cubby hole where she was told that she could sleep. During the night she tossed and turned for many hours as she thought over the things she could say to Gaius. For the first time they all seemed weak and silly. The knowledge that this great fortress with its strong, professional fighting force was commanded by her lover, was overwhelming. Her needs and his ardour so long ago in the shadow of the volcano seemed insignificant against the real world in which he operated. She dreaded to imagine how he might receive her next morning.

She knew that, whatever else, he would not fall into her arms with joy and loving words as she had so often imagined in her dreams.

'I have nothing to say to you.' His voice was cold when Nicomedes showed her into his office late next morning. 'I cannot imagine why you are here or why you thought it proper to follow me here. It is highly irregular, totally unwanted and utterly without precedent. Your presence here is an embarrassment not only for you and for me, but for the men under my command.'

His icy words reverberated around the bare room.

She had waited for over two hours, as though she were one of his regular client dependants in Rome, and Gaius had taken one look at her with shocked, hard eyes and coldly asked her to leave.

Watching his face as he fought with emotions under a deadpan expression, she lost her temper. The other person in the room angered her simply by his presence and she wanted to hit them both and really hurt them.

'You have everything to say to me,' she shouted, her body rigid with fury. 'You will, at least, do me the courtesy of letting me explain how I came to be dressed as I was at our last meeting.'

'You have come all this way to discuss sartorial taste? My dear little lady! As you can imagine, I have no interest at all in such trivial matters. I have been on active campaign since I last saw you.'

'I know that,' she snapped impatiently. 'I do not need a lesson in current events.'

'It seems that you do, or you would not be here. Men have been killed and horribly maimed, a difficult set of negotiations has been completed for a lasting end to the tribal wars against Rome. Naturally, your choice of clothing has been at the forefront of my mind!'

A stifled snort from the other person sounded suspiciously like laughter and her anger grew. She looked furiously at them both, unable to find words to express her disgust.

'I would appreciate it if you would leave. I have business to attend to,' said Gaius, turning to face the mundane green paintwork. 'Imilico – would you please show this . . . lady . . . out?'

The beautiful slave inclined his head gently.

'And you lied to me!' she said bitterly. 'You said you were returning to Italy.'

He smiled slightly and rose from the chair, putting down the roll of papyrus he had been holding.

'I will fetch Nicomedes, master,' he murmured.

Marcella flushed angrily. 'How dare you imply that I require to be thrown out with physical violence!'

Gaius walked around the room, magnificent in his short army tunic and cloak. His face was harsh and more lined from the arduous weeks he had endured. She thought how very dear he looked to her and her body screamed to her not to let him go. She needed to compel him, by whatever means she could find, to make peace with her. She forced herself to calm down and gain control of her emotions. Since he was playing a game of icy logic, she calculated that she must play the same game to win.

'I think you do have an interest in what I have to say,' she said with a boldness and confidence that almost frightened her. She paused for a moment to allow her words to take hold.

'Do you command your men with no thoughts for their welfare? Do you refuse to listen to other people's opinions? Do you punish your slaves without listening to their side of the story?'

He made an impatient gesture and turned to half-face her, a look of slight uncertainty in his eyes.

'It is shredding your emotions to deny me. I want you now, Gaius. And you want me, no matter who else there may be in your life.'

He whirled around to face her fully, his heavy military shoes scraping the floor.

'You may want me, but you are no longer attractive to me. Oh,' he groaned, with an anguish that bit into her heart, 'I admit that I wanted you once. I don't deny the pleasures of that night, the delights of the next morning. I revelled in your body and supped its rare delights.'

'Then why did you run away and why are you sending me away now?'

'Our emotions and physical desires were heightened by the danger and the unsual events. We were thrown together by Fate, but as so often happens, Fate did not expect us to meet again.'

'Not Fate, but Fortuna,' she cried in misery. 'Don't you see that it is our fortune as well as our fate to meet again?'

'That is where you are mistaken. Following me here like this can't make it right or recreate the past. It is wrong for you to be here and will cause nothing but trouble.'

'How can my presence cause trouble unless you allow it to?' She was thinking of Imilico – was Gaius under his spell? Would he allow a jealous slave to make trouble?

'How do you suppose it will look to my men?' he demanded. 'Only the centurions and tribunes are legally allowed to marry and there aren't enough whores in the township to satisfy all the legionaries. Now I have an unchaperoned, unmarried woman in my house! You are

224

tempting Fate with your constant disregard for what is meant to be!'

She saw the bitterness etched into his facial lines, and heard the despair and pain in his voice.

'I know you don't mean that, Gaius. Don't you know that there is so much more for us? We haven't even begun!'

'Our relationship ended the minute I set eyes on you in Rome and saw you for what you really are, with your painted face and your filthy, lust-stained toga, the colour of shame! In the tavern I thought I had found a nymph, a pure spirit with an independent streak who would lead us both to ecstatic heights. Why do you suppose I came in search of you when I decided it was too dangerous to stay in Pompeii?'

She stared at him, rocked by the implications.

'You came to pick up your painting,' she said. 'It was pure chance that I was there.'

'I was not interested in art! I went first to the tavern. Your friend Lydia was there, also searching for you. She suggested you might be with Petronius.'

'But if that is how you felt then –'

'Later, in Rome, I knew I had been totally mistaken in you.' His eyes were glittering with suppressed emotion. 'Where in the name of Hades has Imilico got to?'

'Why don't you throw me out yourself?' she demanded furiously.

'I command this legion and I will not be associated with such a disgraceful scene. I want nothing further to do with you. I am appalled that I set you on this disaster course. I would do anything to put right the wrong I have done you through my lack of personal restraint. You may name your price if you wish to be funded for any respectable business venture. Imilico or my personal secretary will deal with it.'

She stood back and hit his jaw. Hard. He flinched and his body reacted for a split second with the automatic retaliation for which he had been trained. His muscles flexed involuntarily to fight back as if he wanted to smash her into the ground and immobilise her. She knew that in his blind, subconscious mind, he saw her as the enemy and the thought tore through her like a sword in a death-blow.

He controlled himself in an instant, holding his hands by his sides in rigid command of himself.

'A special convoy of four centuries is moving north three nights from now. You may accompany it. The matter is top secret, so keep this information to yourself.'

She turned and walked to the door, slamming it behind her so that the sound echoed through the stone walls of the corridor.

'I wasn't able to find Nicomedes, after all,' said Imilico, unwinding himself from a whicker chair in the corridor and yawning. 'So I'll show you to your room myself. I trust you will find your new quarters comfortable tonight. I had no idea you had arrived last night.'

'I thought you were going to throw me out!' she said as her anger and fear turned to surprise.

'I am very glad to see you,' he said smilingly. 'There was never any question of throwing you out. If he had wanted that, he would have called for his aides, not me or Nicomedes. I thought that I should give you a little time to get through to him and he seemed happy with that. He can be stubborn when it comes to his own good.'

She stared at him, completely reassessing his relationship with Gaius. These were not the words of a lover. These were the words of a devoted slave who approved of her and did not wish to hinder the development of her relationship with his master.

'I have never seen him in such a state,' continued Imilico smoothly.

'He was in total control, not in a state at all!'

'As you know, he is usually very informal in his manner. He displays that sort of cold control only when there is a crisis of massive proportions. That is what makes him a great commander. I think you were right to come here in search of him.'

'You lied to me,' she said grudgingly as she followed him from the HQ building to the adjacent house.

'I certainly did not. I received a message to come south after I left the villa. The military communications system is a hundred times faster than a slow-moving transport wagon, you know.'

He walked her through the house, showing her the locations of the rooms.

'I will have food sent to your room, so you may get back your strength,' he said. 'You may have a battle on your hands, if I have read the signs correctly.'

Chapter Eighteen

Marcella spent the remainder of the day resting after her long journey. In the late evening, she heard the guests going to bed. Gaius called out to several, bidding them have a good night with such lightheartedness that she shook with fury in the darkness. When the moon was high, and the house was quiet, she hastily threw on her dress and crept to the room Imilico had told her Gaius used.

She could hear his regular breathing from the door. She slipped inside and, as her eyes adjusted to the dim light, she could see him asleep, his arms above his head. She had never seen such an ornate bed-head before – it was deeply carved with military scenes and seemed to symbolise the harsh, uncompromising life he led.

'So you think this is wrong, do you?' she said quietly. Her hands were shaking with her fury that he could so easily sleep when she was tormented with need for him. 'You think more of what people would say than of our mutual pleasures?'

Stealthily, she removed the tie from her dress and bound his right arm to the bed through a gap in the design. He stirred, so she quickly tied his left hand in place. Confident that he could not gain his freedom rapidly, she groped around the room, found a taper and kindled several lamps from one that dimly lit the corridor outside.

He remained inert as she stripped the sheets away and hungrily savoured the beauty of his body. She wanted him desperately. She stared at his muscular chest and let her eyes wander down to the slope of his flat hard stomach. It wasn't enough simply to look: she wanted to touch and caress. She straddled him and felt the softness of his penis on her silken labia. The feel of his skin on hers calmed her anger and she was filled with a growing excitement at the thought that, despite his reluctance, he would soon swell and she would force him to penetrate her. Her inner muscles were contracting and softening in anticipatory rhythm as she bent forward and kissed his lips, brushing against his chest.

'I will make you admit that you want me,' she said softly, pulling her dress off over her head. 'You will have to pleasure me because you will be unable to help yourself. Tonight there will be no way you can walk out and work off your frustrations on some other woman.'

His breathing did not falter, but she felt his penis begin to rise and harden under her. She felt him push his pelvis upwards and heard his breathing pattern change.

'So you are awake?'

'Since you first came in the room. I wanted to see exactly how ruthless you are, Marcella.'

'And in the process you proved how ruthless you are. You will take any pleasures a woman has to offer, won't you? So long as you don't need to feel responsible.'

'Not if those pleasures will cause problems for her or anyone else. And, since you are struggling under a misapprehension – I did not work out my frustrations on anyone when I left you in Rome. Or any other time.'

'I don't believe you. I shall make you admit how much we mean to one another.'

'Our union is definitely counter-indicated and certainly forbidden by all the moral codes of the Empire. I

229

do not want to continue the physical relationship we have enjoyed.'

His cool manner infuriated her.

'Liar!' she hissed as her anger welled up again. 'You rely on clever arguments but you behave as badly as any irresponsible drunk! I have seen hundreds of them in the tavern. They laugh about how they have led women on and then discarded them. It is a game with you men, isn't it?' She hit him hard on his chest, wanting to hurt him as much as he was hurting her.

He flinched. 'You have very forceful emotions,' he said evenly. 'You must learn to control them.'

'How dare you pretend to be so cool and in control,' she whispered furiously.

She hit him again and again, beating her disappointments into his hard pectoral muscles. But she wanted to be kissing him, taking him in her mouth, stroking him and being caressed and loved. She fell against him, exhausted and in tears.

'There really is no future for us,' he said sadly.

'Your body does not agree,' she replied indistinctly. She ran her tongue along the line of his jaw and kissed his neck, fluttering her lips against him, tasting the body she craved.

The heat from his body suffused her skin and she could feel that his penis was totally rigid. 'It is responding to the strength of my feelings for you. Besides,' she whispered, sitting up and straddling him. 'You have no choice. For once, you are not the one in ultimate control. I intend to show you how much you want our relationship to continue.'

She slid down his smooth, virile body, delighting in the familiar musky odour that always entranced her senses, and took the hard stem of his masculinity in her mouth. He groaned and tried to move his pelvis away from her, but the bonds held him and the weight of her body constricted his movements.

She sat on his calves and sucked him hard, savouring the power she suddenly had over him.

'You know very well that you are enjoying every moment,' she said. 'Your protests are merely the result of your loyalty to society's moral codes.'

'And my desire to protect you from the condemnation of other people,' he said, gasping the words out as he fought the strong physical instincts she knew were nearly overpowering him.

'I understand that. I, too, do not wish you to suffer because of our passion, but why should anyone know what we feel?'

'Life has a way of firing back. Like local tribesmen, it is unpredictable,' he replied with a groan of sensual enjoyment.

'What would your guests and colleagues say if they could see you now?' she murmured, gently teasing the tip of his penis with her teeth. She caressed the tip with mock-biting movements and simultaneously flicked the cushioned flesh with her tongue.

'And what would your friends say?' he replied indistinctly.

She could see the bonds biting into his wrists as he strained to free himself.

'My friends are all dead,' she said bitterly. 'I don't have to follow convention ever again. I have no status in society to lose. From now on I can do as I please.'

'Untie me.'

'Certainly not.'

'Let me touch you, Marcella.' His voice changed to a softer tone that was almost pleading. 'It is cruel allowing me to see your wonderful breasts so close. I want to take you in my mouth.'

She took her lips from his cock and ran her hands along his thighs.

'You are full of tricks,' she said as she moved up his body till her mouth was close to his. 'You are determined to get your own way no matter what arguments you have to use. I am not taken in.'

The skin of his shoulders felt marvellous and she

231

relaxed against him, savouring the deliciously sensual moment.

Totally without warning of any kind, he threw his legs wide and embraced her body with a hold of iron. She tried to lever herself up but his grip was too tight.

'Let me go, Gaius,' she said, panicking.

'Not a chance, Marcella. You wanted it this way, you have to play by the rules. Are you feeling a fool now that your moment of power has disappeared? You wanted to dominate me. Lots of women have tried, but none have succeeded. Untie me and I might consider letting you off lightly.'

She fought against his strength, but he laughed, his torso firm and hard against her chest. His legs were like a vice around her.

'Let me go! You are only concerned with winning and being in total control. You want me as much as I want you. You can't deny that.'

'This is not the time or the place. There will never be a time or place, Marcella, I have told you that.'

'I have made you admit your need.'

'You'll have to untie me, or neither of us will get what we want,' he said flatly.

She could feel his stiff manhood pressed hard against her stomach. She wanted it inside her. She needed his arms around her and his hands on her breasts. She wanted to hear his breath coming faster and to listen to the little grunts of pleasure he made when he neared his peak.

'And I really want you,' she whispered as she reached up to his wrist and pulled at the bonds. Her breasts brushed against his face and he nuzzled one nipple. She groaned with the pleasure.

'Untie the other hand.'

She fumbled at the belt and he transferred his free hand to her breast, kneading it with infinite tenderness. His legs still held her fast.

She couldn't get the knot free and impatiently, he pulled hard. She heard the wood splinter and he was free immediately. He grasped her wrists and rolled over, crushing her under his weight. With rough urgency, he pushed her legs apart so she could feel that he was hot and ready.

'No.' She bit his shoulder and fought wildly against him. 'You knew all along you were capable of freeing yourself! You manipulative bastard – you were content to let me feel I was in control.'

She could feel his rock hard penis pushing against her pubic mound. Her soft folds were open and moist in readiness. She longed for the pleasures his body held in store; wanted him inside her so badly she could weep with frustration.

'You mean "no" if you aren't the one in total control,' he said harshly. 'But you mean "yes" if we play the game by your rules. You want this as much as I do, but you, too, want it only under the right conditions. These are not the right conditions, Marcella. The situation will never be right for us. We came together in a frenzy of lust – that is the worst basis for a lasting passion.'

He pushed his prick against her, tantalisingly too high and used it to stroke her clitoris till she felt she was going to burst with desire. She began to flex her legs, pushing into the pleasure and kindling sparks of desire deep within her.

He put an arm around her shoulder and pulled her towards him in a rough embrace. He pushed his tongue inside her mouth in a primeval act of possession that left her without dignity or authority. She was unable to move or prevent him from doing anything he wished. His penis continued to stimulate her bud of passion and he held her legs still with his own, so she was unable to move except to tense and relax her muscles with the surges of passionate desire.

She groaned softly as she felt her nipples harden against his chest. The first strong waves of release begin to surge towards a climax. The tip of his penis felt warm and marvellously right against her clit and she gave herself up to her body's urges.

233

Suddenly, he pulled away from her and stood up. He walked over to a chair, sat down and watched her face.

'I have promised myself that I will never possess you again,' he said bleakly. 'I owe that to you, at least. Put a hand to yourself. We can enjoy each other without touching. As you so rightly observed, my body still finds you attractive, even if I do not wish it to be so.'

She saw his hand moving with assurance on his cock as his eyes roamed over the curves of her body.

'You are cruel – why should we not enjoy what we both want?'

'Because it is wrong,' he replied, slightly gruffly. 'But there can be no objections to helping each other if we do not touch. Imagine that it is my hand on your crotch, my fingers inside you.'

'You are confusing things. Compromise that is not acceptable to both sides is not equality,' she said, as angry tears welled up. But her body was treacherous once more. As if hypnotised, knowing that he was forcing her to act out her private lusts in front of him, she put a finger between her legs.

He sighed and she saw his pelvis shudder slightly in response.

'Round and round first. Then up and down, really work the juices out.'

'And you,' she said, watching his penis under his long tapering fingers. 'The feeling is mutual. I want to watch your pleasure.'

Her body began to pulsate into the familiar delightful sparks of bliss. She watched as his erection grew bigger and his hand moved faster. She could feel her breasts almost bursting and she moved so they were pouting upwards.

'You are near your zenith, aren't you?' she murmured as she spread her labia so he could see her womanhood clearly. She ran her fingers along their silky length. 'You want me to climax so you will be free to enjoy your own pleasures.'

'Marcella, push your fingers inside and rub your bud

of love faster, now. Faster! Push yourself into the sensations.'

His voice sounded hoarse and she could see that his hand was massaging his cock in time to her own movements. She felt her excitement rising with his own. The wave crest of their passions was so close that they would surely fall together.

She forced herself to react for the future, not for her immediate fulfilment. She knew that she had to be stronger than she had ever been. To fail now, would be to fail for ever. She took a deep breath and braced herself for the disappointment she was about to endure.

'No, Gaius. You feel responsibility for initiating me into the delights of bodily love, but your guilt is misplaced. I too, feel a responsibility towards you because of the strong passions we have kindled in each other. But our desires are nothing unless they are fuelled on an equal basis.'

She closed her legs abruptly and stood up. She pulled her dress on and saw with satisfaction that his erection was wilting.

'You see,' she said calmly. 'It is not good enough with simply your own hand, is it? You need me. On terms we both agree on from the start. We have achieved that before and we could again. You were right that there will never be a future for us together.'

She saw his expression of pain.

'But there could be a present. And that could be remembered and relived many times in the future.'

She left the room feeling both triumphant and frustrated.

Chapter Nineteen

*S*he walked back to her room, listening to the creaks and clicks of the wooden walls and floors. There were no plants in the courtyard, and no pool or fountain. A few painted busts of emperors, eerily illuminated by the thin moonlight, stood on white marble plinths. The sparse furnishings and the lack of human sounds made her shiver.

As she reached her room a sharp whistle startled her. She whirled around, terrified and shaking in the dark corridor. She could see nothing and there was no sound except the steady drip of water into a bowl. She realised that she had heard an expensive water-clock signalling the beginning of another night hour.

In her room, she lit several lamps and sat down to think and regain her sense of balance. The room was comfortably furnished with no wall decorations and reminded her of her bedroom in the tavern. The furniture was plain: the bed-head was simply a plank of wood, but the cushions and bed covers were of the highest quality and the mattress was thick. She detected Imilico's eastern taste in both the colours and the fabrics and noticed that there were few concessions to feminine needs.

She combed her hair for a long time, wishing she had

a mirror, but taking comfort in the repetitive movement. Eventually she felt calmer.

A pitcher of water and a bowl stood on a small table so she stripped off and washed, adding some perfumed oils that Imilico had given her. She was thinner, after the anxieties of the journey and felt hungry, but she did not have the confidence to summon a slave to bring her something to eat.

There was no sound in the house or from the barracks outside; she snuffed out the lamps and lay down to try to sleep. As she was drifting into uneasy slumber, the water-clock stridently whistled out another hour and she was instantly awake.

The night seemed endless, as she constantly changed position. She calculated that it must be the sixth or seventh night hour when the door opened and she heard his soft breath as he entered.

She was hot from the worry that he would not come and yet, now it had happened, it seemed inevitable. She turned towards him. The moonlight from the tiny window illuminated the upper part of his body and head. She pulled back the blanket and wordlessly he threw off his tunic and slipped next to her, feeling for her womanhood directly.

His tongue moved into her mouth as she opened herself for him and his hard body rocked against her softness in the still, dark North African night.

He felt so right inside her. His body was familiar in its weight and contours and they moved together with accustomed ease. He rolled sideways and held her tightly with a hand on her bottom. He ran a finger between the soft mounds, still keeping up the rocking movement. She put one leg over his body in passionate embrace and he pulled her towards him so he was deep inside her.

His breath came faster and the tips of her nipples rubbed against his heaving chest. As he kissed her gently, his lips felt dry and smooth on hers. She parted them and felt the softness of his breath.

His body ground against hers in a frenzy of confused emotions – anger, passion, distrust, suspicion and, overwhelmingly, need. His pubic bone collided with hers as if he intended to force her to take her pleasures. She put her arms around his neck to draw him close but he rolled over again so his bulk pinioned her to the bed.

Pushing her hips towards him, she gave little involuntary cries as he repeatedly pushed into her, his body beating at hers as though he were trying to escape from some cataclysmic danger.

Marcella met his force as his equal, with an inner strength of her own. She braced her pelvis and flexed her thighs against his. She pulled his head to hers and kissed him deeply, forcing his mouth open and her tongue inside. She drank the nectar of his body and felt him shiver, out of control, unable to stop himself from hurtling headlong into the Olympian heights of ecstasy.

Finally, magnificently, he shuddered against her in orgasmic spasms of release. Gradually, with milder tremors, his body became motionless. They lay together as the sweat of their passion mingled and their bodies relaxed.

Smoothly, silently, he withdrew from her and lay by her side. Marcella snuggled under his arm and placed one leg over his thighs, her breasts against his chest.

Her body was still ready, still tight with desire and the need for fulfilment. She had not achieved even a small release, so great had been her need to give him pleasure. She lay beside him savouring only his presence. She knew that his thoughts were in turmoil and his emotions were torn as he tried to make sense of their mutual attraction that defied all sense, logic and conventions.

She pushed her hot and damp crotch against his thigh, so, when at last he slept, she rubbed herself against him until a small peak of relief enabled her to relax and sleep too.

When she awoke, he was gone. The bed had been straightened around her sleeping body and there was sunshine outside and the sounds of the morning chores. From the barracks behind the house, she could hear parade-ground style orders and the sound of horses' hooves from the cavalry quarters.

She savoured the bouquet of his body on the cushion. She pulled the sheet to her face and breathed deeply into the musk and sweat of the pleasures she had given him, until a servant broke into her dreams by bringing her water and some bread and fruit.

Later that morning, Imilico explained, 'Most of the guests are very highly regarded by the Emperor. I am telling you this because you may be surprised to hear some of the topics of conversation they find commonplace.'

'I will have nothing to say at all in the presence of such illustrious people,' she said apprehensively. 'I can never feel comfortable with people in the top ranks of power.'

'They will accept you easily. I have told them the truth – that you are a friend of my master's cousin Felicius. You have pretty manners and your lack of fortune is of no consequence to them – they simply do not think about such matters. They have gone out on a trip today, but this evening at dinner, you will meet most of them and some of the military tribunes who are permanently stationed here.'

They continued the discussions they had started about oils and perfumes. She was fascinated by the way certain oils could produce different emotional states – some could calm, others stimulate. An idea was forming in her mind and she could see that Imilico was also thinking along the same lines.

Over a light midday meal of bread and cheese, the conversation moved to Gaius.

'He confuses me,' she said. 'He has had no explanation for my behaviour in Rome, and for weeks he believed me to be below contempt.'

Imilico smiled.

'We engaged in a mild power-struggle in his office,

and later, I was definitely the winner. He had every reason to feel humiliated and angry. Yet his instinct told him to believe and trust me, despite everything.'

'There is no doubt,' he said, 'that the two of you have found a rare and precious thing. We can only wait for the gods to show us how they want the future to be.'

As the sun set, Marcella, the military aides and the civilian guests conversed in the sparsely furnished dining room waiting for Gaius to return from HQ. The others all knew one another well and, as Imilico had predicted, they accepted her presence without comment and included her in their conversations. The topics were light-hearted and general, so she relaxed and began to enjoy herself. She eventually felt bold enough to make two small jokes which were greeted with appreciation.

Gaius looked rested when he arrived. He met her eyes evenly but did not smile as he nodded to her and his friends and colleagues.

'There is so much work with the stylus, the wax tablet and the papyrus roll after a campaign! I sometimes think that Rome only asks for these reports in order to keep the clerks busy.'

He lowered himself gracefully to a couch and a servant offered him a bowl of grilled damson appetisers.

'Marcella has been telling us how you got out of Pompeii,' remarked one of the tribunes. 'We had no idea you had been in the disaster.'

'Everyone thought you were in Rome at the time,' said a quietly-spoken man called Lucius.

'You are leading such an exciting life, Gaius. Volcanoes one moment and uprising tribesmen the next! And you have kept us all in the dark – I think you will have to be punished for that! Very severely.' A woman wearing very costly jewellery sparkled at Gaius with glittering eyes. Her tone was not as light-hearted as Marcella would have expected in the situation. She was conscious of wanting to pull her elaborately-dressed hair out and scratch her face to remove the unsettling, faintly threatening expression. From the way the lady was touching Lucius intimately on his arm, and had been leaning close to him on the couch all the evening, Marcella assumed that she was married to him and was trying to make him jealous. His expression of resigned toleration would at any other time have seemed amusing, she thought acidly.

'It was dramatic, Fulvia,' replied Gaius evenly, looking at Marcella for a long moment before transfering his gaze to the smiling woman. 'The sort of thing you don't forget all your life.'

'Fortuna was with you! You were lucky, but I still think you should be punished for not telling us about your adventures,' she persisted.

'Perhaps Fortuna was there – and a lot of other deities besides,' he replied lightly.

The evening was spent in idle and charming chit-chat as the company relaxed after the tense weeks of worry. They were all prepared to be amusing and amused as they enjoyed the luxury foods and drinks that the convoy had delivered. The only barbs were delivered by Fulvia, but even she mellowed as the fine wine flushed her face and neck and she was paid a number of compliments which Marcella thought were contrived and insincere.

Marcella retired to her room before the others and met up with Imilico on the way.

'Are all the guests friends of the Emperor?' she asked. 'Some seem to be making blatant overtures to Gaius, regardless of their domestic circumstances.'

'You mean the lady, Fulvia.' He seemed oddly reserved as he added lightly, 'She is a scandal – he knows all about her. And her husband.'

'He is too tolerant, you mean?'

'That isn't the word I would chose, but it will do,' he said non-committally as they reached her bedroom door and he bid her enjoy a peaceful rest.

Gaius did not come to her that night and she fell asleep well past the eighth hour, her tears dampening the pillow. She imagined him secretly creeping into Fulvia's room and frenziedly rutting with her while Lucius played cards or dice with the other men. She imagined the woman's groans of pleasure and feared that Gaius might find her vulgar, predatory ways charming and sophisticated. She hated the woman and hated him for not coming to her, letting her lie alone with her physical needs near boiling-point.

Next morning, she went into the dining room early, knowing that she could not bear to eat anything. She felt sick and frightened at the force of her own feelings and the need for him and only him.

He was there alone and rose from his couch when she entered. Silently he walked over to her and held her by the shoulders, looking into her eyes. He pushed her gently towards a low stool and, his eyes very serious, he stood her on it and pulled her skirt up, impatiently.

He wore a stern, business-like expression as he put his hand between her legs and gently slid his fingers downwards, inside her. The unexpectedness of his advance made her instantly ready for him and she saw a mixture of old pain and surprised pleasure on his face.

'Gaius – the other guests may come in any moment,' she said wretchedly. 'Why didn't you come to me last night?'

For reply he adjusted his loincloth and slid his penis inside her, holding her bottom so she was steady on the stool.

She held his shoulders tightly, already half-crazed with desire and need. He pushed into her hard, his breath against her neck, his mouth licking and nuzzling her skin. She revelled in the strength and potency inside her.

He put one hand on her breast and teased the nipple through the dress material and she began an incredible journey to the heights in a series of deep, pulsating spurts. Each one was higher and more intense than the one before as he moved into her and then partly withdrew only to enter again. Each time he withdrew she feared it would be the last and she would lose him again.

There was a clatter in the corridor outside and the sound of light, feminine laughter. She tightened her inner muscles convulsively, afraid of the embarrassment if they were interrupted by one of the civilised and educated guests. She was afraid too, of being left physically frustrated. He pulled her closer, increasing his speed and the urgency of his movements, his head pressed to her neck.

'Marcella. Darling.'

The soft, loving words made her erupt into a thousand sparks of light and joy as he shuddered against her. The climax was sudden and bursting with fire and it shook her body with its force.

A voice outside the door called, 'Lucius – come along.'

Lucius shouted back, 'You go on in Fulvia, I'll be along in a few moments.'

A faint smile on his face, Gaius withdrew from her body and set Marcella on the floor. He straightened their clothes and casually picked up a bowl of fruits from the table as the door opened. He held it towards her as though he had been inviting her to choose.

'Ah, Gaius! Greetings to you. This promises to be a good day indeed. Your slave, Imilico, has organised another wagon-ride for us,' cried Fulvia.

Marcella did not like the way the woman said the word 'slave', but she wasn't sure why.

Gaius smiled easily. 'It does indeed promise to be a good day, on the showing so far,' he agreed, his eyes flicking to Marcella. She saw a glint of amused pleasure that reminded her of the time she had met him in the tavern.

'I am sure we will all be able to enjoy ourselves to the full!' Fulvia's tone was heavy with innuendo.

The gleam of amusement was still in his eyes as he handed the woman a bowl of breads.

'I certainly intend to,' he replied without looking at Marcella. 'I haven't had a day off for weeks and a vital message came through last night so I had to spend the entire night working.'

Marcella sighed with relief and understanding.

'Today I shall take my pleasures like any other person. The legionaries are permitted to visit the township so I can allow myself a few hours off duty.'

Marcella was basking in the warmth of his embrace and the veiled promise in his polite words when the door to the dining room opened.

'Where is my wife? Ah, there you are Fulvia!'

A man walked into the room and Marcella felt as if the entrance to the Underworld had appeared and that Cerberus was barking and snapping at her heels with all three of his heads.

Fulvia's husband was not Lucius, he was Caballius Zoticus.

'We are fated to meet.'

His words were infinitely threatening and terrifying. He was speaking very quietly, under cover of the other guests chattering about the plans for the day. The raw masculinity that had first attracted her in the party at Pompeii was now totally abhorrent to her. Her flesh crept with fear and loathing.

'From now on, you will do whatever I want,' he continued. 'Or I shall denounce you for a whore. Here, unlike in Rome, it is clear that not only are you well-known, but you are accepted. Now, you have a great deal to lose.'

She glanced around her and imagined the total indignity and shame that she would feel if Caballius carried out his threat.

Inclining his head towards Gaius, he said, 'You should have told me that he is your lover.'

'He is not.' Her automatic response sounded strangely high-pitched as she tried to fight her fear and revulsion.

'Yes he is. Petro told me on my way out of Pompeii. I am not here by accident – I knew you'd turn up soon enough to be near your boyfriend. I am glad he tipped me off, I can tell you, because the way you are studiously ignoring each other, I would never have guessed. Nobody else has. And Fulvia would hate to have missed out on a tit-bit like that. My wife takes her pleasures in ways that even I find bizarre.'

'You are contemptible,' she whispered, horror-struck.

'You, and a lot of other people, may think I have warped appetites,' he continued smoothly, 'but Fulvia shocks even me sometimes. She the only woman I know who can get an orgasm just watching people being humiliated or having to perform undignified tasks. I should like to let her loose on you – it would be fun to watch.'

'You evil bastard.' She was shaking as she tried to hide her emotions from the rest of the party. 'You are warped. I will see you in Hades before I cooperate with you.'

'Then you will find that Hades is a place on earth,' he said, smilingly.

Chapter Twenty

*H*alf an hour later, Fulvia was sparkling with what Marcella recognised as hedonistic and lascivious anticipation. They were standing on the veranda of the legate's house as the servants placed wooden boxes filled with food and drink in the vehicles, ready for the outing.

The air was still very cool but the woman was wearing a light dress that showed her ample curves. Her silk scarf kept falling from her shoulders and drawing attention to her full breasts.

'They have provided only one military wagon and a decrepit cart pulled by a mule that looks so slow we will be lucky to go more than two thousand paces before dusk,' she said, her light-hearted tone utterly failing to hide her fury. 'How shall we all fit in? Where is the carriage I used yesterday?'

'Gaius is the commander so he must travel in the cart – he can hardly squeeze into the wagon with all of us! We are far too much of a rabble. I haven't had such an adventure for ages – I was so disappointed not to be able to go on yesterday's trip,' laughed one of the wives.

Imilico had told Marcella that she was fabulously rich and connected by birth to the imperial house. She was attended by a young, very blonde slave girl who carried her small, fixed, parasol and she herself was holding a huge peacock-feather fan. Marcella could not even guess at the price. Her flippant good humour sounded out of place to Marcella's shaken spirits, and was a marked contrast to the strange undertone of menace in Fulvia's whole demeanour.

'I, too, enjoy these little hardships,' replied Fulvia unconvincingly. 'It is all part of the fun of travelling away from Rome!'

She climbed ponderously on to the cart and received a look of such intense viciousness from Caballius that Marcella shivered.

Looking magnificent, with his military cloak flung casually over one shoulder, Gaius walked across from the HQ, deep in conversation with Nicomedes. He surveyed the scene dispassionately.

'It was agreed that you should ride in the cart,' said Fulvia firmly. 'I have saved your place for you. We are all waiting!'

Gaius nodded gravely up at her and Nicomedes gave some order to a legionary that she did not hear.

Marcella stood back in shock as she saw that the only space left in the wagon was next to Caballius Zoticus. She glanced towards Gaius and intercepted a glance of pure venom from Fulvia. She frowned with perplexity until, a few moments later, an elegant little open carriage pulled by two very boisterous ponies, drew up in front of her. It was a light vehicle, suited to very rapid travel and the driver was not a cavalryman, but Brutus, the handsome leader of the supply convoy she had travelled with. He leapt down with ostentatious panache, his cloak flapping, and helped her into the carriage. His blue eyes were twinkling with a totally different expression from the austere, disapproving looks he had given her on the road to Theveste. He looked charming, carefree and highly attractive and she hated every handsome, muscular inch of him as he helped her into the carriage. Did Gaius put her into the same category as the Lady Julia for whom he provided delectable male solace so that he could take his own pleasure elsewhere?

As Brutus checked the harness at the animals' heads, Caballius Zoticus got down from the crowded wagon.

'I can manage a couple of unruly ponies,' he said. 'I shall take pride in breaking them to my will.'

He stood close to the carriage and said quietly to Marcella, 'Soon, I shall have you in the total privacy and isolation of the sand-dunes. I can't wait to punish you for your behaviour, knowing that you find my slightest touch loathsome. You are so responsive, you are really enjoyable. Whores pretend if you pay them enough, but I even suspect that some of them actually enjoy being put into undignified positions, so it isn't the same. With you, I will hardly need to exert myself at all, to gain the ultimate pleasures. I will teach you a lesson you will never forget. The first of many.'

Had Gaius planned that she should be stranded in the desert, not with Brutus, but with this twisted inadequate? Immobile from shock at the thought, Marcella watched the scene around her as though it were a theatrical show.

Nicomedes walked away and Gaius was smiling up at Fulvia who fiddled coquettishly with her hair. The lady with the peacock-feather fan sent her blonde slave back to the house on some errand.

Marcella tried to think clearly, but the heavy musk of the monster standing beside the little carriage was paralysing her both mentally and physically.

'No lies you can tell will mean anything to them – I am a nobody!'

'That is true,' he replied appraisingly. 'But Gaius Salvius Antoninus is somebody of considerable significance. It will damage him if the woman he takes to his bed and introduces to his social equals, is accused of being a common whore. This is a close-knit society in which family background is paramount. You don't have even the lowliest of friends or family to vouch for your character. That in itself will make you suspect. Only criminals have blank pasts.'

The young slave girl returned to the wagon and

dropped the parasol as she tried to climb back into the high wagon, holding a long scarf. A slight movement drew Marcella's attention to Fulvia. The woman was clearly anticipating a delicious moment when the girl was disciplined. Her hips were moving in involuntary spasms and Marcella could guess what inner rhythms she was enjoying. She felt sick.

The lady noticed the accident and laughed. When the slave had picked up the sun-shade, she held out her hand and pulled her up beside her. She arranged the scarf over the girl's head to protect her from the sun. The look of sexual disappointment on Fulvia's face was frightening.

The heavy wagon, pulled by sturdy oxen and laden with its happy, patrician passengers, started a series of complicated manoeuvres to face the gateway. Nothing seemed real to Marcella any more. She felt totally and utterly alone.

'What makes you think I am any different from your lover?' Caballius continued, gripping her arm tightly.

'He will take any pleasures he wants from a woman if it suits him. He only needs to smile at them and the bitches feel they are special. But if a woman demands anything more, he will ruthlessly discard her. As you are discovering at this very moment. Commitment is not a word he recognises in his personal life.'

He paused for a moment and looked thoughtful. 'Even my wife is not immune, as you see – though she regards him as a challenge for her contrived little games of dominance and submission. She will have a good time with him today and that will make my life easier, believe me.'

He looked up at her with a repulsive expression of triumph and anticipation and she realised that the most she could do was to buy time by pretending to faint or finding some weak excuse to stay behind.

Caballius took up the reins and prepared to climb into the carriage next to her.

Gaius shouted across, 'Caballius – you drive your

wife. The ponies aren't suited to long trips in the heat of the day so you won't be able to keep up with the rest of the party. I will drive Marcella around the desert for an hour or two – she has never seen the extent of the dunes and you have.'

Caballius looked ready to erupt as he turned and strode to the cart.

Marcella shivered apprehensively in the gentle heat, knowing that his frustration and anger were growing to dangerous proportions.

'You have said only two direct words to me since I left your bedroom,' she said accusingly to Gaius as they passed through the imposing east gate.

Without replying, he glanced at her dispassionately and continued driving, allowing the ponies to work off their excess energy. His physical presence was soothing to her shattered nerves and she began to relax. She was happy simply to be sitting next to him in the heat, knowing that Caballius and Fulvia were well away from them in the opposite direction, on the main road that eventually led to Thamugadi and Lambaesis.

They drove for a long time, the terrain becoming increasingly barren and sandy. The air was pleasantly warm and sweet and there was no sound except for the humming of the wind as it gently moved the sands. No signs of habitation could be seen when, at last, he turned the ponies off the track, gave them nose-bags and secured the reins.

'The desert starts here, but it goes on into infinity,' he said conversationally. 'This will give you an idea of what the borderlands look like. No Roman has ever found the extent of the sands, and they remain as awe-inspiring as the volcano. The heat in the middle of the day is incredible, you have to experience it to understand. This is cool, compared.'

'I borrowed the harlot's clothes because I wanted to pay Caballius back for treating me so shabbily. And I did,' she began, refusing to be fobbed-off with social chat. 'Oh, what is the use – it was all too long ago to be of relevance. And much worse things have happened since then.'

He pulled her into the soft sand. One of the ponies looked around and whinnied softly.

'I don't need to know, Marcella. You do not have to defend your actions to me.'

He looked down, deep in thought and stroked her knee. His touch was enchantment and she felt her mind flying away into a place of Olympian delights.

'I want the truth about us,' he said at last.

He put a hand to her breasts, gently pulling the material so that they stood proud, as he had done the day they first met. It seemed like a thousand years ago.

She lay still against the sand, her body moulding itself to the soft, yielding mineral as he almost absently, stroked her breasts.

'I walked into that tavern in a filthy temper because I had lost my way,' he said, 'and there you were, a steaming little bundle of suppressed passion, desperately wanting to break out of your confines!'

She blushed.

'My father was a man of the old Republican type. Very repressed and unable to love,' he said reflectively, looking out over the far-distant sands. 'When I saw what harm it had done my mother over the years – what cruelty resulted – I swore that I would never leave a woman lost in a web of mediocrity against her will.'

'I have often wondered how you came to be in Pompeii,' she said, embarrassed by the understated force of his emotions and the revelations that she had guessed long ago.

'The Emperor had insisted that I meet up with a couple of my colleagues from Britannia to compare notes on frontier policy,' he said, matching her light tone. 'Pompeii was convenient for us all but I was keyed up because I knew that trouble was brewing in Africa and I wanted to return.'

251

'Is Julia's husband one of the British legates?' she asked and instantly stiffened with embarrassment.

'How do you know about Julia?' He laughed and kissed her gently. 'She is a lovely socialite who is married to an Imperial administrator. Her husband is impotent after an accident, but they are fond of one another so they do not divorce. He tolerates a few discreet liaisons. Sometimes she and I enjoy more than conversation, but it is a casual relationship without commitment on either side. She would hate to be confined to only one lover.'

He bent to kiss her nipples lightly and her intense desire was immediately fuelled. She shifted her position so her hips were closer to him, wanting his touch on her intimate areas, to feel his breath against her neck and on her breast, his tongue on her lips.

She put her hand on his thigh and savoured the smooth skin against her palm. She slid it higher and felt the tangle of pubic hair under his loincloth. He took one hardening nipple in his mouth and teased it. She slid her hand further under his clothing and felt his strong, erect penis. It felt smooth and firm against her fingers. She stroked it gently and his breath came faster.

She wanted him inside her, to ease his pain and her anguish by a tender fusion of their bodies. His hand went to her crotch, pushing gently inside, feeling her desire. He slid his hand to her clitoris and gently circled it so she could feel the oils of her need. He pushed his finger inside again and then out to her bud of pleasure. Time and time again he fired her senses.

He pushed one finger inside while the other hand vibrated her and she writhed with the deep pleasures, feeling the warm sun on her exposed and vulnerable breasts.

He moved down her body, pushing her dress away impatiently, and took her labia in his mouth with a directness of purpose that left her gasping. She felt stranded in the sand, helpless under the touch of his hands. She could feel his tongue inside her. He abruptly parted her legs wide and plunged his fingers inside her

252

as his tongue kept up its insistent movements on her clitoris.

She lay still, savouring the moment, and then plunged her hands into his silken hair.

'Concentrate darling, concentrate,' he murmured. 'I want to taste you when you climax under my lips.'

His voice brought a surge of intense joy to her. She flexed herself fiercely towards him and felt the increased pressure as he met her passion with his mouth. He slid his lips from her and circled her clitoris with his thumbs.

She pushed her hips towards him in an agony of need.

He looked at her very seriously.

'You need me here, don't you? Really need me,' he asked.

She nodded, biting her lip and stroking his shoulders. He bent to kiss her stomach and ran his tongue across the tender lines where her legs met her body. Then he kissed the inside of her thighs, with a soft warmth. He held her legs wide apart with careful hands and she dug her hands into his tousled hair.

He tilted her pelvis so she was exhibited to him squarely. As he ran his tongue down the length of her vulva, she cried out.

'This will take some time,' he said softly. 'Fortunately that is exactly what we have. We need a cushion – we'll have to improvise!'

He scooped handfuls of sand under her, elevating her pelvis and she looked at him in wonderment, feeling totally at ease with the fact that she was completely vulnerable to his caresses. In the desert wastes, he was her sole pleasure and delight.

He stroked each side of her inner thighs, brushing her bottom with his fingers. Then he brought his thumbs up to the satiny skin, stroking with exquisite delicacy.

'I need to taste you and savour your elixir. I can't get enough of you,' he muttered and bent his mouth once more to the nub of her pleasure. His hands were sandy and the roughness on her thighs contrasted keenly with the softness of his mouth.

He gently, oh so gently, sucked and then, just before the sharpness began to bite, stopped and licked her. Then immediately, he sucked tenderly again till she moaned.

His tongue moved down and entered her body, flicking and moving freely around her private folds.

She climaxed with a feverish intensity, but it was not enough. She sat up, throwing herself at his body so her breasts rubbed against his rough, military tunic.

As the uncontrollable ripples of spent pleasure reverberated through her body, he silently lay her down again and entered her with a hard, straight movement of pure passion.

Her body, still recovering from the last onslaught of his passion, leapt into a new orgasmic rhythm. They worked at each other's pleasures, their bodies in unison, straining towards the bliss to come. She climaxed again, almost immediately, and he laughed with pure joy.

It seemed hours later that he was still lying next to her, his strong body hot against hers, his penis still deep within her, his needs not yet met.

'I want you near me always, Marcella,' he said in a strangely matter-of-fact manner. 'I have wrestled with myself so often. I want to set you up in a nice little villa somewhere so I can visit you whenever I want. Somewhere in Africa or Southern Italy, so even when I give up my army post I can easily reach you.'

'I don't want that sort of life,' she said, feeling desperately hurt. 'And I don't want your money.'

'I know both those things. That is why I haven't suggested it. I cannot help my instincts Marcella, but I also don't have to act on them. My deeper feelings scream at me to use everything in my power – money, influence, my body, any argument I can think of, regardless of how unsound it may be – to make you stay in my life.'

She kissed him gently. 'Perhaps now you know how I felt when I had to follow you. I was unable to see logically. I put aside all thought that you might not be interested and had your own life to lead.'

'Passion leads to some strong urges. I can't see a way to achieve it, but I want you near me and involved in my life. I would give anything for that.'

The words, coming so unexpectedly from him, brought on a huge surge of passion inside her.

'I know that I can never be a major part of the life you are destined to lead,' she said. 'You will always have interests and pursuits that I cannot share. The people you know would stifle me with their conventionality. But I want to know you for ever.'

She needed to know that the little part of him she shared was not imaginary. Surely, she prayed desperately to the gods, that was not too much to ask.

'My darling, I do not think that is in question,' he murmured softly. 'You may never want a public role in my life – but you will always be essential to me. I do not know if this extraordinary passion we have for each other will last, but I want to be more than a friend, more even than a lover. Through our passions I feel I am a part of you. That fact can never be destroyed.'

Her inner muscles tightened around him and then relaxed, only to constrict again immediately. She pushed towards him as the spasms continued to increase.

'Gaius,' she whispered. 'My own, true lover.'   They rocked their bodies together with tremendous force in the soft sand, the wind's threnody whispering songs of love. They came together with an unrestrained strength – he rode her as though they were in a race, his hands around her shoulders in a close embrace. She bucked and tossed as though galloping to the end of the racecourse, driven by an urgent, primeval urge. They wallowed in their need and cried to the gods to help them achieve their loving goals.

Their hips pounded and ground their pleasures into the soft powder under the hot sun. She dug her hands into the dunes and pounded his back with her arms, pulled her legs tight around him so he thrust deep inside her, pushing higher and higher into the very depths of her being. She straightened her legs and pushed her thighs against his, feeling the power of his weight and potency meet her own strength and determination.

When it came, the end was so intense that later, she felt that she must have lost consciousness. Lights sparked in a darkness that seemed eternal, her body lifted out of itself, moved like a ship over the sands and fell back as though buffetted by winds. She screamed his name into the dunes and he kissed her deeply, his mouth firm and expressive on hers. He ground out his last spasm of need into her pelvis and she felt his tongue on her lips as he drank in the taste of her pleasures before they lay back, splayed out and defenceless under the sun.

Chapter Twenty-One

*T*hey returned to the fortress long before the rest of the party and bathed separately so they did not cause comment. Scented and relaxed, they lay together in his sparse, military-style bedroom.

'I wonder what happened to Lydia and my aunt and uncle,' she said.

'I should have told you before,' he said sleepily. 'I saw them briefly on-board ship when I finally got out of that hell-hole with the old lady. They have gone to Apulia, if you want to trace them.'

He pulled her on top of him and pressed her voluptuous breasts together, taking both nipples in his mouth.

'Now let us think about us.'

Her body began to respond to him once more and they gently sated themselves in the new peace of their relationship, taking quiet pleasure as friends as well as lovers.

Later that day, when the other guests were resting, Marcella accepted a small goblet of watered Falernian from Imilico in the dining room. Gaius looked relaxed and happy she thought, watching him surreptitiously.

'Marcella and I have had an idea,' said Imilico, resolutely, 'She is unsure whether you will approve, but I know you will. Between us, she and I have enough

257

money to buy my freedom and start up in a small business.'

Gaius' eyes were immediately wary at the sudden change of tempo and Marcella caught her breath anxiously.

'We have discussed the question of your freedom on several occasions,' he said evenly. His eyes took on a remote expression as though he were making complex calculations. 'I thought the plan was to wait until next year when your replacement will be fully trained. What is the hurry? Am I such a harsh master that you need to get free even if it means accepting money from a woman? A woman who will then be destitute, I may add.'

'Master, that is not at all the case. I have no wish to be free earlier than planned, on my own account. My replacement is highly competent and I would not give up all my duties at once. Besides, Marcella will not be destitute -- she has a nice little nest-egg, though it will not last very long unless it is invested wisely.'

'A nest-egg?' demanded Gaius. 'She was penniless in Rome.'

'I wasn't,' she said flatly. 'I have quite a large quantity of gold.'

He frowned.

'That would account for your heavy bag,' he said slowly. 'You must have found it in the villa because that painter had no difficulty carrying it to the cart and it was a dead-weight when I carried it along the road for you.'

She smiled. 'It was in the villa garden. I fought hard with myself, wondering if I should take it. The pieces were scattered over the garden as if they had been dropped in haste. I saw them when the carter left. In the end I decided that Fortuna wanted me to have them.'

'They would have been totally covered by now. I heard that several towns and most of the villas have been submerged under molten rock and ash. Only the tops of the some of the tallest buildings can be seen. Many thousands of people were killed.'

She shuddered.

'Marcella needs to set herself up with an income as soon as possible,' continued Imilico. 'She will be more successful if she has a free man to conduct the front end of the business for her. And one who will pose no threat to her well-being.'

Gaius looked at Marcella, his eyes grave.

'What is the business?' he asked.

'I understand you both met a well-known charioteer, Virius "Invictus" on the road from Pompeii,' went on Imilico. 'Virius has contacts in Syria and we hope that he will supply us with glass jars and bottles. I will mix oils and perfumes to fill them. Marcella will market them to women in the towns and rich villas, with the blessing of the deities and initially using the contacts she made as she travelled with me.'

Gaius gave a short laugh, his eyes glinting, as he walked to the door.

'I have to look into HQ for a couple of hours,' he said. 'Imilico, tell Claudius how much you will need, realistically, and get him to arrange the details in the usual manner. Marcella will not take any money from me, but she can hardly deny you your traditional rights!'

He paused at the door. 'This will mean, Marcella, that we will be legally and financially bound together for years to come, forced to meet at regular intervals, though free to lead our own lives.'

'For as long as Imilico stays in your household,' she replied carefully. She knew that Gaius could get out of the deal by simple means.

He shot her a look of pure, affectionate amusement as he left the room.

'Everything is going well,' said Imilico smilingly as he hugged her.

'Who is Claudius?' she asked. 'He evidently has a great deal of power if Gaius leaves such decisions up to him.'

'He does. As Gaius Salvius Antoninus' personal secretary, he will never better his situation in life. And my

259

master will never better him, so he will not willingly let him go,' he replied with a smile. 'Claudius is also the reason I shall remain in this household.'

In the evening, the guests and officers reclined in the dining room gorging themselves on the fine foods and vintage wines and discussing the day trip. Caballius and Fulvia seemed reserved but good humoured. Marcella hoped that they had taken out their frustrations on each other during the afternoon. Three legionaries provided a quiet, highly accomplished, musical background and the conversation centred on the finer things in life. Marcella was enchanted by the way the cultured guests were as familiar with philosophy, art, music and literature, as the men in the tavern had been with dice.

Towards the end of the meal the party became more informal, as a juggler made them all laugh with rude jokes and tricks. Caballius wandered over and sat on the floor by her couch. His glance flickered to Gaius.

'You will be interested to know,' he said in a low voice, 'that I bought back that portrait of your intimate charms. I had to sell it as a short-term measure, but I always knew it had true potential. I intend to auction it at dinner tonight. Unless you cooperate, of course.'

She looked at him, appalled. 'You wouldn't do that,' she said bleakly. 'If you make out that I am a whore, then it proves that you must associate with whores. Your wife would find that humiliating.'

He laughed. 'It was Fulvia's idea to buy it back and come to the fortress to wait for you. She is very quick to see opportunities. One thing I have in common with my dear wife is that I've been waiting for years to pull Gaius Salvius Antoninus down.'

'You bastard,' she said in a low voice. 'I will never cooperate with you.'

'You will have to,' he simply. 'You are in a desert fortress, at night, with no means of transport out. Even if you managed to seduce some legionary into letting you creep out, you wouldn't last an hour before the locals picked you up and had some sport.'

'Go to Hades. You have no sense of common decency at all,' she whispered venomously, but she was shaking with fear and her mind felt blank of ideas or initiative.

'And there is no way that you can shield yourself or your lover from this humiliation – unless you do what I want. And what Fulvia wants, of course. You brought this on yourself, you know. She was livid that he snubbed her in public by driving out with you. She was determined to take it out on me, so I had to divert her attention. She was prepared to let me off – so long as she gets some fun with you! She fancies a threesome – the sort of thing you saw in Pompeii. Except that unlike the male slave on that occasion, you would be unwilling. And I would also be participating.'

Marcella shuddered in total revulsion. 'To prostitute myself to your filthy antics is not only unthinkable to me, but Gaius himself would never forgive me.'

'So, either way, I win. The timing is perfect,' Caballius whispered. 'Fulvia and I will have the pleasure of seeing the two of you humiliated in public once and for all, or just you – many, many times, in private. I can't decide what I would prefer.'

She could see Fulvia watching as Caballius wandered back to his own place and the juggler concluded his act.

Caballius immediately announced, 'I have a treat for you all. I can offer a piece of art for sale.'

Marcella prayed to Minerva and Juno, in their capacities as patronesses of women, to help her, but she had no faith in her supplications.

'Art?' Gaius sounded casually interested.

'A very special painting.'

Caballius gestured for the board to be brought forward. The auctioneer was Brutus, looking particularly well-groomed and attractive, his blue eyes sparkling.

'I have offered the painting to Marcella, who is very much an art connoisseur, but she doesn't want to pay the asking price. Unless she changes her mind, I am able to offer the picture now. What is it to be Marcella? This is your last chance before it is unveiled.'

From the corner of her eyes she could see that Fulvia was enjoying this moment as much as her husband. Her hips were moving slightly as they had done when she was watching the blonde slave. She pushed them against the long bolster that divided her part of the couch from the man next to her and fumbled at her breasts under cover of wiping her mouth with her hand towel.

'I think Marcella should pay up,' she said in an unnaturally loud voice.

Marcella could see Gaius' gaze moving from her to Fulvia, his expression very thoughtful. For the very last time, she looked into his eyes and saw their mutual passion and respect untainted by the horrific revelations that were about to begin.

He had saved her life and protected her from harm. He had introduced her to his eminent guests and agreed to release Imilico early. In return she was about to bring a degrading and embarrassing scene upon him.

With tears in her heart, she remembered the tumultuous emotional times they had shared: his fierce anger, borne of desire for her well-being, and his tenderness. He had many times whispered loving words as she reached the zenith of her pleasures. He had spanked her soundly, and cut her short with cold contempt. He had wanted her to stay near him for ever and yet, when she first arrived in the fortress, he had coolly told her to leave with the special, secret convoy that was departing in three days.

The convoy.

She shook slightly at the realisation that the three days were up – the convoy would be leaving that night.

There was a way out for them both: she could take the painting and hide in one of the military wagons without anybody knowing. And she would never have to pay Caballius. All she needed was time.

'Well, hurry up and decide,' prompted Fulvia.

'I'll buy the painting,' she said as lightly as she could. 'Why not? It is extortionate, but I will pay your price.'

Caballius laughed. 'I knew you wouldn't be able to resist.'

Fulvia looked at Marcella with an unpleasant look of triumph and relaxed against the bolster, breathing heavily. Marcella wanted to retch.

'That was bad business policy, Caballius,' said Gaius, throwing a few grapes into his mouth. 'One of us might be prepared to pay more!'

Marcella stared at him, totally appalled.

'The deal has been concluded. I have bought it,' she said sharply.

'If you insist,' he said with a smile. 'But I would still like to see your taste in art. I shall be interested to see what you consider worth buying. It isn't often that we have any cultural diversions in this wasteland. In any case, to abide by the rules, I ought to know about any deals that are made on army premises.'

'No, my darling, Gaius.' She hardly knew what she was saying. 'It is not what it seems. You don't understand.'

She saw the guests and military aides looking at her, clearly surprised by the intimacy her words implied.

'You are so right,' said Caballius nastily, the cruelty glinting in his eyes. 'One of the guests at this meal will never be the same in your eyes again and you have the right to know about it.'

Brutus was looking to Gaius for his orders and Marcella watched helplessly as her lover gestured his approval and the cloth was pulled from the board. Marcella put her head in her hands, unable to look.

There was a long silence and a few gasps, as if people could not believe what they were seeing. One of the women began to giggle.

Lucius gave a bark of laughter. 'The lady has excellent taste, Gaius! And a great sense of humour! What did you pay for it, Marcella? I'll bet it wasn't less than an aureus! If you'll sell it to me, I'll double that.'

'I'll triple it,' shouted one of the military tribunes.

'No, I must have this one. I want to show it in Rome. It will be a sensation,' cried Lucius. 'I bid ten gold coins!'

'You stupid fool, Caballius! You will pay for this! You are a laughing stock! And me with you.'

Marcella heard the total contempt in Fulvia's voice and the promise of future penalities for her husband. She stole a look at the painting. It was a picture of Caballius himself, drawn in the grotesque style that she had occasionally seen in Pompeii. The head was too large for the body and a row of harlots was lightly depicted in the background. His cock was painted in bright colours and considerable detail, so nobody could miss that it was the main feature of the painting. But it was exaggeratedly tiny.

And completely limp.

Late that evening, when the party was breaking up for bed, Marcella went to the staff quarters with a purse of gold from Lucius' final bid. Imilico, Brutus and Nicomedes were drinking quietly in a corner, looking pleased with themselves.

She sat down, unbidden and ladled herself some of the best wine from the mixing bowl.

'Who is the painter?' she asked quietly and she sipped the perfectly warmed liquor.

The two soldiers looked at each other and then at Imilico who looked sheepish.

'Caballius couldn't resist bragging about his trophy to me,' said Brutus. 'He said the girl in the portrait was you, though I don't think you are at all like that. She looked an ingenuous little thing and you have a definite air of sophistication and maturity.'

Marcella sipped the wine to hide her expression.

'I had only been here a day,' he continued, 'and I had already had my fill of him and Fulvia, so I discussed the matter in confidence with these two and we decided that he deserved to be taught a real lesson.'

'Apparently some whore humiliated him at one of the

vulgar contests he enters – the whole of Rome had heard about it by the time we left, and I had no qualms about passing the information on. The entire Roman world probably knows by now,' explained Imilico. 'It was Nicomedes' idea to add a row of harlots and remind Caballius of his worst hour.'

'We didn't know till the last moment that he would auction it,' said Nicomedes, laughing. 'That was an added bonus, as it turned out, because he was totally disgraced.'

'I owe you,' she said, placing Lucius' gold on the table. 'This is something on account.'

'Let's call it quits,' said Nicomedes. 'Even though you couldn't have been the girl in the picture, there is no doubt Caballius would have embarrassed both you and the legate. None of us wants him in trouble – it reflects badly on the legion as a whole.'

Much later, Gaius came to her room. He undressed in silence and sat on her bed. She took her clothes off slowly, watching his face. His eyes dwelt lingeringly on her full breasts.

'What was going on this evening?' he asked eventually.

'You don't want to know the details. Believe me.'

'Brutus, Nicomedes and Imilico have been plotting something during the last few days. They have been behaving very strangely and Fulvia and Caballius were so furious over that fiasco, that I told them they could leave tonight with the special convoy. They will be well on their way by now. You are evidently involved, so what was it all about? How did the man come to display such a degrading picture of himself?'

'I don't have Lucius' gold any longer, and I didn't pay for the picture,' she said firmly. 'That is all you need to know. The matter is closed.'

'If I didn't know better,' he went on reflectively, 'I would say it was painted by Imilico – he always was very artistic, though I haven't seen him try a portrait before. He usually does garden scenes with birds and flowers. You should see the room he helped decorate in the town house in Sabratha! You feel you are in the depths of the country.'

She lay back on the bed and his gaze flickered over her body with a dark, insistent expression of hunger and longing.

'I think we should stop talking,' she said, gruffly, pulling him towards her and kissing him hard on the mouth. She pushed her tongue between his lips and the taste made her shudder with a deep, passionate desire. She felt that there was no way she could ever tire of him or feel complete without him.

He straddled her and put a hand on her breast once more, kneading her and squeezing the nipple gently. He bent to kiss her but she slid down the mattress under him and took his penis in her mouth, holding his balls delicately in her hands. She felt heady with the pleasures she knew she was giving him.

'Oh, Marcella, darling.' He groaned.

She mouthed him and licked the tip, sucked hard and then ran her hands over his silky skin.

She grasped his thighs in her arms and pulled him towards her so he was deeply embedded in her mouth.

He groaned again and tried to escape, but she moved with him down the bed, determined to give him pleasure this way and to taste his ecstasy.

'No,' he cried hoarsely. 'You mustn't do this – I want, I want – '

But it was too late for him to protest and she drank down the juice of his passion, supping from the cup of desire until she was intoxicated with their ardour.

He fell sideways on the bed and pulled her close.

He slept into the night and she lay beside him listening to the melody of his body and breathing in the marvellous male aroma. She felt privileged to be close to him in his hours of vulnerability.

She awoke to find him kissing her, watching her face as he vibrated the bud of her pleasure with a gossamer touch.

'You have been dreaming about this,' he said smilingly. 'I have been watching your face as you gradually became aroused. It was so lovely to see your pure enjoyment. So innocent. You have an extraordinary air of purity Marcella, so strange in one with such wanton urges.'

Her womanhood was on fire as his fingers worked her as though she were a musical instrument, strumming the depths of her pleasures. She thrust her body towards him, crossing her ankles and pressing her legs tightly together so her clitoris was prominently exposed.

'Such a tiny little blossom and yet so powerful,' he said softly, his hand still working at her.

She opened her mouth to kiss him, and he lightly brushed her lips with his. The waves of passion surged through her like an ocean of power and she erupted immediately. Before the ripples of passion receded he moved on top of her and pushed into her with a deep thrust of tranquility, kissing her and fluttering his tongue against her neck. Her body responded with intense spasms of passion.

They worked together in their ardour, their bodies rocking in unison as if to hidden music. He pushed at first slowly then with increasing speed and force until her body was rocked with his strength and the spasms of pleasure shook small cries of pleasure from her. She gripped him tightly as her body took control.

They rocked together for an age, for ever, for eternity. Time and space ceased to matter as she whirled round in a pool of sensual delights that rippled through every muscle of her body.

Finally, ecstatically, she felt she was bursting into a thousand small pieces of lust and love, desire and relief. She smiled at him in their mutual pleasures as her mind was lost in peace, happiness and joy.

BLACK LACE NEW BOOKS

Published in July

COUNTRY MATTERS
Tesni Morgan

When Lorna inherits a country estate, she thinks she is set for a life of pastoral bliss and restfulness. She's wrong. Her closest neighbour, a ruthless businessman and a darkly handsome architect all have their own reasons for wanting to possess her, body and soul. When Lorna discovers that paganism is thriving in the village, the intrigue can only escalate.

ISBN 0 352 33174 7

GINGER ROOT
Robyn Russell

As the summer temperatures soar, art gallery director Eden finds it harder and harder to stick to her self-imposed celibacy. She starts to fantasise about the attractive young artists who visit the gallery, among them a rugged but sensitive sculptor who she sets out to seduce. It's going to be an exciting summer of surprises and steamy encounters.

ISBN 0 352 33152 6

Published in August

A VOLCANIC AFFAIR
Xanthia Rhodes

Pompeii. AD79. Marcella and her rampantly virile lover Gaius begin a passionate affair as Vesuvius is about to erupt. In the ensuing chaos, they are separated and Marcella is forced to continue her quest for sybaritic pleasures elsewhere. Thrown into the orgiastic decadence of Rome, she is soon taking part in some very bizarre sport. But circumstances are due to take a dramatic turn and she is embroiled in a plot of blackmail and revenge.

ISBN 0 352 33184 4

DANGEROUS CONSEQUENCES
Pamela Rochford

After an erotically-charged conflict with an influential man at the university, Rachel is under threat of redundancy. To cheer her up, her friend Luke takes her to a house in the country where she discovers new sensual possibilities. Upon her return to London, however, she finds that Luke has gone and she has been accused of theft. As she tries to clear her name, she discovers that her actions have dangerous – and very erotic – consequences.

ISBN 0 352 33185 2

THE NAME OF AN ANGEL
Laura Thornton

Clarissa Cornwall is a respectable university lecturer who has little time for romance until she meets the insolently young and sexy Nicholas St. James. Soon, her position and the age gap between them no longer seems to matter as she finds herself taking more and more risks in expanding her erotic horizons with the charismatic student. This is the 100th book in the Black Lace series, and is published in a larger format.

ISBN 0 352 33205 0

To be published in September

SILENT SEDUCTION
Tanya Bishop

Sophie is expected to marry her long-term boyfriend and become a wife and mother. Instead, she takes a job as a nanny and riding instructor for the wealthy but dysfunctional McKinnerney family. Soon, a mystery lover comes to visit her in the night. Is it the rugged young gardener or Mr McKinnerney himself? In an atmosphere of suspicion and secrecy, Sophie is determined to discover his identity.

ISBN 0 352 33193 3

BONDED
Fleur Reynolds

When the dynamic investment banker Sapphire Western goes on holiday and takes photographs of polo players at a game in the heart of Texas, she does not realise they can be used as a means of revenge upon her friend's cousin, Jeanine. In a world where being rich is everything and being decadent is commonplace, Jeanine and her associates still manage to shock. Dishonesty and double-dealing ensue. Can Sapphire remain aloof from her friends' depraved antics or will she give in to her libidinous desires and the desires of the dynamic men around her?

ISBN 0 352 33192 5

If you would like a complete list of plot summaries of Black Lace titles, please fill out the questionnaire overleaf or send a stamped addressed envelope to:-

Black Lace, 332 Ladbroke Grove, London W10 5AH

BLACK LACE BOOKLIST

All books are priced £4.99 unless another price is given.

Black Lace books with a contemporary setting

FEMININE WILES £7.99	Karina Moore ISBN 0 352 33235 2	☐
AN ACT OF LOVE £5.99	Ella Broussard ISBN 0 352 33240 9	☐
THE SEVEN-YEAR LIST £5.99	Zoe le Verdier ISBN 0 352 33254 9	☐
MASQUE OF PASSION £5.99	Tesni Morgan ISBN 0 352 33259 X	☐
DRAWN TOGETHER £5.99	Robyn Russell ISBN 0 352 33269 7	☐
DRAMATIC AFFAIRS £5.99	Fredrica Alleyn ISBN 0 352 33289 1	☐
UNDERCOVER SECRETS £5.99	Zoe le Verdier ISBN 0 352 33285 9	☐
SEARCHING FOR VENUS £5.99	Ella Broussard ISBN 0 352 33284 0	☐
FORBIDDEN FRUIT £5.99	Susie Raymond ISBN 0 352 33306 5	☐
A SECRET PLACE £5.99	Ella Broussard ISBN 0 352 33307 3	☐
A PRIVATE VIEW £5.99	Crystalle Valentino ISBN 0 352 33308 1	☐

Black Lace books with an historical setting

THE SENSES BEJEWELLED	Cleo Cordell ISBN 0 352 32904 1	☐
HANDMAIDEN OF PALMYRA	Fleur Reynolds ISBN 0 352 32919 X	☐
JULIET RISING	Cleo Cordell ISBN 0 352 32938 6	☐
THE INTIMATE EYE	Georgia Angelis ISBN 0 352 33004 X	☐
CONQUERED	Fleur Reynolds ISBN 0 352 33025 2	☐
JEWEL OF XANADU	Roxanne Carr ISBN 0 352 33037 6	☐
FORBIDDEN CRUSADE	Juliet Hastings ISBN 0 352 33079 1	☐
ÎLE DE PARADIS	Mercedes Kelly ISBN 0 352 33121 6	☐
DESIRE UNDER CAPRICORN	Louisa Francis ISBN 0 352 33136 4	☐
THE HAND OF AMUN	Juliet Hastings ISBN 0 352 33144 5	☐
THE LION LOVER	Mercedes Kelly ISBN 0 352 33162 3	☐

A VOLCANIC AFFAIR	Xanthia Rhodes	☐
	ISBN 0 352 33184 4	
FRENCH MANNERS	Olivia Christie	☐
	ISBN 0 352 33214 X	
ARTISTIC LICENCE	Vivienne LaFay	☐
	ISBN 0 352 33210 7	
INVITATION TO SIN	Charlotte Royal	☐
£6.99	ISBN 0 352 33217 4	
ELENA'S DESTINY	Lisette Allen	☐
	ISBN 0 352 33218 2	
LAKE OF LOST LOVE	Mercedes Kelly	☐
£5.99	ISBN 0 352 33220 4	
UNHALLOWED RITES	Martine Marquand	☐
£5.99	ISBN 0 352 33222 0	
THE CAPTIVATION	Natasha Rostova	☐
£5.99	ISBN 0 352 33234 4	
A DANGEROUS LADY	Lucinda Carrington	☐
£5.99	ISBN 0 352 33236 0	
PLEASURE'S DAUGHTER	Sedalia Johnson	☐
£5.99	ISBN 0 352 33237 9	
SAVAGE SURRENDER	Deanna Ashford	☐
£5.99	ISBN 0 352 33253 0	
CIRCO EROTICA	Mercedes Kelly	☐
£5.99	ISBN 0 352 33257 3	
BARBARIAN GEISHA	Charlotte Royal	☐
£5.99	ISBN 0 352 33267 0	
HOSTAGE TO FANTASY	Louisa Francis	☐
£5.99	ISBN 0 352 33305 7	

Black Lace anthologies

PAST PASSIONS	ISBN 0 352 33159 3	☐
£6.99		
PANDORA'S BOX 2	ISBN 0 352 33151 8	☐
£4.99		
PANDORA'S BOX 3	ISBN 0 352 33274 3	☐
£5.99		
SUGAR AND SPICE	ISBN 0 352 33227 1	☐
£7.99		
SUGAR AND SPICE 2	ISBN 0 352 33309 X	☐
£6.99		

Black Lace non-fiction

WOMEN, SEX AND	Sarah Bartlett	☐
ASTROLOGY	ISBN 0 352 33262 X	
£5.99		

---------- ✂ --------------------

Please send me the books I have ticked above.

Name   ....

Address   ....

          ....

          ....

          .... Post Code   ....

Send to: Cash Sales, Black Lace Books, 332 Ladbroke Grove, London W10 5AH.

Please enclose a cheque or postal order, made payable to **Virgin Publishing Ltd**, to the value of the books you have ordered plus postage and packing costs as follows:

UK and BFPO – £1.00 for the first book, 50p for each subsequent book.

Overseas (including Republic of Ireland) – £2.00 for the first book, £1.00 each subsequent book.

If you would prefer to pay by VISA or ACCESS/ MASTERCARD, please write your card number and expiry date here:

....

Please allow up to 28 days for delivery.

Signature   ....

---------- ✂ --------------------

WE NEED YOUR HELP ...
to plan the future of women's erotic fiction –

– and no stamp required!

Yours are the only opinions that matter.

Black Lace is the first series of books devoted to erotic fiction by women for women.

We intend to keep providing the best-written, sexiest books you can buy. And we'd appreciate your help and valued opinion of the books so far. Tell us what you want to read.

THE BLACK LACE QUESTIONNAIRE

SECTION ONE: ABOUT YOU

1.1 Sex (*we presume you are female, but so as not to discriminate*)
Are you?

Male ☐
Female ☐

1.2 Age

under 21 ☐   21–30 ☐
31–40 ☐   41–50 ☐
51–60 ☐   over 60 ☐

1.3 At what age did you leave full-time education?

still in education ☐   16 or younger ☐
17–19 ☐   20 or older ☐

1.4 Occupation _____

1.5 Annual household income
     under £10,000   ☐   £10–£20,000   ☐
     £20–£30,000   ☐   £30–£40,000   ☐
     over £40,000   ☐

1.6 We are perfectly happy for you to remain anonymous;
     but if you would like to receive information on other
     publications available, please insert your name and
     address

     _____

     _____

     _____

     _____

SECTION TWO: ABOUT BUYING BLACK LACE BOOKS

2.1 How did you acquire this copy of *A Volcanic Affair*?
     I bought it myself   ☐   My partner bought it   ☐
     I borrowed/found it   ☐

2.2 How did you find out about Black Lace books?
     I saw them in a shop   ☐
     I saw them advertised in a magazine   ☐
     I saw the London Underground posters   ☐
     I read about them in _____
     Other _____

2.3 Please tick the following statements you agree with:
     I would be less embarrassed about buying Black
     Lace books if the cover pictures were less explicit   ☐
     I think that in general the pictures on Black
     Lace books are about right   ☐
     I think Black Lace cover pictures should be as
     explicit as possible   ☐

2.4 Would you read a Black Lace book in a public place – on
     a train for instance?
     Yes   ☐   No   ☐

SECTION THREE: ABOUT THIS BLACK LACE BOOK

3.1 Do you think the sex content in this book is:
      Too much   ☐   About right   ☐
      Not enough   ☐

3.2 Do you think the writing style in this book is:
      Too unreal/escapist   ☐   About right   ☐
      Too down to earth   ☐

3.3 Do you think the story in this book is:
      Too complicated   ☐   About right   ☐
      Too boring/simple   ☐

3.4 Do you think the cover of this book is:
      Too explicit   ☐   About right   ☐
      Not explicit enough   ☐

Here's a space for any other comments:

SECTION FOUR: ABOUT OTHER BLACK LACE BOOKS

4.1 How many Black Lace books have you read?   ☐

4.2 If more than one, which one did you prefer?

4.3 Why?

SECTION FIVE: ABOUT YOUR IDEAL EROTIC NOVEL

We want to publish the books you want to read – so this is
your chance to tell us exactly what your ideal erotic novel
would be like.

5.1 Using a scale of 1 to 5 (1 = no interest at all, 5 = your
ideal), please rate the following possible settings for an
erotic novel:

Medieval/barbarian/sword 'n' sorcery ☐
Renaissance/Elizabethan/Restoration ☐
Victorian/Edwardian ☐
1920s & 1930s – the Jazz Age ☐
Present day ☐
Future/Science Fiction ☐

5.2 Using the same scale of 1 to 5, please rate the following
themes you may find in an erotic novel:

Submissive male/dominant female ☐
Submissive female/dominant male ☐
Lesbianism ☐
Bondage/fetishism ☐
Romantic love ☐
Experimental sex e.g. anal/watersports/sex toys ☐
Gay male sex ☐
Group sex ☐

Using the same scale of 1 to 5, please rate the following
styles in which an erotic novel could be written:

Realistic, down to earth, set in real life ☐
Escapist fantasy, but just about believable ☐
Completely unreal, impressionistic, dreamlike ☐

5.3 Would you prefer your ideal erotic novel to be written
from the viewpoint of the main male characters or the
main female characters?

Male ☐ Female ☐
Both ☐

5.4 What would your ideal Black Lace heroine be like? Tick as many as you like:

Dominant	☐	Glamorous	☐
Extroverted	☐	Contemporary	☐
Independent	☐	Bisexual	☐
Adventurous	☐	Naïve	☐
Intellectual	☐	Introverted	☐
Professional	☐	Kinky	☐
Submissive	☐	Anything else?	☐
Ordinary	☐	_____	

5.5 What would your ideal male lead character be like? Again, tick as many as you like:

Rugged	☐		
Athletic	☐	Caring	☐
Sophisticated	☐	Cruel	☐
Retiring	☐	Debonair	☐
Outdoor-type	☐	Naïve	☐
Executive-type	☐	Intellectual	☐
Ordinary	☐	Professional	☐
Kinky	☐	Romantic	☐
Hunky	☐		
Sexually dominant	☐	Anything else?	☐
Sexually submissive	☐	_____	

5.6 Is there one particular setting or subject matter that your ideal erotic novel would contain?

_____

SECTION SIX: LAST WORDS

6.1 What do you like best about Black Lace books?

_____

6.2 What do you most dislike about Black Lace books?

_____

6.3 In what way, if any, would you like to change Black Lace covers?

_____

6.4   Here's a space for any other comments:

_____
_____
_____
_____

_____

Thank you for completing this questionnaire. Now tear it out of the book – carefully! – put it in an envelope and send it to:

Black Lace
FREEPOST
London
W10 5BR

No stamp is required if you are resident in the U.K.